# THE VOICE OF THE DOLLS

Only one more thing happened that night. Jennie had a nightmare again and woke screaming, "Don't! Don't do it!" When Sarah went in to her her eyes were wide open and glazed with terror. It was quite five minutes before she could bring her back to consciousness and another half hour before she went back to sleep. But she would make no explanation about her dream.

"I don't remember. I don't know why I cried," was all she would say.

Cuddling the thin nervous little body in her arms, Sarah had a feeling of desolation herself. It was the late hour, being woken suddenly from sleep, thinking how quiet the attic was. This house was getting on her nerves. And who was to comfort her if she cried?

# The Voice of the Dolls

Dorothy Eden

CORONET BOOKS
Hodder Paperbacks Ltd., London

Copyright 1950 by Dorothy Eden
First published 1950 by Hodder & Stoughton Ltd.
Coronet edition 1966
Second impression 1972
Third impression 1974

---

Printed and bound in Great Britain for
Coronet Books,
Hodder Paperbacks Ltd,
St. Paul's House, Warwick Lane,
London, EC4P 4AH
by Hazell Watson & Viney Ltd,
Aylesbury, Bucks

ISBN 0 340 16035 7

# I

"IF YOU'RE not going to marry," Sarah said to herself, repeating Aunt Florence's conversation, "you've got to find a profession. And painting wild flowers isn't a profession, it's an attractive hobby, nothing else."

Sarah scuffed irritably and somewhat unhappily at the champagne-coloured leaves already beginning to litter Aunt Florence's neat paths. A conversation of that nature with Aunt Florence, intimate on Aunt Florence's part and guarded on her own, left her feeling like a child, which was ridiculous and humiliating. She had to admit that she couldn't go on living alone in a cottage in Sussex, tramping the downs each day with her sketch-book, now the summer was over. Also it had been lonely since daddy had died; and one knew that apart from the financial question, one couldn't go on living that way indefinitely. But it was unfair of Aunt Florence to assume that at the age of twenty-five she was unlikely to marry. The fact that she stood five feet ten inches in her stockings, took size six in shoes and had a mind of her own surely wasn't going to scare all men.

She could, as Aunt Florence suggested, get a job as nature-study mistress in a girls' school. "And this, girls," she practised aloud ironically, "is the daisy by which you tell your fortune—he loves me, he loves me not. Oh, hell! And again, hell!"

Aunt Florence had a charming garden. The bricked walks, flanked by bright borders of dwarf geraniums and French marigolds, led to a small arbour where there were chairs and a table and a garden swing in which one could recline with the greatest comfort. At the end of September, irrespective of the weather, Aunt Florence considered the summer over and the garden draughty. But for Sarah's marked preference for the swing, it would have been dismantled by now and put away for the winter. As it was, Sarah spent every fine afternoon there, reclining on her back, studying the delicate skeleton within each hammered gold leaf of the oak tree arching above her, and listening idly to voices over a brick wall which divided Aunt Florence's house from the adjoining one.

She hadn't begun to be interested in the people next door. Aunt Florence hadn't talked of them. In London it seemed that neighbours were not any more personal than houses, and one might just as well nod to individual door knockers along Kensington Walk as speak to the people who lived behind them. So the inhabitants of the tall elegant Georgian house next door, with the blue door and blue shutters, were no more than a blur of voices on a sunny autumn afternoon.

At least they had been for the whole of Sarah's ten days' stay with Aunt Florence. But this afternoon she had scarcely settled back in the swing before she heard a light vague voice saying with complete distinctness,

"I think this corner's the best, Jennie. Now it's getting late in the year it's warmer here. And I think it's going to rain soon. Bring your dolls. Can you manage them all?"

"Yes, thank you, Aunt Venetia," a child's voice answered politely.

"Though what you want with so many I just can't think."

"I have to have them all, Aunt Venetia. They're a family."

That child, Sarah realised at once, doesn't laugh enough. She's too serious and mature.

"Oh, all right. But people in families do die sometimes."

There was quite a long silence. The ragged leaves shone yellow as honey against the low grey clouds. Sarah flicked a drifting leaf off her skirt and found herself raising herself on her elbow to listen.

Finally the child answered in her clear mature voice,

"Yes, Aunt Venetia. Like my mother."

Sarah was aware of an undefined feeling of distress, almost as if she could see the shocked face of the woman, as if, indeed, the simple statement were shocking. Then Aunt Venetia said,

"Oh, I didn't mean that, Jennie. I was just saying—well, look at the bother carrying six dolls into the garden every day. But if you like to do it I guess that's all right. Don't sit on the damp grass, and come in when Mrs. Hopkins calls."

"Yes, Aunt Venetia," came the expected docile response.

Sarah knew that Aunt Venetia drifted off then, for the sound of her footsteps was as vague and listless and somehow undirected as her voice had been. For a few moments she could hear Jennie talking in undertones, evidently as she arranged her six dolls. She eyed the wall ruefully, regretting its height. Even standing on the table she wouldn't be able to see over; and she had a great longing to see the grave child and her family.

Then suddenly, in a voice quite unlike her own, Jennie (who else could it have been but Jennie?) said, "Why don't you want Tim to come, Oliver?"

In another tone, surprised but genial, a caricature evidently of the person called Oliver, the answer came, "I not want Tim to come? My dear old chap, what a peculiar imagination you have. I can assure you I'm looking forward with the greatest of pleasure to his visit. After all, an explorer from the Antarctic isn't someone one meets every day. I may write a play round him. Ha! ha! ha!" The laugh, in the child's voice, was the most precociously clever thing of all. It gave the impression of being good-natured and benevolent. Oliver, according to Jennie's interpretation, sounded a nice person, a person whose company one would enjoy. "Anyway," the voice went on, "Jennie is looking forward to his coming. In fact, she's so excited Mrs. Hopkins says she can't do anything with her. Isn't that so, Jennie?"

Sarah waited with interest for Jennie to answer in her own voice. When she did it was almost startling, so real had been her mimicry.

"Yes, Uncle Oliver. Because he's my mother's brother, isn't he? He'll be like mummy, won't he?"

"I've never met him, kitten. Your father has. Ask him."

"I don't remember him very well, Jennie." That was the other voice, peculiarly repressed and tired. "Yes, I think he was a little like your mother."

"You'll know him by his nose," came another voice. The child had difficulty in making it harsh and autocratic, yet one sensed it was. "All the Flemings had long noses."

"And Tim's followed his for so long it's probably got out

of bounds by now," said Oliver's jolly voice, and again came the clever imitation of a rollicking laugh.

"Mary didn't have a particularly long nose"—that was Venetia's vague slightly peevish voice—"did she, Eliot?"

"Not particularly." That was the tired voice again. "Jennie isn't a great deal like her."

There was a slight thud. One of the dolls obviously had fallen down. There was "tch-tch" from the child. "Venetia can't you sit properly? Why must your back be so wobbly? And now your hair ribbon's off."

Sarah drew an unconscious sigh of relief. This was an ordinary small girl playing with her dolls. The other, absorbing as it had been, was too uncanny. The child was far too clever, and she evidently spent too much time alone. Perhaps this Uncle Tim, whoever he was, would remedy that.

A spatter of rain suddenly fell from the heavy clouds. There was a stirring of wind, then more rain. Sarah waited for sounds of Jennie gathering up her dolls to rush into shelter.

"Jennie!" called a voice from the house. "Come in out of the rain."

"Yes, Mrs. Hopkins," Jennie answered absently, not stirring.

After a few moments the same voice, more impatient now, called again, "Jennie, do for goodness' sake come in. Oh, you're here, Mr. Oliver. Can you make Jennie come in? She's out there with her dolls, lost as usual. Probably doesn't even know it's raining."

"Jennie!" That was a deep masculine voice, easy and good-natured, the male equivalent of the rollicking one Sarah had heard from Jennie's lips. "What are you doing, kitten? Oh, a tea-party." The voice was much nearer now, and Sarah heard footsteps on the bricked path. "Isn't it too bad about the rain. Never mind, let's finish it in the nursery."

"Yes, Uncle Oliver." The blitheness had gone out of Jennie's voice. She was now a well-mannered, colourless child.

"I'll help with this family. Hasn't it grown since I last saw it?"

"It's always been the same, Uncle Oliver."

"Has it, then? I thought you must have sneaked one in on me. This little one, for instance."

"That's baby Robert."

"Baby Robert! But, kitten—"

"I know he's dead, really," Jennie answered in her precise adult voice, "but I like to pretend he isn't. And my mother, too."

There was a moment's silence. Then Oliver said uneasily, "Well, I declare! Which ones shall I carry?"

"I can carry them all, thank you. I'm used to it."

"Jennie, you're a wonder. If you don't grow up and become the mother of ten I'll be most disappointed."

"We'd better hurry," said Jennie sedately. "It's wet."

Sarah heard first her light footstep then the heavier one of Uncle Oliver going down the path. Forgetting her own increasing wetness she considered. Oliver tried hard with Jennie, but for some reason the child didn't respond. She shut herself in the moment he appeared. Did she behave like that with everyone? And if so, why? Why did she have to escape into her world of fantasy?

Sarah ached with curiosity. But, she reflected soberly, she would have to go on aching. For she wasn't likely to find out what went on next door nor do anything to improve matters.

To work off her restlessness she dressed in raincoat and brogues and took the Tube to Holborn to spend the rest of the afternoon in the British Museum. That proved successful to a point. She spent a long time over illuminated manuscripts and Chinese porcelains. Then she came upon a worn, almost shapeless rag doll owned and loved by some Egyptian child in a forgotten dynasty. And Jennie, the living child in the house in Kensington who escaped from what surely must be an unhappy reality to her world of fantasy came back sharply and irresistibly. Why should she connect Jennie Foster with a long-dead child playing with her doll in another civilisation? Was it because she seemed as lost as the child who had been dust for centuries?

Sarah sighed and turned and walked out of the museum. Somehow she had to follow her hunch that all was not as it should be and find out what went on next door.

When she reached home the rain had stopped and there was

a primrose-coloured sunset that made a light like flaring gas jets in the windows of Aunt Florence's house and the house next door. Birds were singing and the garden with its wet green smell was enticing. Aunt Florence called that tea was ready, but Sarah remembered that she hadn't covered the swing and went down the garden to do it. That wasn't her main reason for going down. She thought that the cessation of rain might have brought Jennie out again.

Sure enough there were footsteps on the brick path. But they were heavy and measured. And there were two people there (one of them must have been walking on the grass for there was only one set of steps audible) as she knew almost at once by the deep tones of Oliver saying,

"There's only one thing to do, Eliot, if she can't go to school. She must have a governess."

"Ah!" said Eliot. His voice was dry and restrained, and undoubtedly the one Jennie had imitated earlier in the afternoon. "Can you afford it?"

"Of course, old chap. The play's doing damned well. Anyway, Venetia would be only too pleased—"

"I tell you I won't live on Venetia's money."

"But, my dear fellow, there's utterly no question of that. A while back, I admit, it was touch and go, but now, with this play doing well and another practically ready . . . Reid, by the way, was telling me he wants to start rehearsals as soon as possible. There isn't a thing to worry about. Jennie can have a brace of governesses, if she has a mind."

There was quite a long silence. Then Oliver went on, "It was the small doll that shook me. Baby Robert, she was calling it. Did you know she had it?"

"No," Eliot answered sharply. "Why should she be doing that?"

"Jennie was nearly seven years old when her mother died. She probably felt it more than we realised."

Again there was a silence.

Then Oliver said, "Venetia must do more for her."

"It's nothing to do with Venetia," Eliot burst out in a thin hard voice. After his previous restrained tone the vehemence was somehow shocking. "Jennie is my child."

"But, my dear fellow!" Sarah knew by Oliver's sympathetic concerned tone that he had his hand on Eliot's shoulder. "Venetia and I want to help. We always have wanted to. You mustn't shut us out like this. After all, Jennie, so far, is the sole descendant of the family, and that makes her very important. You mustn't let your pride come before her welfare."

"Oh, for God's sake, Oliver, don't be so pompous!"

"I say, old man, you're extraordinarily touchy today. You'd better go and work it off."

"And that would please you very well, too."

Oliver laughed good-humouredly.

"Work's good for the soul. Apart from that, Jennie gets a governess because the child is becoming an introvert. And those aren't comfortable people to have around. Our home's a happy home."

"My God!" Eliot ejaculated. "Why don't you hang up a sign 'God bless this house'. Or do you think it's so happy it can dispense with a heavenly blessing?"

"For jeepers' sake!" Oliver's deep voice came tolerantly. "You're getting touchier every day. I think you ought to have a word with Lionel about your nerves."

At that moment the doves which frequented the tall trees at the bottom of the garden and which had been silent during the rain began a belated cooing, and there was a flutter of wings.

"Those damned doves!" Eliot's voice had a taut barely-controlled anger. "Can't they be quiet? They stop me working all day and now they start in the evening."

There was a short silence while both men apparently listened to the contented purring sound from the trees. Then Oliver said, "Don't be so imaginative, old man. You'll develop a phobia."

Eliot made an impatient exclamation. A moment later Sarah heard his quick irritated footsteps receding in the distance. As they faded away she heard another sound, the low good-natured chuckling of Oliver, the tolerant amusement of an elder brother for a trying younger one. It was not unlike the crooning of the doves. It had the same cosy well-content quality.

That evening when they were seated companionably at the fireside, Aunt Florence with a half-finished patchwork quilt spread over her knees, Sarah sprawling ungracefully in her chair, her hands clasped behind her head, Sarah said thoughtfully, "Who are the people next door?"

Aunt Florence, prim and dignified, said repressively, "One doesn't become familiar with one's neighbours in London, dear."

"But you must know who they are."

"Oh yes, I know their name. Foster."

"What does Oliver do? The one with the jolly laugh."

Aunt Florence looked pained.

"Sarah, you've been listening over the wall."

"One can hardly help it in the garden."

Aunt Florence sighed.

"All I know, dear, is that Oliver is a playwright; his play *Meadowsweet* is running in the West End now. It's very successful, I believe. His wife is Venetia. She's supposed to be delicate. His mother, a quite impossible old woman, lives with them. I believe she has her own apartment on the second floor. And the brother Eliot lives there, too."

"And Jennie?" Sarah said eagerly.

"Jennie is Eliot's child. Her mother is dead."

"And Tim is her mother's brother?"

"Yes, I believe there is a brother who has been with a scientific expedition somewhere in the Antarctic. He hasn't been home for five years."

Sarah looked at Aunt Florence with raised brows. Aunt Florence had the grace to twinkle.

"All right, then, I'm inquisitive, too. That family's been next door for two years and all I can discover is that Venetia's money bought the house, and, apparently, marrying Oliver she took on that dreadful old mother and Eliot and his wife and child as well."

"Oliver married her for her money?" Sarah enquired.

"Oh, I wouldn't say that. She has looks, and she's a perfectly nice person."

"And Jennie's mother," said Sarah. "Why did she die?" As she spoke she experienced again that queer sensation of shock that she had had in the garden when Jennie had spoken of her mother's death.

"Oh, that was simple enough. Childbirth."

"Women don't die of that nowadays," Sarah said sharply.

"My dear, there are exceptions."

"They shouldn't," Sarah muttered. She couldn't understand her rejection of the fact that childbirth had been the cause of Jennie's mother's death.

"Well, this one did. The baby, too. I expect that's why the brothers live together, so Venetia can look after Jennie."

"Jennie's unhappy," Sarah said.

Aunt Florence looked at her with eyes unexpectedly sharp in her mild well-bred face. Then she said, "I've always suspected that; but it's nothing to do with us."

"She plays with her dolls too much."

"I know she does. It isn't healthy. Perhaps when the brother comes he'll do something."

"I wonder why they don't want him to come," Sarah speculated.

"Eavesdropping is a most undignified habit, Sarah," Aunt Florence said reprovingly. She selected a patch and tried the colour against its proposed neighbour. "My only regret is that my own hearing isn't acute enough. What else did you hear?"

"I heard Oliver and Eliot quarrelling. Or they would have been if Oliver would play."

"Poor man," said Aunt Florence sympathetically. "I think he has quite a time with that brother. Neurotic, I should say. But Oliver's wonderfully patient. I expect he can afford to be. He has so much more than Eliot—a good home, a good-looking wife, success. As far as I know Eliot composes music without any success at all. I expect he suffers from frustration."

"Why, darling, you're getting positively modern."

"Oh, I keep up to date with your jargon. You use different words and think your intuition is amazing, but we knew those things in my day, too. Well, why don't they want Tim to come?"

"I haven't the faintest idea. I must admit I'm fearfully intrigued."

"You should be more intrigued with your own future, not with the folks next door."

Sarah's eyes sparkled. She stretched her long legs and studied them with interest.

"Aunt Florence, does that extra couple of inches really put me out of the marriage market?"

"The odds are against you. The men tall women marry are usually quite nondescript. I hope you have too much character to choose one of those. And don't call it a market. It's much more a tenancy agreement these days."

Sarah threw back her head with enjoyment.

"Dear darling aunt, what are you doing with a patchwork quilt over your knees and the expression of a Victorian maiden aunt? If you ask me, you're a wolf in sheep's clothing."

"Dear, try not to laugh quite so heartily. A pretty soft laugh is always so much in a girl's favour."

"But we've ruled out the marriage market, Aunt Florence, so my guffaws can be completely uninhibited. No, I forgot. I guess it wouldn't be too becoming for my new profession."

"Sarah!"

"Yes, Aunt Florence?"

"You're planning to be a governess!"

"How right you are."

"But, dear child, are you suited—I mean, such a cramping profession to a person with your love of freedom."

"This particular job won't be cramping. At least, I have a hunch it won't." The laughter had left Sarah's face and her grey eyes were suddenly intense. "Maybe I'm crazy, but I've got to get into that house next door. I've got to find out about Jennie. You said there was nothing we could do, but you see there is. They want a governess for Jennie and I'm going to get the job if it's the last thing I do."

"But, Sarah! A governess! I hardly think it's the kind of thing your father would have approved of for you, even if you can remember your seven times table, which I doubt."

"So do I, but I know all my wild flowers. And as for daddy not approving, would he have stood for a child's unhappiness? You see, we're the only people who know about that, so it's up to us to do something."

"This Tim," Aunt Florence said uneasily; "he'll fix things."

"An explorer? He probably hasn't even seen a child for ten years, much less diagnosed their state of mind. I place no faith whatever in the great Uncle Tim. Eliot will probably find an excuse to get rid of him in a couple of days."

Aunt Florence produced her last defence.

"They mightn't have you."

"They'll have me," said Sarah definitely.

It rained hard for the next two days, and the garden next door was silent except for the drip drip of drenched leaves. Sarah had made several journeys to the arbour to find out. On the evening of the second day Tim arrived. She knew that by watching from Aunt Florence's bedroom window and seeing the taxi drive away, and catching a glimpse of umbrellas and the wet and rather battered hat of a tall man going up the steps to the front door. She could hear the confusion of excited voices, then the blue door shut and the voices ceased. She felt as if a chapter of a story were going on from which she was excluded.

The next morning Aunt Florence, without a word, put the *Daily Telegraph* in front of her. An insertion in the Situations Vacant column had been heavily outlined with pencil. It was an advertisement for a governess for a delicate child, and the address at which applications were to be made was that of the house next door.

## II

LATE in the afternoon of the same day Sarah walked up the steps to the blue door with its polished knocker shaped like a lynx's head, and rang the bell.

She felt very tall and conspicuous in spite of her dark worsted suit and her flat-heeled shoes. She hadn't got a hat at all (whoever was crazy enough to wear hats living in the country?) and there hadn't been time to go and buy one. Her hair which grew upwards in short curls was, daddy had used to say, the colour of the shy red squirrel that flashed like the movement of light up the trunk of a tree. He used to ask her if she had got her nuts in for the winter, although he knew she had none of the squirrel's propensity for preparing for the future. Her eyes were clear grey and full of light, her nose slightly tilted, her mouth wide, soft and blithe. There were freckles on her cheekbones. She had the look of a cheerful urchin, and her instincts were similar—to take what came and worry about neither past, present nor future. She had never truly been in love and didn't expect to be, but neither was she reconciled to getting nothing out of life but a career. She was quite sure her attempt to be a governess would be a sorry failure. It didn't matter about that so long as she discovered what ailed Jennie Foster and put the matter to rights.

Of course there was the chance, as Aunt Florence had pointed out, that she might not be engaged. Someone else may have got there first, or the Fosters might be allergic to squirrel-red hair. But whatever happened she was going to see inside the house, she was going to get beyond this highly respectable door. And that, at least, was something.

The door was opened by a rather untidy maid with loose moist lips who stared and said, "Oh! You're another of those, I expect," in a listless voice.

"Have there been others?" Sarah asked, suddenly afraid that she might be too late.

"Only one. And I shouldn't think Mr. Oliver would take her. Negligent, that's what Mrs. Hopkins said she was."

"Negligent? Mrs. Hopkins?" Mrs. Hopkins was the voice that had called Jennie in from the rain, the one she didn't always obey. "Oh, I expect she meant negligible," Sarah said.

"I don't know what it means anyway," said the maid in her indifferent voice. "But Mr. Oliver wouldn't like you if you're that, that's what Mrs. Hopkins says. Being theatrical, you see. Come this way, miss. If you'll wait in the library I'll see if Mr. Oliver will see you. I shouldn't be surprised if you get the job because you're the one Mrs. Hopkins saw in her teacup."

"Her teacup?"

"Reading the leaves, miss. She's awfully good at it. Quite scares me. Someone tall with red hair, she said, and probably stands no nonsense."

16

Sarah frowned, then realised she was doubly fulfilling Mrs. Hopkins's prophecy.

"I'll tell Mr. Oliver you're here, miss," the maid said hastily, and withdrew.

The library with its book-lined walls was rather dark. It must be where Oliver wrote his plays. There was a Sheraton writing-desk at the window, and it had pens, an ornate bronze inkwell and sheets of manuscript paper on it. There was also a silver vase with three over-blown roses in it. They were the only flowers in the room. The hall had been light and pleasant, with its Persian rugs, gilt-framed mirrors, oyster-coloured walls and staircase. But this room was a little sombre. And cold, too. Sarah repressed a shiver. She didn't let the atmosphere of rooms affect her; she never had the instantaneous impression that seized some people at certain places that an evil deed had been committed in that particular spot. Nothing, surely, could be further from evil than this respectable book-lined room with its one dramatic vase of flowers. Yet an odd shiver of apprehension went over her. She was sure the rest of the house was much more cheerful. She wished Oliver would come.

A little later there was the sound of loud whistling in the hall. The door of the library opened and a large man with very broad shoulders and thick rather long blond hair came in.

"Ah!" he said, smiling genially. "Sit down, my dear. I'm Oliver Foster. What is your name?"

"Sarah Stacey."

"And I understand you're enquiring about the position of governess."

"Yes, Mr. Foster."

He sat down opposite Sarah. He was dressed carelessly in shabby brown corduroy trousers and a yellow sweater. His hair was inclined to stand on end as if he frequently rumpled it. His light-blue eyes were lazy, yet had a curiously observant watchful quality; there were lines tilted upward from the corners of his mouth as though he laughed a lot. He had no superfluous flesh although his height and extremely wide shoulders made his presence seem overwhelming. He was entirely different from what Sarah had expected him to be.

"Do you know," he said with a candour that got under her guard, "I've never interviewed a prospective governess before. I'm damned if I know how to go about it."

"But I thought—the maid said—"

"The servants in this house talk too much. They get away with everything but murder. Yes, there was another candidate, but she obviously had adenoids. One thing I couldn't tolerate is Jennie speaking with a superfluity of b's. How old are you?" He caught Sarah's expression and his mouth curved upward in an amiable grin. "Is that a question one doesn't ask? Skip it then and tell me where your last position was."

"I'm twenty-five," Sarah answered composedly, "and I haven't had a previous position. I've never governessed before. But my father was a professor of languages and my education has been quite complete."

"Tell me, then, what made you apply for this job?"

"I have to work during the winter."

Oliver nodded as if he understood perfectly.

"Ah! You're not the hibernating kind."

Sarah laughed. "What I meant is I paint during the summer. I get commissions to do wild flowers. But they don't bloom in the winter."

"So you come indoors." Oliver regarded her approvingly. "I think we may get on very well. I confess I was horribly scared of having to sit down to meals with some poker-backed genteel creature. Governesses as a race are completely foreign to me."

"Me, too," Sarah wanted to say, but restrained herself in time, and the next moment the sound of a piano caught her ear. She listened disturbedly, identifying the desolate sound of Sibelius. It was so right, it matched so well the atmosphere she would only half admit she was aware of, the sense of lostness that lay beneath the veneer of the pleasant hall and the pleasant manners of the man in front of her.

"That's my brother, Eliot," Oliver explained. "He composes. He has his piano in the attic, as far away as possible, but not quite inaudible."

"He plays beautifully." Harsh winds wailing, snow, birds high in the frozen sky. . . . What had that to do with this small luxurious but completely conventional house in the heart of London?

"He's quite brilliant, but there's just something lacking, some driving impulse, or the ability to recognise and seize the right opportunity—just that thing that gives one success in this horribly competitive world. You'll understand, perhaps, when you meet him. Jennie is his child, but he's completely hopeless over business matters. So this sort of thing is left to me. My wife helps, too, but she isn't very strong. She's in bed today, as it happens."

"Nothing serious, I hope," Sarah said.

"No, just a chill. But she has them frequently. As a matter of fact I'd like you to assist a little with social duties, too. We have a lot of people coming in, and when Venetia isn't well it would be a tremendous help if you could take over. Would that be agreeable to you?"

"Perfectly. I should like it."

"That's grand. You'll find our guests interesting, I think. They're a mixed bag—actors, producers, writers. The main thing is to see they don't start running the house."

"But are you engaging me so quickly?" Sarah asked. "Don't you want any sort of reference?"

"I like your voice. Voices are important. If Jennie learns to speak like you do we shall all be perfectly satisfied. Can you start at once? Is that too much to expect?"

"Actually I could. I'm staying next door with my aunt."

"Next door! Well, what a coincidence! Is your aunt the little woman who looks like Queen Victoria?"

"She does, a little," Sarah agreed.

"Well, that, surely, is all the reference you need. I must make your aunt's acquaintance." Then he added, "I should be grateful if you could start at once. Jennie hasn't been strong enough to go to school this year. She's a perfectly normal child mentally, but she's been alone too much and grown a little introspective. I find her morbid, almost. Absurd. But she'll like you. You'll do wonders."

"Why do you think that, Mr. Foster?"

He looked at her with his bright genial eyes.

"Intuition, Miss Stacey. You have a look of well-being.

You'll do us all good, I shouldn't wonder. We need brightening up. Will you bring your bags over this afternoon? Mrs. Hopkins will show you your room. Mrs. Hopkins is cook-housekeeper and a treasure."

"I'll go and pack and come back in an hour or so, Mr. Foster."

"Fine!" He held out his hand. "I hope you'll like it here, Miss Stacey. As I say, we've never had a governess around before, but don't mind us. Just go your way as everyone does in this house. If you want a hand with your bags give a yell."

Sarah didn't need to give a yell because when she came in with her single bag a thin tall young man dressed in a faded khaki shirt and blue trousers and with a pair of gardening shears in his hand appeared from round the side of the house and said with a strong Cockney accent,

"Help you with that, miss?"

"It's perfectly all right, thank you," Sarah said. "It's not heavy."

"You the new governess, miss?"

"You the gardener?" Sarah wanted to retort. Instead she said, "I seem to be. It's all rather sudden."

"Well, and you'd expect that with this household. Blimey, if they ain't queer. What with this playwright and this composer and now this explorer—" He gave his shears a sharp click. His long thin face was gloomy. "If you want my advice, miss, I'd say don't come. But I couldn't expect you to take notice of me."

"No," said Sarah rather sharply. She realised it wasn't quite the thing to be having an intimate conversation with the gardener at this stage of her career. It was only that he had such quick bright eyes. They held her against her will. With a little education and someone to work with him over that accent— Anyway, what business was it of his to be giving her advice?

He seemed to realise he had been forward, for now he said.

"Better be getting on with the 'edge. Wish you luck, miss."

"Thank you," Sarah answered, and picking up her bag she went up the steps.

This time the door was opened by a stout woman in a clean white apron. She had beautiful round blush-pink cheeks and a face like an elderly cherub. Her little mouth was like a ripe cherry.

"Miss Stacey?" she said. "I'm Mrs. Hopkins. Mr. Oliver told me you would be coming, but I knew anyway. I saw it in my teacup."

"How do you do, Mrs. Hopkins," Sarah said. "Are you good at reading teacups?"

Mrs. Hopkins made a deprecatory movement with her plump little hands.

"Well, some folks think so. And I do say I see a lot of things that come true. I saw about Mr. Tim coming home, and I saw you plain as plain. Petunia, that's the housemaid, is quite nervous about it, silly child. She thinks I might see something queer about one of her boy-friends, I daresay. Jennie, now—well, she can do it almost as well as I can, the minx, but she makes it up. She mimics something uncanny, as you'll soon find out. Come this way, Miss Stacey. I'll show you your room and then Jennie's waiting for you."

Mrs. Hopkins led Sarah up two flights of stairs and finally opened the door of a small but attractive bedroom.

"That's yours," she said. "Jennie's next door, and then there's the nursery. I suppose you'll call it a schoolroom now. Old Mrs. Foster has her rooms on this floor, too. There'll be just the three of you. Mr. and Mrs. Oliver and Mr. Eliot are on the floor below. And the guest-rooms, of course. I'd better mention there's a couple of attic rooms above you where Mr. Eliot does his composing—I hope the piano won't worry you. I'm saying this because he never will. Wrapped up in his work he is, and thinks everyone else should be. Mr. Oliver is, too, of course, but he's more—well, good-spirited about it. Dear knows what would happen to this household if it weren't for Mr. Oliver."

"And where do you sleep, Mrs. Hopkins?"

"I have a room in the basement. I like to be handy to my kitchen, especially since—" She stopped suddenly, her little ripe lips pressed together. Sarah waited expectantly. "Well, you'll see soon enough," Mrs. Hopkins finally vouchsafed.

Sarah felt curiosity stirring again, but she sternly quelled it. This was not the time and Mrs. Hopkins was not the person of whom to ask questions.

"Is Petunia in the basement, too?" she asked.

"Yes."

"And the gardener? Does he come by the day?"

"He did. He gave notice last week, which is as well as he'd got beyound it, poor old man. We haven't got one at present."

"But I saw one in the garden. He wanted to help with my bag."

Mrs. Hopkins looked surprised, then her plump face creased.

"Oh, him," she said tolerantly. "Enough cheek to sink a ship. Now if you'll leave your things, dear, we'll go and find Jennie."

Jennie was standing at the window of the ex-nursery with her hands clasped behind her back. She was small for her age and her hair hung down her back in two thin dark plaits tied with tartan ribbon. She looked as Sarah had imagined she would, Alice-in-Wonderlandish, wistful and lonely.

"Jennie," said Mrs. Hopkins, and the child turned.

Sarah, who had been prepared to open her arms and let the lonely little creature run into them, stopped abruptly in her gesture. For the face looking up at her was neither wistful nor childish. From beneath coal-black brows a pair of disconcertingly intelligent eyes stared at her assessingly. The rest of her face was quite plain—pale cheeks, short nose, gnomish wide mouth.

"This is Miss Stacey, Jennie," Mrs. Hopkins went on.

"Hullo, Jennie," Sarah said.

"How do you do," Jennie replied coldly.

The fierce pride in those dark brilliant eyes rejected any advances. This, indeed, was the last thing Sarah had expected.

"You and Miss Stacey will be getting on grand," Mrs. Hopkins went on, as if Jennie were a completely ordinary child. "You'll have to be firm with her, Miss Stacey. She dreams and forgets to come in out of the rain. Just like her father. Well, I'll leave you to get acquainted because I've my work to do. Dinner's at seven. Mr. Oliver says you're to eat with the family."

"Thank you, Mrs. Hopkins. Jennie can tell me anything I want to know."

"She'll tell you, all right. Nothing much going on that she misses." With which remark Mrs. Hopkins left them.

Sarah, wondering how to deal with the inimical stare in front of her, said tentatively,

"You must show me your things, Jennie. Have you got any dolls?"

"No."

The uncompromising denial again left Sarah at a loss.

"But I thought most little girls had dolls."

No comment was forthcoming so Sarah (why should she be ill-at-ease because a precocious eight-year-old was staring at her?) began looking round the room. It was low-ceilinged with a red brick fireplace and windows facing north. It would make a very pleasant schoolroom. There were even cupboards which would be grand for school paraphernalia set in one wall. Sarah opened one at random and saw the dolls.

She knelt down to examine them. They had obviously been puppets—someone must once have given Jennie a puppet set, probably for a miniature theatre—for they were dressed as men and women, the two men in scarecrowish suits, the two women in crushed and grimy crinolines. Their paint-daubed faces and startling eyelashes were grotesque. There was a fifth one propped in the corner. It was smaller than the others and was wrapped in a piece of white curtain lace for a shawl.

"Jennie," said Sarah quietly, "you told me you hadn't got any dolls. Why did you say that?"

She expected the child to be truculent, but instead the vivid eyes became expressionless.

"Those aren't dolls," Jennie said.

"Then what are they, dear?"

"They're people. They're my family. And I don't care to talk about them."

"Very well, we won't talk about them just now." Sarah shut the cupboard. Her voice was quite calm, but inwardly she had a peculiar sensation of trembling. Don't get the jitters, she admonished herself, just because this is more realistic than you had expected. The child's talented, that's all. She's theatrical like her Uncle Oliver.

But there was something more to it than being theatrical, Sarah knew that instinctively. She looked at the shut cupboard and thought she could see the puppets through the wood, grinning and life-like. And here was their spokesman and their life-blood standing beside her like a small sphinx, her brilliant eyes full of secrets.

Oliver was right, it was extremely uncomfortable having a morbid child in the house.

Sarah got to her feet briskly.

"Come along," she said. "Help me to unpack and then tell me about where you have your tea and the time you go to bed."

The next hour was quite unrewarding. Jennie did as she was told, too obediently, and vouchsafed no information at all. When Sarah said, "I hear you've got your Uncle Tim visiting," the child answered stolidly, "Yes, he came Wednesday," and there was nothing at all in her closed face to show that once, in the garden, she had talked excitedly about him. Nor whether he had come up to her hopes and expectations. Sarah found her way down to the kitchen and brought up Jennie's tea on a tray. Jennie previously had used to eat in the kitchen at a corner of the table while Mrs. Hopkins and Petunia prepared the dinner, but from now on she would have her meal properly upstairs.

She made no comment about this change beyond saying "Mrs. Hopkins saw you in her teacup." And then what was her most natural remark so far, "I didn't have to have a governess if I didn't want one."

"Did you want one?" Sarah asked.

"I didn't care," Jennie said indifferently. "I'm not good at mathematics. Before I was ill last year I used to be bottom of the class. I didn't care."

"I'm not very good at them either," said Sarah. "We'll both have to learn. Drink your milk, Jennie. I'm going to run your bath."

But as she turned to go out of the room a man appeared in the doorway.

"Is that your job?" he asked. "To run Jennie's bath?"

Sarah knew at once who he was by his eyes, black and with the moody brilliance of Jennie's. His face was long and narrow and seemed to be set crookedly on his shoulders, but this, Sarah realised, was caused by one shoulder being slightly higher than the other. He had the same look of brittle delicacy that Jennie had. Heavens, thought Sarah, two neurotics in one house! Thank goodness that Oliver at least was cheerful and sane.

"I hardly know yet what constitutes my job," she answered cheerfully. "But I'm perfectly happy to see Jennie gets her bath. You're her father, aren't you?"

He nodded.

"Oliver told me he'd engaged you. Oliver does impulsive things, as you'll find out."

Did that mean, in that first glimpse, he disapproved of her? Then why didn't he exert himself and take an interest in his daughter's life himself? He had the look of being able to say cutting and sarcastic things like that remark in the garden, "God bless this happy home!"

"Do you disagree with your brother, Mr. Foster?" she said.

His black eyes were on her frankly and quite impersonally.

"I thought he shouldn't have chosen so quickly. But this time he may be right, after all. I hope my piano won't worry you. It's just over your head. I often play at nights, quite late. It doesn't disturb Jennie. She's used to it."

"I expect I'll get used to it, too," Sarah answered good-naturedly.

"You'll have too, I'm afraid, if you stay here."

He said that, Sarah realised, as if he didn't expect her to stay. He underestimated her determination. She wasn't going to be put off either by a piano played all night or a pupil who could, when she desired, look like a basilisk.

"I must have something," he went on, and now there was almost a suspicion of a whine in his voice. He stood a moment lost in thought, his mouth bitter, then he roused himself and went across to Jennie at the table.

"Good night, my dear," he said, touching her head with his long thin brittle hand.

"Good night, father," Jennie answered unmoved.

"Has Miss Stacey seen your dolls?"

"Yes."

The brief answer sent Eliot's eyes to Sarah.

"I hope that Jennie will be too busy soon to spend quite so much time with her dolls," he said. "She's getting too big for constant escapism."

So he didn't like the dolls, either. Was it because among them was represented his dead wife and son? It was cruel and pathetic of Jennie to have done that.

"I expect we'll be quite busy," Sarah answered politely.

"Good. Well, I shall see you at dinner."

When he had gone Sarah waited to see if Jennie would comment on his visit or give any indication whether she cared for her father or not. But all she said in a tone that was mild yet clearly an ultimatum was, "I always take Baby Robert to bed with me."

"Do you," said Sarah. "I'll get him out while you undress."

The child flashed her a look that was half suspicion, half incredulity. It was the first expressive look Sarah had seen on her face.

"Don't you think I'm too old," she demanded belligerently.

"Of course you're not too old, dear."

"Perhaps you don't know that I'm eight."

"Yes, I do. I'm twenty-five, but I'd still take a doll to bed with me if it comforted me."

The fierce eyes confronted her.

"It's not because I need to be comforted."

Sarah touched her shoulder.

"I'm sorry, I used the wrong word. It's someone to talk to in the dark that you like. And who better than Baby Robert, I'd like to know."


### III

SARAH took pains dressing for dinner that night. It wasn't in the matter of deciding which dress to wear, because she had only one suitable—the black with the square neck which set off one of her best features, the very pure white skin of her throat

26

and shoulders. But she brushed her hair hard, arranging the short fly-away curls into some order, and toned down the freckles on her cheek-bones with a careful application of make-up. Then she sat back in her chair, wondering why she was taking this care.

Venetia obviously would not be down to dinner, there would only be Oliver and Eliot, and of course Tim, the explorer, who no doubt was a bearded giant used to dining in fur-lined jacket and parka.

Why was she taking this care? Was it because of Oliver? Because she wanted him to see that his impulsive choice had been right? Or because she hoped he would see something in her looks to admire?

Dragging her thoughts out with her usual honesty, Sarah gave a disgusted exclamation.

"Watch your step, Sarah, my girl. You're not Jane Eyre."

A tap at the door caused her to start.

"Come in," she called.

The door began to open and Sarah was conscious of a wheezing sound like that of an obese spaniel. She watched fascinated as an elderly lady of very great bulk, leaning on a stick, filled the doorway. She was dressed in grey silk, and a large cameo brooch rode like a small boat on her vast bosom. Her pendulous chins were tucked against her throat, her nose and mouth and small sharp bright eyes, no doubt of normal size in a normally sized face, were so diminished by the breadth of her cheeks that her face had an odd look of distortion. Her beautiful white hair was elaborately dressed and ornamented with a jewelled comb. She stood staring at Sarah and continued to breathe like a wheezy puppy.

Sarah collected herself.

"You're Mrs. Foster," she said.

The lady inclined her head.

"I am. I wanted to take a look at you before I go down. No one tells me anything in this house."

"I'm Sarah Stacey," Sarah said, not quite knowing how to cope with this old lady—"that dreadful old Mrs. Foster" whom Aunt Florence had talked about.

27

"Didn't you know Jennie was to have a governess, Mrs. Foster?"

"Oh, I heard them talking about it. Behind my back, of course. Everything is done behind my back in this house. Well, you're an upstanding young woman. Bit on the thin side. Like my son Eliot. Not like Oliver." She chuckled breathlessly, the cameo on her bosom dipping and rising. "Oliver enjoys life. But Eliot—well, he's never been the same since Mary died. I can't think why, he wasn't all that crazy about her. He hasn't it in him to be completely crazy about any woman. And his daughter's just like him, so far as I can see. Shut-in. Has secrets. I hate people with secrets!" She thumped her stick emphatically. "I hope you're not the secretive kind, Miss Stacey. I hope we can have a chat now and then."

"Why, of course, Mrs. Foster."

"Well, that will be a change, I must say," the old lady rumbled in a pleased tone. "Someone to talk to. The boys are always too busy, and Venetia—between ourselves, Miss Stacey, one might as well talk to a fashion plate in a magazine as talk to my daughter-in-law. Not a brain in her head; and there's Oliver becoming one of the most brilliant playwrights in London. Well, there's no accounting for tastes. It's five minutes to seven."

Sarah stared. The abrupt change in conversation was beyond her.

"Dinner's at seven, didn't they tell you? We mustn't be late. There's rum trifle tonight. Mrs. Hopkins told me. I'm partial to sweet things. Do you eat well, Miss Stacey?"

"Yes, I think so."

"Good! I like to see a person enjoy his food. Shows he's got discrimination. Always put food as the prime pleasure in life and you won't get too many disappointments. Your stomach's far more faithful to you than men ever will be."

It was easy enough to sum up Mrs. Foster. She was a lonely old woman greedy both for food and gossip. In a household where there was intrigue she could be dangerous. Sarah made a mental note to use discretion with her. But she was grateful now to have the old lady to accompany her downstairs.

When they walked into the dining-room, a cheerful and

28

charming room with a blazing fire, a large bowl of mauve Michaelmas daisies in the window recess, cream walls and blue rugs on the parquet floor, there were four men, not three, to greet them. Oliver, large and handsome in a dark suit but with his mop of coarse fair hair still attractively ruffled, came forward.

"Ah, Miss Stacey. I believe you've met my brother Eliot. Let me present Burgess Reid, my producer."

Sarah shook hands with a thick-set short-statured man, with a very high brow and a belligerent jaw. He looked both intelligent and aggressive. She could imagine beginners weeping in the wings and even hardened old stagers walking in fear of him. But his smile was suave and charming.

"And this," Oliver went on, "is Tim Royle. Just back from —where the devil are you back from, Tim? All I can think of is icebergs and penguins."

"The Auckland and Campbell Islands, south of New Zealand," said the cultured voice of the tall thin young man who, two hours previously, had offered in rough Cockney to carry Sarah's bags up for her. "How do you do, Miss Stacey." His eyes were alive with mischief. His skin was deeply tanned and fitted his skull bones closely so that there were no curves, only angles and hollows. One of his eyebrows lifted slightly higher than the other when he smiled. It gave his face an irresponsible look that was both likeable and irritating.

Sarah collected her wits.

"How do you do, Mr. Royle," she answered. The crooked eyebrow seemed to represent a challenge. She knew in that instant that she would inevitably have to respond to any challenge from Tim Royle. "Did you finish the 'edge?"

"Finish it! Crikey! 'Ow many 'ands do you think I got?"

"What are you two talking about?" Oliver demanded good-naturedly. "Tim, is that horrible accent affected or are your good manners just a veneer?"

"Don't be silly, Oliver," old Mrs. Foster said. "Tim's father was a clergyman. He married Mary and Eliot; surely you remember."

And at that all Sarah could think of was the cliché that it was like a stone flung in a calm pool.

Tim's brows drew together so that they were perfectly symmetrical. With the absence of the slightly lop-sided look his face was cold and hard and a little frightening. He was two people in one, Sarah thought. She felt faintly repelled. He must have cared for his sister a great deal, but he couldn't blame Eliot that she had died in childbirth. Eliot must feel badly enough about that without having to bear the weight of guilt also. Though indeed just now he looked as if he were bearing it. His nostrils were pinched and his eyes dark with suffering. When Oliver unobtrusively laid a sympathetic hand on his shoulder he drew away sharply, with a movement of rejection. He must have spent the last year very alone in his grief. But that apparently was what he preferred to do.

"Mary looked so sweet," Mrs. Foster was going on, either unaware of the disturbance she had caused, or deliberately enjoying it. "She had one of those madonna faces, Miss Stacey. Not a bit like Tim's. It was a charming wedding, Mary in white satin carrying lilies of the valley. So pure." She sniffed loudly. "Do you cry at weddings, Miss Stacey?"

"I never see that there's anything to cry about," Sarah said bluntly.

Oliver said mildly but firmly, "Mother, that's all over now, and getting maudlin does no good. Miss Stacey, what would you like to drink?"

"Now don't waste time drinking," grumbled Mrs. Foster. "I'm starving. Pour your drinks and sit down at the table with them."

Sarah sat between Burgess Reid and Eliot. She was not a shy person and usually not at a loss for conversation, but these two men made her feel uncomfortable. She would infinitely have preferred to be beside Oliver, who sat at the head of the table and carved the chicken with meticulous skill, or even Tim, who was opposite and who had got back his look of mocking disrespect.

There was no need, however, to make conversation, for Oliver's genial voice dominated everyone else's. He handed out plates of chicken like a king distributing largesse.

"Women can't carve a bird," he said. "That's why I don't allow it to be done in the kitchen. There's an art in it if one takes the trouble to learn. After all, one doesn't get anywhere with anything if one doesn't take the trouble to learn. Look at me, developing a one-track mind about play writing. Well, Burgess, break the news. How much longer is *Meadowsweet* going to run?"

"We'll probably take it off in a month," Burgess answered. "You can't complain. A year in the West End with a first play is quite a feat. The critics will judge you when you've repeated the success. How's the new play coming along?"

"Oh, splendidly. You'll have the completed manuscript shortly."

"I was counting on that," said Burgess. Then he added casually, "Rachel Massey's on her way back from America. I think we may be able to get her to play Alexandra."

Oliver looked curiously naïve with pleasure.

"Rachel Massey! That's marvellous. With her reputation and my small one we've surely got a winner. Do you think she'll accept the part?"

"Well, you're not a Terence Rattigan yet, but—yes, I think she'll take it."

There was a small clatter as Eliot put his knife and fork down.

"I don't think she would be in the least suitable for the part," he said in a tight voice.

Oliver looked at him with interest.

"Why not, old man? I've never met Miss Massey personally, but I've seen her act. Good heavens, Eliot, how can you say a girl like that wouldn't be suitable."

"She isn't the type," Eliot persisted.

Oliver shrugged good-naturedly.

"Well, you're entitled to your opinion. But I would remind you that Alexandra's my creation. I ought to know who can play her. When will you see Rachel, Burgess?"

"As soon as she arrives, in a day or two."

"Am I making a mistake," put in Mrs. Foster, "when I seem to remember Rachel Massey was a friend of that Lexie Adams? Didn't she give evidence or something?"

Sarah noticed that Eliot picked up his glass and swallowed the contents in one gulp. He kept his eyes on the table. He didn't look up again. Neither did he make any further comment. His face had a peculiarly drawn look. Sarah had the impression that if he looked up his eyes would be full of fear. But what would that mean? He seemed a poor spiritless creature, anyway. And for some reason he didn't like Rachel Massey. What could she possibly have done to him?

Oliver, on the other hand, seemed to be enjoying a private joke. His lazy eyes were gleaming.

"Rachel and Lexie were very close friends," he said. "Wasn't that so, Burgess?"

"I believe it was, Rachel's not very happy about the whole thing."

"Who is this Lexie?" put in Tim suddenly in his bland voice. "Someone I ought to meet?"

"No," said Oliver pleasantly. "Not now. You're too late, old man. Miss Stacey, another helping of chicken? Come along, I'm hoping you'll share my good country appetite that I've carefully nurtured in the city."

"Yes, eat up, girl, eat up," encouraged Mrs. Foster, the high jewelled comb in her hair nodding. "I'm having another helping. Here's my plate, Oliver." She passed it up and leaned back in her chair, breathing heavily. "But I wish they'd discovered who the other man was."

Sarah looked at her in surprise. Was she wandering?

"Seen going up to Lexie's flat," she went on, enjoying Sarah's interest. "They never did find him. It was such a mystery. I adore mysteries, don't you, Miss Stacey? But they drive me quite mad when there's no solution."

"Here's your chicken, mother," Oliver said in an authoritative voice.

"She was leading a double life, of course," old Mrs. Foster continued unperturbed. "I suppose all actresses do. This Rachel Massey will be the same."

"Nonsense, mother," Oliver said. "What a suspicious mind you have. Yes, Petunia, what is it?"

The maid Petunia had appeared at the door and was saying that Doctor Forsythe had called to see Mrs. Oliver.

"Good," said Oliver. "Will you excuse me a few minutes, please. I'll just have a word with Lionel before he goes up."

He went out, and the tension, with the breaking of the conversation, relaxed. Burgess Reid began chatting to Sarah about the Sussex countryside and Tim and Mrs. Foster started a conversation about the diet of penguins. Presently Oliver came back, and the rest of the meal was uneventful.

As they rose from the table Oliver said to Sarah,

"Venetia wants to meet you. Will you come up now?"

"Is she well enough, Mr. Foster?"

"Yes, she's much better this evening. She'll enjoy seeing a new face."

Upstairs, Oliver showed her into a large bedroom luxuriously furnished and full of flowers. Venetia lay in a low wide bed with pale blue brocade hangings and sheets of paler blue satin. She had quantities of very soft fine pale-gold hair spread on the pillow. That was her chief beauty, for her face, small and pale, had only a rather empty prettiness. The only sign of illness Sarah could detect was the slight dilation of her blue heavily-lashed eyes.

"Hullo, darling," Oliver said softly. He went across to kiss her with tenderness. "This is Miss Stacey. I told you I would bring her up. My wife, Miss Stacey."

Sarah put out her hand to take the languid one offered her from the bed. She felt very large and healthy standing there looking down at the delicate creature.

"How do you do, Mrs. Foster," she said, "I'm sorry you're ill."

"Oh, I'm much better tonight, thank you. Lionel says so."

"Yes, he told me so," Oliver said. He sat on the bed possessively, holding one of his wife's hands. "That's grand, isn't it? You'll be up and about tomorrow."

"Yes, I expect so. I'm so glad you've come, Miss Stacey. Now Jennie's off my hands—I confess I just couldn't manage her. She wore me out. She's such an odd child and inclined to be hostile. I do everything I can, but she just doesn't respond." Her mouth drooped petulantly. Now Sarah could catch a glimpse of the spiritlessness old Mrs. Foster so much despised.

"I know you do, darling," Oliver said. "But you had the jealousy element to contend with. Jennie remembers her mother too well. And she's dead, poor soul, and you're alive."

33

He clasped her hand tightly, and Venetia, looking up at him, smiled.

Sarah had a queer feeling, suddenly, that the room had too much sticky sweetness in it; all those flowers, carnations, roses and gardenias, heavy with perfume, the over-luxurious bed, and Venetia giving her anxious sweet smile to her husband.

"I think Jennie and I will get on very well," she said to make conversation.

"I'm sure you will," Venetia answered. "You're the type she needs, I can see. Someone to shake her out of herself. I think lots of outdoor exercise, the kind I've never been energetic enough to take."

Oliver rubbed his fingers up and down her arm.

"And lessons to keep her mind occupied. Eliot agrees."

"Poor Eliot," said Venetia. This time her languid voice had a ring of sincerity. For the first time Sarah felt a faint liking for her. She wondered how the prickly Eliot responded to that sympathy.

"We must go now," said Oliver. "We mustn't tire you."

"Who's downstairs?" Venetia asked.

"Oh, Burgess, Tim, Lionel's staying for a drink. Miss Stacey is going to help out with hostessing when you aren't feeling fit, darling. Don't you think that's an excellent arrangement?"

Sarah felt Venetia's eyes on her assessingly. Their indifference changed to appeal. With a slight stir of surprise Sarah was aware that she was liked.

"Oh, excellent, Oliver. I'm sure Miss Stacey—what's your name? I can't call you Miss Stacey always."

"Sarah."

"That's nice. And I'd like you to call me Venetia. Don't let's stand on ceremony."

"Grand idea," said Oliver heartily. He was beaming with satisfaction because his plans were approved. "We've no ceremony in this house, as Miss Stacey has probably discovered already. And now, darling—"

"Just let me show Sarah my new robe. It's in the wardrobe, Sarah. I love new things, don't you?"

Sarah opened the wardrobe and took out the heavy champagne-coloured silk robe.

"Bring it here," Venetia said.

She took it to the bedside, and Venetia ran her hands over the silk, smoothing it sensuously. It was as if she were stroking a cat. Her face was rapt.

"Isn't it lovely?" she said. "Don't you love the feel of silk?"

"It's beautiful," Sarah said politely.

"Yes, Oliver bought it for me. He knows I love new things. He spoils me. Don't you, darling?"

"Shockingly," Oliver agreed. He stood up, stretching his big frame. "We mustn't neglect our guests. I'll be up to say good night. Come along, Sarah."

Sarah was aware, with a sense of pleasure, of his easy adoption of her first name. She felt suddenly happy, sure she was going to enjoy her new job, intrigued and interested by everything she saw. Even if she did unconsciously draw a deeper breath when she got out of the stifling sweetness of Venetia's room her happiness was not abated.

She went downstairs, eager to hear what was going on. The men were in the drawing-room now. It was a long high room lit by candle-shaped lights. The furnishings, in shades of lavender and delphinium blue, were in perfect taste. Again a fire burned brightly, and before it stood a neat dapper man with a small dark moustache who was introduced to Sarah as Doctor Forsythe. He was drinking whisky, and looked very much at home.

"Well, what do you think of my patient?" he said. "She's a great deal better tonight. I understand you're going to live here, Miss Stacey. You must take good care of Venetia. Very good care. Isn't that so, Oliver?"

Oliver had gone to the piano in the corner, and spreading his large mobile hands on the keys began to play. Over the sound of the notes he said, "Yes, indeed that's so." Then he began to sing in a loud rollicking voice,

'I love sixpence, pretty little sixpence.
I love sixpence better than my life . . ."

35

Tim rose from one of the low chairs where he had been in conversation with Burgess Reid and sauntered towards Sarah.

"Did she like it?" he asked.

"Like what?"

"Your face."

"Don't be so asinine," Sarah said stiffly.

"You mean she didn't? But all women are jealous. I like it, anyway. Particularly those clusters of freckles—like Sirius, or the Sign of the Plough. You know, the thing I liked most about coming home was seeing familiar stars again. After the Southern Cross and a steely sky, and that uncanny aurora borealis, that looked so rosy and warm and yet was as cold as the devil. The reflection of the sun going down on ice. That's why I like my familiar stars." His eyes rested on her cheeks, and she felt the colour rising in them. What an impossible and ridiculous person he was.

"*I brought fourpence home to my wife . . .*" sang Oliver.

"Have you seen over the house?" Tim was asking.

"Not completely."

"Then come out here and I'll show you something to be careful of. If I don't do it no one else will think of it, and we'll have you breaking your neck."

He led her out of the room and across the hall. Through the open door of the dining-room Sarah caught a glimpse of the bulky form of old Mrs. Foster furtively scraping out the trifle dish. There was an avidity and concentration in her actions that was repellent. So that was her secret vice. It may be worth knowing for the future. On the other hand how could it be, for however inverted and bitter Eliot might be, and in spite of the tragedy of Mary's death, the basis of this house was happiness, Oliver's and Venetia's.

Tim had opened a door on the right side of the hall towards the kitchen.

"Look here," he said.

As she came forward he gripped her round the waist.

"Not too far. That's a steep drop."

Sarah drew back, startled. The open door showed a flight of steps, almost vertical, leading to a cellar. Like a lot of old

36

houses in London there was no introduction to the steps. They fell sharply from the threshold, a trap to the unwary.

"You see," said Tim, "you need to be warned. People don't always think, and there can be accidents."

"But everyone living here knows about them," Sarah said nervously.

"They should. Mary apparently didn't."

"Mary!"

"She had a fall down here they tell me."

Sarah drew in her breath in horror.

"When the baby was coming?"

"Two months before it was expected."

Oliver's voice from the drawing-room came low and caressingly,

> "I spent nothing, I lent nothing,
> I love nothing better than my wife . . ."

"And so she died," Sarah whispered.

"It brought on premature birth," said Tim's grim voice. "They both died."


## IV

SARAH'S adaptability for sleeping soundly in strange beds deserted her that night. She heard the clock strike one, then two. A little after that she thought she heard the floor creaking above her and sat bolt upright, perspiration on her brow. Her nervousness made her impatient with herself. This household certainly wasn't an ordinary one, but there was nothing in it about which to get nervous. It was merely the strain of the evening and now the lateness of the hour that made her exaggerate things.

Then the piano above her began to play. So the creaking had been Eliot going up to the attic. She certainly didn't appreciate his tendency to compose music in the middle of the night, but if that was all that was going on upstairs it was nothing to worry about.

All she could think of now was that musicians were awkward and uncomfortable people if inspiration attacked them in the small hours. She would have to get used to this and sleep through it.

But she didn't think she ever would because she would always think of the taut unrelaxed sadness of Eliot's face, and wonder if it was that rather than inspiration that drove him to his piano.

Mary must have known about those steps. If she had been living in the house she must have known. If she had just been visiting it would have been different. Even then she could have tripped and fallen. Tim was simply looking for melodrama. Angry at his sister's death he wanted someone on whom to pin the blame. But who was the Lexie Adams they had talked about and what had happened to her?

The piano above her was playing a simple melody over and over again. Sarah found herself fitting words to it, *You'll never find out, you'll never find out.* Resolutely she turned over and willed herself to sleep.

Petunia brought her tea in the morning. She put the cup down and said, "Mrs. Hopkins says you oughtn't to expect it, but since I have to bring it up to Mrs. Foster you might as well have a cup. She says to turn it three times and she'll read the leaves for you."

"Thank you, Petunia," Sarah said. "Tell Mrs Hopkins that's very kind of her."

"Though I wouldn't believe too much what she sees, miss," Petunia said, pushing a straggle of hair under her cap. "It can be downright upsetting. She keeps seeing new men for me and I've been going steady with Jimmy for six months. What do I want with new men?"

"What indeed?" Sarah murmured. Petunia, in spite of her thinness and her air of coming unstuck at the edges—her cap was crooked, her hair inclined to stray, her mouth was never entirely closed and the hem of her dress drooped unevenly— was not unattractive. "What does Jimmy do?"

"He's a bus conductor. Works awful late sometimes. Picks up queer language, too. Gets it from all those idle women who ride up and down from Richmond to Kensington and Knightsbridge and Oxford Street. If they calls him anything he answers back. He'll do the same to me if I marry him. Maybe I should look for a new man like Mrs. Hopkins says. It might teach him a lesson. I hope she sees a good-looking one in your cup, miss."

"I hope nothing of the kind," said Sarah. "I have a job."

When Petunia had gone she got up, bathed and dressed, then went in to Jennie's room. Jennie was not there but in the schoolroom sitting on the floor with two of the dolls. She was dressed and her hair, except for a slightly crooked centre parting, was neatly braided. The dolls were a man and a woman. The woman had a piece of crumpled blue satin draped round her shoulders, and Jennie was saying in her precociously clever imitation of Oliver's jolly voice, "You see how much I love you, my darling."

Then, in Venetia's nervous excitable voice, she said, "Oh, I do, Oliver. It's so sweet of you. You know how I love beautiful things."

"Good morning, Jennie," said Sarah calmly.

The child started sharply, showing how absorbed she had been in her play-acting. She looked up at Sarah and her face was a little exasperatingly unreadable mask.

"Good morning, Miss Stacey." She picked up the dolls possessively.

Sarah wanted to ask her if she deliberately eavesdropped because of the way she seemed to know all that went on in the house, even the intimate things. But she was afraid of antagonising the child completely. Even now it was going to be hard enough to gain her confidence.

'You're very clever at mimicking, Jennie," she said. "Where did you learn it?"

"Nowhere. I just do it."

"Well, it's quite a talent, but you want to be careful how you use it."

"I don't make things up," Jennie said in her shutting-out adult voice. "I just do things that have happened." ·

"Such as what?" Sarah prompted.

"Uncle Oliver gave Aunt Venetia a new robe to celebrate

39

the three-hundredth performance of his play. I was just doing that."

"Well, put the dolls away now."

Jennie obediently did so, packing them into the cupboard silently. Then she turned her stolid face.

"Are you going to forbid me playing with them?"

"No, of course not, Jennie."

"Father said you would. Aunt Venetia said so, too."

Sarah wondered involuntarily how long it would be before Jennie trusted her. Unless she went very carefully now it would be never. Jennie's dislikes would last a long time. It seemed very important, more important than anything else, to gain her confidence and love.

"I don't mind you playing with the dolls," she said carefully, "and mimicking people, too, so long as you're not cruel. Remember never to be cruel."

Jennie closed the cupboard door and stood up. It seemed to Sarah that her face was a little less guarded. She said primly,

"Breakfast is at half-past eight and Uncle Oliver doesn't like anyone to be late because he goes into his study to work at nine o'clock."

"Very well, then let's go down," Sarah said briskly, "because our work begins at nine, too."

Oliver was the only one in the dining-room when they went in. He had on a tweed jacket and canary-coloured sweater. His blue eyes were bright and happy.

"Ah, good morning," he said. "Come and sit down. We never wait breakfast for anyone. Eliot frequently doesn't have it, and Tim's as lazy as hell. How ever he organised an expedition is beyond me. But there you are. Most people are surprised to hear I work hard, too."

"How is Venetia this morning?" Sarah asked.

"Oh, much better. She'll be up later. She's all right, you know. She just has a slight chest condition we have to watch."

Petunia came in with the coffee, and milk for Jennie, and they all sat down.

"I start work at nine sharp," Oliver said. "I shut myself up for four hours. I've had to make rigid rules about it. If you know anything about writing, Sarah, you'll understand how

40

one has to be driven to it. At first I had to get Mrs. Hopkins to lock me in. But now I've got discipline. I do my four hours without a murmur." He spoke with simple pride in his achievement and gave his friendly smile. "And what about you two? Have you planned a time-table?"

"I'm drawing one up this morning," Sarah answered.

"Good. Get some outdoor stuff into it, too. There's a café in the Gardens where they make little cakes with currants and bits of ginger. Jennie likes them. Don't you, kitten?"

Jennie answered, "Yes, Uncle Oliver," in her prim voice.

Sarah had the impression that Oliver liked them, too, that he often went there and would appreciate her company. But that surely was wishful thinking on her part. If it were true it would merely be because he liked someone to talk to and the house got lonely when Venetia was ill and Eliot at his solitary work.

She looked up and caught Oliver's eye, blue and twinkling, began to blush, then was saved from embarrassment by Tim's sudden appearance at the door and his laconic voice saying,

"Good morning, folks. Am I late?" He looked from Sarah to Oliver, his eyes deliberately innocent. "Have I interrupted something?"

Sarah felt the colour in her cheeks again, this time from anger. She wanted to tell this impertinent young man just what she thought of him. Before very long she would.

"Jennie's curriculum," Oliver answered. "Isn't that a grand solemn word. What do you think of it, Jennie?"

"I think time-table would be easier," Jennie answered.

Tim put his hand on her head and ruffled her smooth hair.

"Out of the mouths of babes," he said; but to Sarah's astonishment she saw a dawning smile on Jennie's face, and a glimmer of softness in her eyes. Curiously, she had a feeling of anger and jealousy that Tim should have found the way behind Jennie's mask so soon. But of course that was explained by Jennie's eagerness to like him. She had talked herself into it, no matter what Tim was like. Sarah remembered her pathetic conversation with her dolls in the garden and felt that that explained everything. Her response to him was simple auto-suggestion.

After that breakfast was quite uneventful. Oliver ate rapidly, looked at his watch, and seeing that it was ten minutes to nine excused himself. Sarah heard him run up the stairs two at a time, and a moment later the door into Venetia's room open and shut.

"The devoted husband," Tim observed behind the *Daily Mail*.

Without reason his mild impersonal voice irritated Sarah.

"And why not?" she asked coldly.

"Darling, I must now toil for four long weary hours so that I can buy you more beautiful clothes!" Tim's left eye appeared round the paper. He added in his normal voice, "You're perfectly right to look heated, my dear. Oliver's a nice fellow, and it's quite time I relearnt my manners. One loses them down south. Only penguins to talk to, and they don't hesitate to tell you what they think of you in the rudest language. You should hear the language I've learnt from them. Petunia's Jimmy has nothing on me."

Jennie giggled and instantly smothered the small surprising sound. Was it possible she could be a normal child after all?

"Finish your milk, Jennie," Sarah said.

Jennie drank obediently, her eyes over the edge of the glass on Tim all the time.

"I," said Tim, behind his paper, "have a busy day ahead of me. The morning with my tailor, then lunch in Soho. Do you enjoy finding new restaurants, Sarah?"

"It hasn't been one of my hobbies."

"Lack of opportunity, probably. It's quite fascinating. I vary my nationalities as much as possible, Greek, Swiss, Jugoslav, Chinese, Indian, Spanish. Maybe it's the result of a long diet of seal. Or maybe I'm adolescent. What do you think?"

Sarah, supervising the finish of Jennie's breakfast, made no answer.

The whole of Tim's face appeared round the paper.

"You don't like me much, do you, Sarah?" Before she could reply, if she could have thought of a suitable reply, he went on, "Don't let it worry you. I usually have that effect on people at first. But I grow on them. Maybe I'll grow on you. Stranger things happen. One day we might even be making violent love in *The Highlander*. Speculation's fascinating, isn't it?"

"I could think of a better word," said Sarah. "Come along, Jennie. We've got work to do."

Jennie proved to be a co-operative but uninspiring pupil. Sarah, fumbling her way through unfamiliar and almost forgotten reading, history and geography books, had one eye automatically on the door. She fully expected a visitor. Old Mrs. Foster, at least, would not be able to resist finding out what was going on. Probably Eliot would be interested to see the steps being taken in his daughter's education. It was too much to expect that Oliver would make an exception and break off his work to come up. But someone would surely look in to see Jennie sitting primly at her small table, her head bent over her exercise book. At eleven o'clock, sure enough, there was a tap at the door, but when Sarah called, "Come in," the only person to appear was Petunia carrying a tray.

"Your elevenses, miss," she said. "Mrs. Hopkins said as how you'd probably enjoy them, and Jennie always has her milk now. Oh, and Mrs. Hopkins said to tell you as how she saw a real lovely man in your cup. Very close, too, if he ain't here already. You should be hearing from him any day. Ain't it exciting?"

"I think Mrs. Hopkins has quite an imagination," Sarah said.

"Oh, it's all true, miss. She saw my Jimmy two days before I met him, and that was the day he overcharged me. Eightpence to Hyde Park Corner he wanted, when of course it's only four. We was both so mad we was going to call the police when suddenly it happened."

"What happened?"

"Why, we discovered we were soul mates. Or as near as makes no matter."

Puzzled as to how a wrong bus ticket could cause Petunia to arrive at so dramatic a conclusion Sarah waited for her to go on, which she obligingly did.

"It was the look in his eye," she said dreamily. "We've been going steady ever since. Mrs. Hopkins's teacups comes true. You wait and see."

Lunch, too, was a disappointing meal. Eliot was there, but he was quite uncommunicative beyond explaining that Oliver

43

had gone into town to lunch; there was no sign of Venetia, and old Mrs. Foster was too engrossed in her food to do more than fling a few questions at Sarah. Sarah decided to take Jennie on a nature-study walk through Kensington Gardens in the afternoon and perhaps have tea at the place Oliver had mentioned.

Before going she took the ribbons out of Jennie's hair and unbraided it.

"Wait till I get a brush," she said. When she had brushed the long straight silky locks until they gleamed and tied a ribbon with a frivolous bow on top of Jennie's head, there was colour in Jennie's cheeks and her eyes were very large.

"Look at yourself in the mirror," Sarah said.

Jennie did so, staring at herself as if she saw a stranger.

"I look sissy," she muttered.

"You look pretty," Sarah insisted. "How would you like a party?"

"A party! I wouldn't know how to be at a party."

"Indeed you would. When all the other children came."

"What children?" she asked flatly, and Sarah realised that she had no contact at all with other children.

"Oh, the ones Aunt Florence and I know. We know lots who'd love to come."

"Do you?" Jennie looked at her guardedly. It was impossible to tell whether she was pleased or not, but at least she wasn't hostile. "What would I wear?"

"A party dress, of course. I'll speak to your father myself."

Jennie gave her a long reflective look. She still didn't show any eagerness. Obviously she was weighing up the advantages of a party as against retaining her lonely state.

Then she said primly, "It would have to be Uncle Oliver you asked."

Sarah decided to call in on Aunt Florence on the way. Aunt Florence obviously had been expecting it, for she showed no surprise. She looked hard at Jennie, said, "So this is the child," then patted her on the shoulder and said, "Run along to the kitchen. It's the second door on the right. Ask Bertha for a piece of cake."

Jennie looked at her unmovingly.

"We're going to the café for tea, thank you."

"Then go and play with Hamlet. But don't rub his fur the wrong way, he doesn't like it."

"Who's Hamlet?" Jennie asked.

"He's a large elderly rather bad-tempered cat. He'll most likely hate you on sight. On the other hand I think the two of you might have something in common. Go and see."

Looking more human in her bewilderment, Jennie went. Aunt Florence took Sarah into the drawing-room.

"What a little gargoyle," she said. "Looks right into you."

"I know," said Sarah ruefully. "I haven't any secrets from her. I don't think anyone else has in that house."

"But they must have, my dear. A child can't know everything." She sat down and folded her hands in her lap. She looked composed, mid-Victorian and as gentle as a dove. "Tell me all," she said eagerly.

It was a relief to talk, not only because Aunt Florence was an interested and intelligent listener, but because talking seemed to arrange the household next door in better perspective.

"So Mary had an accident," Aunt Florence said. "Poor girl. Anything else?"

Sarah remembered about the actress, Lexie Adams, but what had happened to her or what she had to do with the Foster household she didn't know.

"I don't think there's anything wrong," she said. "They're just rather unusual people. Eliot is brooding on his wife's death, and he's not had any success so far with his music. Venetia isn't strong and I would think likes pampering. Jennie should be a natural child when she's had some normal life. Oliver's the one who keeps things on an even keel. Oh, and there's Mrs. Hopkins. She reads teacups. She's already seen the man in my life. Petunia and I think it's a joke."

"It's not a joke," came Jennie's voice suddenly and startlingly behind her. "Mrs. Hopkins sees real things. She says there's death in the house. And she doesn't mean my mother and baby Robert. She means someone else. You wait and see."

The child's large eyes, completely lacking in warmth, her sombre face and the conviction in her voice were unreasonably disturbing. Unreasonably, because it wasn't sensible to take seriously the fiction told to an imaginative eight-year-old.

"Good gracious!" murmured Aunt Florence. "What a ghoulish creature you are. Did you like Hamlet?"

"Yes, I did, but I don't know whether he likes me. Bertha says he takes time to get used to strangers. I was thinking—I wondered—" for the first time Jennie's composed voice quivered, her face showed emotion.

"Yes, child?" said Aunt Florence.

"—if I could see him sometimes. Then he'd get to like me, maybe."

"And what's to stop you," said Aunt Florence kindly. "I'll have Hamlet set aside an hour any afternoon Sarah can spare you. It'll do him good, having company. Is that all right with you, Sarah?"

"I should think it's perfectly all right, Aunt Florence." She could read the expression in Aunt Florence's eyes perfectly. The poor lonely child looking for someone to love her, even an animal. Somehow it irritated her because Jennie didn't need to be that lonely. Certainly her father wasn't much help, but she had Oliver and Venetia.

"Now we'd better go," she said briskly. "Do you want to say goodbye to Hamlet?"

"I've said it," Jennie answered. For the first time and quite spontaneously she put her hand in Sarah's. Sarah caught Aunt Florence's eye. Now she was getting caught up in this sentimental emotion herself. But there was something moving about this first friendly action of Jennie's, something that told her of the intense warmth beneath the unpromising exterior.

Jennie had insisted on taking baby Robert with his gangling legs walking with them. She carried him importantly in both arms, but she remained sufficiently childlike to scuff leaves and even to chatter a little. Sarah chattered back light-heartedly. After all it was much too early to make a lot of headway with a child like Jennie. She was advancing slowly and at least was gaining her confidence, if not her affection.

She half expected to find Oliver at the café, but instead there were Tim and old Mrs. Foster, wearing a persian lamb coat and an imposing hat with quills, eating buns.

"Well, well," said Tim. "This is a popular spot today. Are you two having tea?"

"Yes," said Sarah shortly.

"Then come to our table. I saw you coming and waited."

"I was too famished to wait," called old Mrs. Foster, her cheeks bulging. "These buns are very good. I often come over here and try them."

Tim brushed his finger lightly over Sarah's forehead.

"Don't scowl," he whispered. He turned to Jennie. "Which do you like best, cakes or buns?"

"Cakes, thank you," Jennie said.

"Then take two of these and go out in the sun. It's much better for the baby."

Jennie smiled up at him, her face all at once tender.

"It is, too. He doesn't get enough sun. I'll be out here, Miss Stacey."

As she went Sarah said, "You shouldn't encourage her to think that horrible bit of wood is alive. She's daft enough about it already."

Tim smiled pleasantly.

"Everyone has to have their method of escape. Jennie has her family, I have penguins. As it happens, our conversation isn't going to be for Jennie's ears."

"No, it isn't," Mrs. Foster agreed, brushing crumbs off her lap and helping herself to another cake. "Tim's just been asking me who Lexie Adams was."

In a queer way the slight cold that came into the Kensington house at the mention of that name seemed to come in here, too. Sarah suddenly wanted to say that she didn't want to know, that knowledge would be a complication she would prefer to be without.

"Was?" she heard herself saying questioningly.

"Well, she's been missing for long enough."

"Missing!" Involuntarily Sarah looked at Tim and saw that he was watching Mrs. Foster intently. His face looked sharpened, as if the skin had tightened over it. She wondered what concerned him so much now about Lexie Adams when last night he had been completely indifferent. Or had he?

"Yes," said Mrs. Foster, cutting her cake into precise little squares. "Goodness knows what's happened to her. The story is she went away with a man, but I'm guessing he strangled her or tipped her over a cliff."

She put one of the squares into her mouth and chewed neatly, with obvious pleasure. Then she looked up with her bright little eyes, eager to savour Sarah's shock.

"That would be rather untidy," Tim murmured. "Who was the man she went away with?"

"They never found out. Such a to-do there was. Didn't you see it in the paper, Sarah? They gave her a paragraph because she was just coming into prominence on the stage."

"We took *The Times*," Sarah said, since she seemed to be expected to say something. "You wouldn't notice a missing actress much in *The Times*."

"Well, there it was," Mrs. Foster went on. "The girl vanished and the only evidence was that of the porter of the flats where she lived. He said he'd seen her go out with a man. He'd seen this particular man with her on several occasions. But none of her friends knew anything about him. She must have been living a double life. Not that she explained anything even then. She just wrote a note to her manager saying she'd decided to take a long holiday and was breaking her contract. Just like that. I thought it looked decidedly fishy, but Oliver said something about the course of true love."

"We haven't ordered your tea," said Tim to Sarah. He beckoned to the waitress.

Sarah leaned across the table.

"I don't follow all this, Mrs. Foster. Lexie was Rachel Massey's friend, and Rachel, I gather, was in the States when she disappeared, or chose love and obscurity, or whatever it was. But what has it to do with the Fosters?"

Mrs. Foster's eyes glinted.

"The reason for that is a little surprising. Tim, I hope you won't mind this, but it's life, the kind you won't find down with your penguins. Lexie Adams was Eliot's friend—" she winked with rich appreciation, "that kind of friend, I should think."

"Eliot's!" Sarah exclaimed.

"Yes. That surprises you, doesn't it? You'd think it would be Oliver, wouldn't you? He's the one the ladies notice. But no, it was Eliot who found her. Apparently they began with music in common. Eliot used to visit her a lot. That was before Oliver had married and we were all in the house in Pimlico. It wasn't nearly such a nice house as Oliver has now—dark and rather damp, and in a poor neighbourhood. But it was the best we could do then—my husband died when the boys were young and we'd had a struggle."

"And this was while Mary was alive?" Tim said. His voice again had that disconcerting grimness that made him two separate people.

"Yes, of course. I said we were in the Pimlico house and it was the Kensington house she died in. She knew nothing of it, poor child, until afterwards when rumours, about Lexie's private life were made public. But it wasn't Eliot Lexie went off with. The porter swore to that. He was most explicit." She helped herself to another square of cake, and went on in her rich voice, "He could have been lying, of course. Some people were suspicious. Her family even called the police in. But they never traced her. And of course Eliot had nothing to do with it. My younger son may be a failure, but he's no bigamist."

Sarah couldn't help wondering how Mrs. Foster would have behaved had she really believed her son had abducted a woman. She almost thought the old woman would enjoy it as a sensation. She would have appreciated the discovery that Eliot was not completely spineless after all. Spinelessness and a failure to appreciate the joys of the gourmet were, to her, the chief sins. It was small wonder that Oliver was the favourite son.

But Eliot involved with another woman before his wife's death, Eliot who was posing as the bereaved inconsolable husband—that was another thing. . . .

Sarah, deep in her shocked thoughts, was aware of Tim indicating her untasted cup of tea. She looked up to see his narrow mocking eyes.

"Don't let a small thing like a murder put you off your tea," he was saying.

"Tim, don't be idiotic. She wasn't murdered. She merely disappeared. Hundreds of people disappear, a lot of them purposely."

"Yes," said old Mrs. Foster in her rich relishing voice.

"Lexie's disappearance was made to look like being on purpose with that letter and all. But if you ask me she was murdered. Those kind always are."

Sarah pushed back her chair, feeling distaste not so much for the story as for Mrs. Foster's relish in it. As she moved Jennie came in from outside.

"It's starting to rain, Miss Stacey. Shouldn't we go home?"

Sarah gladly seized the chance to go.

"Yes, we must. We'll run. Goodbye, Mrs. Foster. Goodbye, Tim."

Tim grinned and said imperturbably,

"I'll come with you. Jennie can get under my coat."

Mrs. Foster settled herself comfortably in her chair.

"I shall stay here until the shower is over. I'll see you both at dinner."

Before they were half-way across the park the rain had stopped and Jennie slipped out of the shelter of Tim's coat and ran on ahead. Then Tim tucked his arm in Sarah's in a completely possessive way.

"There's no need to hold my arm," she said stiffly. "It's not dark. I don't have to be supported and we're not lovers."

"Let's come out," he said gaily, "when all three things are true."

The autumn trees made a yellow light against the grey sky. The air was sharp and clean, with a feeling of cool water in it. Sarah thought of the charming house in Kensington Walk, of the bowls of flowers in the hall and lounge, of the firelight on the walls, and the air of graciousness and ease. She thought of Venetia with her large blue eyes and uncertain air and beautiful clothes. And Oliver, good-natured, amusing and tolerant, with his voice that could be as fascinatingly soft as the crooning of doves. And of the sound of Eliot's music.

None of that could be connected with an actress mysteriously disappearing or with a pregnant woman accidentally falling down a steep flight of stairs. It was out of character. It didn't belong in that house.

"Tim," she said abruptly, speaking for the first time, "I'm so sorry you had to find out that way."

He looked down at her—she hadn't realised the satisfaction

of walking with a man tall enough to look down at her—even if it were only Tim Royle.

"Find out what way?" he asked. His voice was mild.

"About Eliot, of course. Poor Mary, it must have been a dreadful shock to her. With the baby coming, too. I mean, that's a time when a wife would expect her husband to be quite faithful. She must have been very sensitive. And she must have loved him very much."

"So what?" said Tim. There was a new note in his voice that Sarah didn't choose to hear.

"Well, you did wonder how her fall could have been an accident. Obviously it wasn't."

She was startled to feel Tim gripping her arm. His face was taut, his eyes narrowed and fierce. He was all at once the other person, the one she didn't know at all and of whom she was a little afraid.

"Never let me hear you say that again," he told her. "Mary didn't kill herself. She was my sister. I knew her as well as one person can know another. She wasn't the kind to go out of this world leaving one child and taking another with her. She was quiet and sweet and soft, but she had guts. Do you understand?"

Sarah dragged her arm from his grip. Her own temper was rising. She hadn't meant to insult his sister and he knew she hadn't.

"I'm sorry if I've jumped to conclusions," she said stiffly. "It seemed obvious to me. Then what do you think? That someone pushed her?" She spoke scathingly, for a moment not remembering that she was talking about a real person whom Tim had loved, but some theoretical character.

She wasn't prepared for Tim's reply.

"Perhaps," he said softly between hard lips. "Perhaps."


# V

IT ALL, Sarah thought afterwards, seemed to be a tissue of suppositions, Mrs. Hopkins' unfounded and baseless predictions,

Eliot's apparent fear of what Rachel Massey might discover, Tim's startling suspicions about Mary's death. She personally would refuse to read anything significant into any of the events. Eliot had a guilty conscience, his illicit love affair having been dragged into unpleasant publicity. That was all.

When they got in, Petunia told Sarah that Mrs. Oliver wanted to see her. She looked as if she wanted to make further confidences, but Sarah, not waiting to hear them, went straight up to Venetia's room. There she found Venetia sitting on the stool in front of the mirror dressed in her new negligee and brushing her hair.

"Oh, Sarah," she said, "are you good at new styles of hair dressing? I should go into town and get mine done, but I don't feel equal to it since we're going out tonight. Did you hear about it, by the way? Oliver's taking us all to the theatre. You're to come, of course. And I believe he's asked your aunt, too. He says we should get acquainted, being next-door neighbours."

"How kind of him!" Sarah exclaimed.

"Oh, Oliver's always kind," Venetia said casually. "Being married to a writer isn't all fun, but it has its compensations. Look what he's just given me."

In her palm sparkled a pair of diamond ear-rings.

"How perfectly lovely," Sarah said. "How lucky you are."

Venetia put them back in their box.

"I have a weakness for pretty things. Oliver knows and he spoils me. I expect it's very bad for me."

She lifted her large soft blue eyes and Sarah thought that there was something very attractive about her. No wonder Oliver liked to buy her expensive presents.

"I can't do anything but a simple hair style," Sarah said.

"That doesn't matter, so long as it shows my ear-rings to the best advantage. Oliver would be disappointed if I don't show them off." She smiled then, her lips curving slowly, her eyes secret. Was she thinking of Oliver's caress when he had given her the gift?

Sarah picked up the hairbrush and began to brush Venetia's hair rather violently. The world was divided into two classes, the women who were given things and the ones who had to buy them for themselves. She belonged to the latter and she liked it. She didn't have to say thank you to anyone.

"Is Eliot coming tonight?" she asked.

"Oh, yes, Oliver insists. He says Eliot's getting morbid. Poor boy, I'm awfully fond of him, I do what I can, but one gets a little impatient with him all the same. It's not fair to the other people going round with a long face all the time. Now he and Oliver are having a row because Oliver's invited Rachel Massey to come with us. She arrived in London today. She and Burgess are coming here for drinks before we leave. I really can't think why Eliot is taking this attitude. He's growing into a recluse."

Sarah looped up the long shining strands of Venetia's hair into ringlets. She had come here to be Jennie's governess, not Venetia's maid. No, that wasn't true. She had come because her long nose scented a drama and she had never been able to keep it out of trouble. Now the drama was developing because an actress from America was being introduced into the household. What old trouble was Rachel Massey stirring up?

"Who else is coming tonight?" she asked.

"Oh, Oliver's mother. Isn't she a frightful old woman? But one has to put up with her, of course. Burgess Reid, we owe him a party and he can partner Rachel. Tim, of course. How do you like Tim, Sarah?"

"He's—oh, I suppose—"

Venetia gave her light pretty laugh.

"Say no more. He is quite odd, isn't he? But being Mary's brother we have to be nice to him. Never mind, he'll be off to the South Pole again before long. And you can bear him tonight, can't you?"

"Of course," Sarah said politely.

"Then there's your aunt. I'm longing to meet her. Oliver says she's quite adorable. Sarah, that style looks wonderful. How clever you are. Oliver will rave over it."

Sarah was aware that Venetia was perfectly well able to do her own hair, but she had wanted to show off the ear-rings. Now that was done Sarah could go. She went out, planning to hurry up to Jennie. But again she was detained by the telephone ringing and Petunia calling to her that she was wanted.

It was Aunt Florence.

"Sarah, imagine me being included in your party tonight. That was Oliver. Isn't he a charming man? He just walked in as if he'd known me all his life. And he spoke most highly of you."

"Did he?" Sarah murmured, pleased.

"What are you going to wear, dear?" came Aunt Florence's voice.

"Oh, my grey. It's all I have, Aunt Florence."

"It's very becoming dear, but you ought to get some more dresses. You ought to become more clothes conscious now."

"Darling, I'm only the governess. Grey is appropriate."

"No, indeed, according to Oliver you're much more than the governess. You must dress to suit these occasions. I shall wear my black velvet and my diamonds."

More diamonds! Sarah said helplessly, "But, Aunt Florence it's a very small party."

"Definitely my diamonds," came Aunt Florence's stubborn voice.

When Sarah, dressed for the theatre, went downstairs she found, to her surprise, that Eliot was playing the piano in the drawing-room. Venetia was listening to him. There was no one else in the room. As he played he seemed to relax, the tautness going out of his face so that it had an empty receptive look as if he had achieved the ability to live entirely in this pool of quiet lovely sound. When he stopped Venetia said warmly,

"That was beautiful, Eliot."

The warmth in her voice brought, surprisingly, an answering warmth to Eliot's face.

"I'm glad you liked it."

"But I always like your playing. I wish you would do it down here more often instead of shutting yourself upstairs. No one uses this piano except Oliver, and he just for his ridiculous strumming. Unless, of course, you invite me up to the attic to hear you."

"Would you care to do that?"

"But of course. I get rather bored with you and Oliver both

shut away working, and now Sarah has Jennie. I'd sit very quietly."

Sarah felt uncomfortable before the glow in Eliot's eyes. Venetia was only doing this because she was kind and a little bored and occupationless. But Eliot, frighteningly alone, with no common ground between himself and his brother, and unaware of how to approach his own child, was in a dangerous emotional state. It was perfectly simple to see that. He could so easily misconstrue Venetia's kindness, and when he discovered his mistake the result could be tragic.

Before he could say more, however, there was a bustle in the hall, the sound of voices, and Oliver appeared at the door. He was dressed in evening clothes and he looked very handsome and obviously in the best of spirits. He turned to say something to someone out of sight, then put out his hand and led into the room a tall dark-haired young woman wearing a mink coat over a black dinner gown.

"Let me present," he said dramatically, "a very famous and beautiful lady. Miss Rachel Massey."

"Hullo, everybody," Rachel said in a warm vibrant voice.

She was very good-looking and perfectly at ease. Her strong features, prominent nose and wide mouth were assets for which any actress would be grateful. In that first glance at her Sarah could read both character and ruthlessness in her face.

Oliver went on to perform the introductions singly. Everyone had come in now, Tim and Burgess Reid and Aunt Florence and old Mrs. Foster. In the buzz of conversation Sarah only heard odd sentences spoken in Oliver's hearty voice.

"She hasn't read the part yet. Of course, one doesn't expect miracles, but one hopes for them. Tim, you may have something in common with Miss Massey. She loves sea travel. And this is my brother, Eliot. . . ."

Sarah turned from her conversation with Aunt Florence to watch them. She saw Eliot's pale tense face grow even paler as Rachel said in her warm voice,

"I've been wanting to meet you. You knew my friend, Lexie Adams, didn't you? You know that's the queerest thing, the way she went off without a word. I believe there's something phoney about it and I'm determined to find out what happened while I'm over here. I'm counting on you to help me."

Sarah saw Eliot's tight lips move. Then old Mrs. Foster's raucous voice sounded above the rest.

"Lexie Adams, did you say? You're not expecting to find her alive, are you? She's murdered, sure as fate."

The play was Gertrude Lawrence's latest, and Sarah had never seen her act. She should have been entranced, but other things kept niggling at her. Jennie's question as she had tucked her in, "Miss Stacey, did you remember to ask Uncle Oliver about my party?" indicating for the first time that after all Jennie was interested in the party; the dramatically handsome pair Oliver and Venetia in evening clothes made; also how unexpectedly distinguished Tim looked and how unexpectedly quiet he was, as if he were working out a problem; Eliot's taut controlled face as Rachel had talked to him about Lexie Adams, his agony kept beneath the surface; and all the time how the diamonds, Venetia's ear-rings and Aunt Florence's brooch and ring with its single superb stone sparkled, like tiny mocking stars, to keep one's mind from being absorbed in the play.

When they arrived home the table in the dining-room was lighted by candles in branching crystal candlesticks, and the flickering light danced on the silver and made wavering pools on the polished surface of the table. There was a scent of burning logs and roses. It seemed to Sarah as if they were still in the unreal and make-believe atmosphere of the theatre.

The ladies went upstairs, and Sarah coming down first found Oliver standing alone in front of the fire.

"I had something to ask you for Jennie," she said, seizing her opportunity. "She would like a party, and I think it would be a good thing for her. She should have some friends. She's—"

Oliver interrupted her with a humorous glint in his eye.

"Now, Sarah, don't start bringing out all your arguments before you know whether I'm going to refuse or not. As it happens I think you're entirely right. Jennie should have a party."

Venetia and Eliot came into the room just then and Venetia,

catching the last words, said interestedly, "What's this about a party?" She came over to Oliver and tucked her hand inside his arm. Her cheeks were flushed and she looked excited and happy.

"Sarah's been saying Jennie should have one," Oliver explained.

"Oh! Somehow she's not the sort of child one associates with parties? Who would she ask?"

"I think we could soon find some children," Sarah said.

"What do you think, Eliot? You're her father." Oliver's voice was perfectly genial but—was it Sarah's imagination—she seemed to be aware of a contemptuous note in it. Or was that because of the quick resentful flash that darkened Eliot's face.

"Since I imagine the expense of the party will be yours," he said, "the arrangements had better be yours, also."

"Oh, come now," said Oliver. "I'm more than happy to give the child a party."

"Of course we are, Eliot," Venetia said. She smiled her sweet kind smile. Eliot muttered something and turned away. But it was true, Sarah noticed, with a feeling almost of fear, that Venetia's kindness affected him deeply. Sympathy was dangerous to him in his melancholic condition. He was ready to fall in love with the first good-looking woman who noticed him. And that woman, unfortunately, was his own sister-in-law.

Rachel Massey came in then and Oliver began pouring drinks, talking in his hearty paternal voice all the time.

"You're looking very grand tonight, Sarah. Did you enjoy the play? Gertrude Lawrence has got something, hasn't she? But wait till they see our Rachel."

"Mrs. Hopkins wants to know when we sit down to dinner," came Tim's voice. "She says in another five minutes the turkey will be spoilt, but nothing can prevent it because she foretold such an event this morning. And one can't alter the leaves."

"You mean tea leaves?" said Rachel. "You mean she reads cups? What an enchanting person she sounds."

"Oliver! Eliot!" The raucous cry came from the doorway. Old Mrs. Foster was standing there, the jewelled comb in her hair quivering importantly. Behind her Aunt Florence, obviously distressed, was willing her not to make an announcement.

"Say nothing," she whispered.

"Say nothing, indeed! When there's been a theft? Oliver, Miss Stacey has had her diamond ring stolen."

Oliver took a step forward.

"What! Is this true, Miss Stacey?"

Aunt Florence twisted her hands together in distress.

"I'm sure it's just lost."

"I should think so," said Venetia practically. "Stolen indeed! What nonsense. There's no one in this house would steal a ring."

Mrs. Foster looked put out about the calm reception of her statement.

"Well, it's disappeared, anyway," she muttered. "Explain that, will you?"

Tim came forward.

"Where did you take your ring off, Miss Stacey?"

"I took it off to wash," Aunt Florence answered agitatedly. "Then I went in to peep at Jennie. I hope you don't mind, Sarah. If she had been awake I was going to talk to her for a minute. But she was asleep. Then I remembered I had left my ring in the bathroom so I went to get it."

"And it had gone?"

"Yes. But it must be somewhere. Please don't bother about it now."

"Perhaps it dropped on the floor and rolled into a corner," suggested Rachel. "Let's all go up and look."

"We've looked thoroughly already," old Mrs. Foster said. "The ring's been stolen, I tell you."

"Mother, please!" Oliver said firmly. "Of course the ring hasn't been stolen. It's a misunderstanding. Are you sure you didn't absentmindedly slip it in your bag, Miss Stacey?"

"I shall look again," Aunt Florence was perfectly courteous, but now Sarah detected a slight note of coldness in her voice. "I'm really quite sure it isn't there."

"The servants should be questioned," said Eliot abruptly.

Sarah was sure neither Mrs. Hopkins nor Petunia had been

upstairs in that short interval. So if the ring were really stolen it must have been done by someone in this room. Suddenly she was realising that for the first time and the knowledge was a little horrifying. Her eyes went over the group; Eliot—what would he want with a ring, with both wife and lover dead; Tim with his nonchalance; Oliver disturbed but not yet seriously worried; Burgess Reid expressing well-bred disfavour; Rachel sauve and handsome; Venetia showing the concern of a hostess at a misadventure in her house.

"That Petunia should be questioned first," insisted old Mrs. Foster. "I don't like the look of that girl, and she goes about with a bus conductor. He probably spends all his money on football pools and can't afford to buy her a ring."

As if she had heard her name at that moment Petunia appeared at the door. She instantly sensed something was wrong and her mouth hung open a moment before she spoke.

"Please, sir, Mrs. Hopkins says if you wait another five minutes—"

"There won't be no dinner," Tim finished pleasantly. "What about it, Oliver? Hadn't we better eat?"

Oliver ignored him.

"Petunia," he said, "have you been up to the bathroom on the first floor or have you seen anyone else go up within the last ten minutes?"

"Why, no, sir. I've been in the kitchen with Mrs. Hopkins. She can bear me out. Except for just as you all arrived. Why—" Her voice quavered. She looked round helplessly. "Is there something wrong?"

"Please!" Aunt Florence interrupted beseechingly. "Please, Oliver, don't bother any more about it."

"Bother!" exclaimed old Mrs. Foster. She was a warhorse hearing the guns. "If you ask me it's becoming a matter for the police."

"Don't be absurd, mother," said Venetia with surprising presence of mind. "Sarah will go upstairs and have a quick look. Won't you, Sarah? And the rest of us will start dinner."

Thankful to get out of the room Sarah nodded and went.

Of course there was no sign of the ring in the bathroom. She hadn't expected there would be, though she hadn't begun to

59

think of an alternative solution. She searched the stairs carefully and the passage to Jennie's room.

Jennie was sound asleep. Sarah could hear her quiet breathing as she stood at the door. There was a distant roar of buses along Kensington Road and someone's footsteps on the street without. But no sound came from downstairs. Were they all eating their turkey in a well-bred way while the roses, too late and delicate for the warm room, shed their petals, and the candles winked on Venetia's diamonds, and Oliver's benevolent good-humoured glance went over his guests.

Someone at that well-ordered dignified dinner table had Aunt Florence's diamond ring because it was impossible to suspect either Mrs. Hopkins or Petunia. One of the party was a thief.

Sarah felt an arm round her waist. She started violently.

"Hullo, little one," said Tim affectionately.

Little one! "If you think that's funny——" she began indignantly.

"A term of endearment only. You're a fine woman, Sarah. If only you'd love me a little."

"Tim, for heaven's sake! You don't even like me."

"On the contrary I admire you a great deal."

"Well, anyway, this is neither the time nor place for a sentimental conversation. Something serious has happened, and why aren't you having dinner, anyway?"

"I've come up to help you. Any luck?"

Sarah said slowly, "Did you expect me to have?" and somehow was grateful for the complete sobriety of his reply,

"No. Frankly I didn't. Sarah, there's something odd going on. I don't particularly like it."

"What do you mean? Something besides Aunt Florence losing her ring?" She was almost afraid to put that question.

Tim nodded. When his face was lean and serious like that she respected him a great deal more. But he had a slightly dangerous look which surely the circumstances didn't warrant. He was getting an obsession about his sister's death.

She tried to laugh.

"Aren't you just being a little superstitious? Because your sister died here you think the house is bad."

He didn't appear to hear her. He was pursuing a thought of his own.

"There's a tension. Aren't you aware of it? No one's happy. Eliot looks on the verge of melancholia. Venetia, beneath all her poise, is as nervous as a kitten. She takes refuge in ill-health. The old lady drugs herself with food. And you've seen what they've done to Jennie."

"Oliver?" Sarah questioned automatically.

"Oliver may just have an innocent happy nature—or else his ways are devious also. There's something."

"It's tied up with that mystery about Lexie Adams," Sarah said involuntarily.

Tim nodded. "You may be right. Tomorrow I'll do a little research."


# VI

BEFORE breakfast in the morning Aunt Florence telephoned Sarah.

Sarah had been up early because at four-thirty Eliot had begun playing love songs and was still doing so. Even down on the ground floor she could hear the faint gentle sound of the piano. When she learned to sleep through these disturbances and read no significance into them—such as the type of music Eliot played being a guide to the state of his mind—she would be much better. Just at present, from strain and lack of sleep she had reached the state of imagining things and wondering if the satisfying of her curiosity was worth the sacrifice of her health.

Aunt Florence probably hadn't slept either. Sarah said,

"Good morning, darling. How are you? Did you manage to get some sleep last night?"

"Sarah," came Aunt Florence's voice on a disturbingly sober note, "you may not believe it, but I have my ring back."

"What, did you find you had it after all?"

"No, dear. It was left here this morning."

"By whom?"

"Oliver, from the description Bertha gave. She said the man

61

simply handed her an envelope with the ring in it, and said to apologise to me for the worry I had had. That's all."

"How odd!" said Sarah.

"What am I to do about it?"

"There's nothing you can do."

"But shouldn't I thank someone?"

"I don't know," said Sarah slowly. She looked round to make sure that she was alone. "It almost seems as if questions might be embarrassing."

"That's what I thought, too. Sarah, there's something queer—"

"I know," Sarah agreed quickly.

"You must stay and find out what it is, dear. For Jennie's sake."

She added that about Jennie, but Sarah knew Aunt Florence's curiosity was almost as great as her own. At this stage she wouldn't have been able to bear not finding out what was going on.

"Of course I'll stay," said Sarah, "if I can stand enough sleepless nights."

She started as she realised that Oliver was at the door. She wondered how much he had overheard. He was smiling his familiar friendly smile. He looked bright-eyed and handsome as if he had slept well.

"Good morning, Sarah. Did I hear you say Eliot's playing had kept you awake? With all due respect for his genius we can't let that go on happening. I'll speak to him."

"No, please don't," Sarah said quickly. She had an intuition that to take Eliot's playing in the night from him would be dangerous. It was apparently his only form of escape. "It won't disturb me when I'm used to it." Then she added flatly, "Aunt Florence says she has her ring."

"Yes, I believe she has." Was he going to say no more than that? He behaved as if it were no more than a hair ribbon Aunt Florence had lost.

"But—did you find it on the floor after all?"

Oliver laid his hand on her shoulder.

"We'll say no more about it, shall we?" he observed pleasantly. "Your aunt is gracious enough to understand how upset

Venetia and I were at having such a thing happen in our house. Where's Jennie? Are we all ready for breakfast?"

Sarah realised, to her chagrin, that she was to hear no more. Whom was Oliver protecting? Or had the ring been on the floor all the time?

Well, if Oliver expected her to show curiosity she would disappoint him. She went out of the room saying over her shoulder, "How's Venetia this morning?"

"Oh, she's not so well. Her cough's troubling her a little. But she's coming down to breakfast. It's more cheerful for her than staying up in bed alone."

Venetia did come to breakfast, but Oliver had been right when he said she didn't look so well. There were hollows under her eyes as if she hadn't slept and the rouge stood out on her cheeks. But when Sarah asked her if she felt all right she said, "Yes, very well, thank you," and began to toy with a piece of toast as if she had no appetite.

Tim came in with his usual cheerful nonsense, but for once it didn't irritate Sarah. She was grateful for something to break the uncomfortable tension.

"Where are you taking me today, Jennie?" he asked. "Shall we ask Miss Stacey's permission to go to the waxworks, or would you prefer something more morbid?"

"Jennie's going to have a party shortly," Oliver chose to announce in a jolly voice. "She has to get a party frock. Perhaps you'd like to take her shopping, Venetia?"

Venetia looked up. Sarah fancied she winced slightly.

"Oh, not today, Oliver."

"And why not today?" Oliver enquired cheerfully.

"I really don't feel up to it."

"You don't mean you're still worrying about last night's episode? But that's all cleared up, I told you. We can now forget about it, thanks to the generous view Miss Stacey took of the affair. Venetia's foolish enough to have let it give her a bad night. Of course, it's an unpleasant thing to have happen in one's house even when the explanation is perfectly innocent."

Venetia's large tired eyes were on Oliver. She began to cough a little in a strained way. She did seem rather ill this morning. Had Oliver told her anything of how the ring had been found? Did he enjoy keeping people in the dark?

Sarah realised suddenly that Eliot was standing at the door watching, his face like a cat's, thin and concentrated. He's a little queer, Sarah thought uneasily. Heaven knew what he might do if he had fallen in love with Venetia.

"Miss Stacey!" That was Jennie's urgent whisper. "Miss Stacey, am I really to have a party?"

Sarah nodded.

"But it's not even my birthday."

Tim caught the whisper and leaned across the table.

"It's mine next Wednesday. You have the party and I'll grow the year older. How's that?"

Jennie looked up at Sarah. Her face was eager. She looked almost like a normal child.

"Could I, Miss Stacey? Could I have my party on Uncle Tim's birthday?"

"Ask Aunt Venetia, dear."

"Could I, Aunt Venetia?"

"Next Wednesday," Venetia said vaguely. "Why, I daresay. Sarah, will you—"

Sarah said, "Yes, I'll arrange everything." She understood now that Venetia had moods, she was a little neurotic, she couldn't take things in her stride the way Oliver could.

Then Eliot came in. He hadn't said anything and remained silent as he poured coffee and sat down. His face had its usual brooding look. He didn't look like the kind of person who would have been playing love songs half the night.

Jennie wanted to go and tell Mrs. Hopkins about her party. She slipped out to the kitchen and burst out with the news.

"Mrs. Hopkins, I'm to have a party on Uncle Tim's birthday next week, and I'm to get a new dress, and will you make me a cake?"

Mrs. Hopkins's kindly eyes met Sarah's over Jennie's head. They were full of approval.

"Indeed I'll make you a cake."

"I've never had a party before," Jennie went on. "Miss Stacey thought of it. Mrs. Hopkins, will you see what it says in your cup about my party?"

"Well, now, dear—" Mrs. Hopkins was obviously reluctant. "I've finished my tea. I've poured the leaves out."

"Have some more," begged Jennie. "But please!" She was dancing on her thin legs, her eyes were sparkling. Sarah had never seen her so animated. Neither had Mrs. Hopkins, for reluctantly she lifted the teapot and poured another cup of tea.

"I swore last night I'd never do this again," she said to Sarah.

"Neither you should," said Sarah. "Not after the things you've already been telling Jennie. Death in the house and things like that. As if the arrangement of tea-leaves shows the future."

"Well, I saw about the turkey getting spoilt last night, and that nice man for you who'll come along, never fear. It's more than the leaves, dear," she went on earnestly. "It's something that comes over me. I see things perfectly plain as if I'm an instrument." For a moment her eyes were curiously opaque. Then she said briskly, "Don't let it worry you. If it's to come it'll come no matter what. You can't change destiny."

"Mrs. Hopkins, don't waste time talking," Jennie said impatiently. "See what the leaves say about my party. Please!"

Mrs. Hopkins looked at Sarah. She shook her head helplessly.

"I can't disappoint her, can I? I daresay it won't hurt for this once."

Sarah didn't answer. She found herself suddenly tense as she watched Mrs. Hopkins drink the tea, telling herself the whole thing was nonsense, that there was no possible way of telling the future by the way the tea-leaves lay in the bottom of a cup. Though of course it wasn't the leaves Mrs. Hopkins read. It was the way that staring at them seemed to make her project herself into the future.

Mrs. Hopkins tipped the dregs of the tea out and turned the cup carefully in the curved palms of her hands. Jennie hopped on the other leg, her face shining.

"Well, then," said Mrs. Hopkins portentously.

Don't! Sarah begged silently, then was glad she hadn't spoken the word aloud. What a fool she was growing, letting Mrs. Hopkins's superstitions worry her.

Mrs. Hopkins stared at the interior of the cup. She seemed to hold it interminably.

"Well, what?" Jennie demanded impatiently. "What do you see?"

"Just wait." Mrs. Hopkin's voice was curiously thick. She held up one plump hand. To her dismay Sarah saw that it was trembling.

"Stop it!" she whispered then, and now her voice was audible. "Stop it, Mrs. Hopkins."

Mrs. Hopkins put the cup down clumsily.

"But you're not saying anything," Jennie said. "What did you see?"

"I saw you in a white frock, very sweet and lacy, like a little princess."

Jennie gave a skip.

"And am I having a nice party?"

"Very nice, dear. Now run along."

"Yes, run upstairs," said Sarah. "Get out your books. I'll be up in a moment."

"Miss Stacey, I must be going to have the party if Mrs. Hopkins saw the dress. Do you think Aunt Venetia will buy me a white dress?"

"I expect so. Run along."

Jennie went, skipping light-heartedly, and Mrs. Hopkins said feebly, as if she had to say something. "I've never seen her like that before, so full of life. You're good for her, Miss Stacey."

"Maybe," said Sarah absently. She went across to the table and picked up the cup Mrs. Hopkins had set down. It had nothing in it but a meaningless sprinkle of leaves, nothing to make Mrs. Hopkins tremble. The woman had fancies, that was all. And morbid ones at that. "Mrs. Hopkins, what did you really see in the cup?"

"Never mind, love."

"But something frightened you. What possibly could in this?" She pointed to the leaves contemptuously. "You're letting your imagination run away with you."

"It's not the leaves, love. It's something that comes over me."

"Then what came over you this morning?"

"I can't explain. A sort of darkness. There was Jennie in a white dress and—and—" Mrs. Hopkins clutched Sarah's arm in a painful grip. There was perspiration on her forehead. "Oh, I said I wouldn't do this again, didn't I? It was Jennie who inveigled me into it. A child's party, what could be more harmless, I thought."

"Jennie in a white dress," Sarah said urgently. "What else? You've got to tell me what else."

"I can't. I can't, I tell you. I don't know. Just a sort of darkness." Her grip on Sarah's arm grew more painful. "But don't let her have that party, Miss Stacey."

Sarah at last extricated herself from the hard grip. She was trembling a little herself, she realised. So foolish—an old woman with a teacup—and the dark mystery it contained.

"I think you need another cup of tea, Mrs. Hopkins. You mustn't take these things so seriously."

"But don't I always see them right? Didn't I see death before poor Mr. Eliot's wife had that fall? Didn't I see Mr. Tim's visit long before they'd even heard from him. And then you with your red head. Who was to know Jennie would get a governess with red hair?"

"I think," said Sarah a little unsteadily, "your resolution to not read your cup any more is a very good one. It's too upsetting."

"It is that. But it's getting almost that I have to. Do you see what I mean? If things could be prevented by my giving warnings—"

But by now Sarah was getting a grip on herself.

"What things?" she asked. "Nothing's going to happen. You're letting your imagination run away with you."

Mrs. Hopkins shook her head slowly.

"I wish I could believe that. But I can't. And if you'll take my advice you'll make it up to Jennie some way, but you won't let her have that party."

Sarah had made a decision to set Jennie a lesson that morning, and then slip out for an hour on a private errand. Oliver might not have approved of the liberty she was taking, but she could neither ask his permission nor explain.

67

She took a bus over to Pimlico. She had a deep curiosity about the house where the Fosters used to live when Eliot married Mary and Oliver was still unmarried. She wanted to see how much they had risen in the world. Old Mrs. Foster had given her the address, 57 Birchell Street. You walked a couple of blocks from the bus stop and it was the second house from the corner of Northumberland Street.

It was not a very good neighbourhood, consisting mostly of dingy boarding houses and grimy-windowed flats. The uniform grey was depressing. None of the houses had seen paint for a very long time. Scarcely had that thought come to Sarah when she realised that one of them was receiving a coat of paint now, and it was, oddly enough, the house at 57 Birchell Street. Workmen's ladders were out and the new white of the walls was in startling contrast to the surrounding drabness.

She stood still to watch, and a hand was laid heavily on her shoulder.

"Two minds with but a single thought," came Tim's voice.

"Tim! What on earth are you doing here?" Sarah snapped, still unnerved by his method of indicating his presence.

"The same as you, I should think. Poking my inquisitive nose in. I've come to look for the writing on the wall. Let's go over the place, shall we?"

"How can we?"

"Easy. Come and I'll show you."

Tucking his arm into hers in a proprietary way he led her up to the house. There was only one workman visible, and he was at the top of his ladder painting the second-floor window frames. The bright red of the sills looked gay and bold and defiant in the dreary street, like the painted lips of a girl among the dim tired faces of old women.

"Hi!" yelled Tim.

The man looked down, holding a paint pot that dripped crimson.

"Is the front door unlocked?"

The man took a few steps down the ladder.

"Who are you?"

"Mr. Oliver Foster gave us an order to view. We hope we're the new tenants."

"Didn't know they were letting tenants see the place yet. It's been empty long enough. Nigh on two year, they tell me."

"Well, isn't that wicked, with the housing shortage the way it is," Tim said in a shocked voice. "My wife and I have been desperate, I don't mind telling you. Especially with the prospect of an increase in the family."

"*Tim!*" Sarah whispered angrily.

"Lots of couples like you in that position," the workman commented. "The old world's had it, if you ask me. Guess it's all right for you to go in. Fred's inside somewhere. He'll tell you the way round."

"Thank you," Tim called. "Come along, darling. Mind the step."

Once inside Sarah jerked her arm away from him.

"Tim, you fool! I believe you did that deliberately."

"Well, it got us in, didn't it."

"There would have been other ways."

"Maybe. I liked that way." He looked at her with his bright merciless eyes. "Didn't you?"

"Believe it or not, I didn't."

"Ah, darling, what are you? A child hater?"

He said that as seriously as if she were, in fact, carrying his child. How utterly asinine he was! As if she would ever— Without finishing her thought, which had brought the hot colour to her cheeks, she said sharply, "Well, let's look at the place now we are in."

It proved to be as dreary inside as its outside appearance indicated. Looking at the dark rooms and darker passageways Sarah thought briefly of Jennie living her babyhood in these gloomy surroundings. She thought of Eliot's wife Mary trying to brighten the rooms and make them warm and homelike. More disturbingly she thought of old Mrs. Foster's heavy footsteps on these creaking stairs and how Mary must have winced at their approach. Followed by Tim she went from one room to another, wondering which one Oliver had chosen to write in, which one had been Mary's and Eliot's.

"How glad they must all have been to go over to Kensington," she said. "It was awfully generous of Oliver to shift his whole household."

"Generous of Venetia to have them, too," Tim commented. "The queer thing is I have a hunch Mary wouldn't have wanted to go."

"Because it wouldn't be her home?"

"She must surely have wanted some life with her husband alone."

"And he with her. And he doesn't like living over there now, that's pretty clear. I wonder what made him go."

"I wonder," said Tim. "Well, this isn't telling us much. Let's go out in the back garden."

The moment they opened the back door they heard the doves. There was a soot-grimed pear tree at the bottom of the narrow garden and in it the white and grey and beige-coloured doves fluttered and cooed.

"How odd!" Sarah murmured, fascinated.

There was a small toolshed in the garden and, at the sound of their steps, a man, apparently Fred, appeared.

"My name's Maxwell," said Tim. "This is my wife. We're prospective tenants."

"Ah!" said Fred. His hands were crusted grey with cement. "What's that shed you're working in?"

"Coal shed, tool shed, anything you like. It's been an old air-raid shelter enlarged. I'm putting in a cement floor. Beautiful job it is. You'll find it's a better floor than the kitchen has, ma'am."

"Really?" said Sarah. Her eyes were still on the fluttering shapes in the pear tree. "Where do all those doves come from?"

"Oh, there's a dove cote somewheres near. They fly over. Drive you crazy, wouldn't they, that crooning all the time. Like a blinking woman with a baby."

Eliot hated doves yet he had had the sound of them in his ears all day the whole summer long when he had lived here. Hadn't it driven him crazy?

"Come and see this floor," Fred invited. "Smooth as glass, it is."

Tim followed him, and presently Sarah, stepping over the long weeds, did so, too. The shed had bins for coal and a workbench, and plenty of room for gardening tools. It would be extremely useful to whatever tenants came here. But Sarah wasn't particularly interested in it, nor did she share the pride of Fred for the fine floor he had laid. While Tim poked about displaying an unusually keen interest in the shed's possibilities she stood listening to the doves and wondering why Oliver and Eliot had neglected for so long to get a tenant for the house. Was money so immaterial to them now?

"Do you know, it's funny," she said on the way home, "but I feel as if there's something I've overlooked."

"Are you thinking that the stairs are dark and treacherous enough there for Mary to fall down if she were inclined to go about falling downstairs?"

Sarah noticed the absence, at last, of badinage in his voice. She answered seriously, "No, it wasn't that. You might think I'm just being fanciful, but I feel it's got something to do with those doves."

# VII

SARAH decided not to go to Madame Tussauds with Jennie and Tim in the afternoon. After his disconcerting behaviour that morning the thought of a whole afternoon in his irritating presence was too much. So he and Jennie went off together, and she found herself with an afternoon on her hands. It had begun to rain, a fine cloudy drizzle that left the amber trees in the park like fog-bound lamps. The dahlias in the garden drooped. It seemed very silent without the sound of the pigeons in the trees. Where did they go on a wet day? Sarah wondered. To shelter in the nooks of ancient buildings round St. James's Park and Trafalgar Square? The silence they had left made it seem they had taken the summer with them.

She stood with her nose flattened against the window pane, watching the drifting rain and thinking a little wistfully of spring in English hedgerows. She could close her eyes and imagine herself back in a Sussex lane, the shoulder of a hill hunched behind her, the sky as fragile as a harebell flower over the green fields. She would go back as soon as it was spring. By then Jennie, she hoped, would be a more normal child and strong enough to go to school. Oliver's new play would be running. Tim most likely would be off on another expedition. Eliot would still be getting his queer lonely satisfaction from playing half the night in the attic, and Mrs. Hopkins would be having her alarums and excursions from imaginary calamities in her teacup.

Death in the house indeed! The only death likely to occur was that of old Mrs. Foster from overeating.

The rain continued to spin a grey web round the trees and the leaves to detach themselves with precision and drift through the mist to the ground.

Old Mrs. Foster came to the schoolroom to see what Sarah was doing.

"Where's Jennie?" she asked.

"She's gone with Tim to Madame Tussauds. I'm working on a curriculum." (That was Oliver's word—he seemed as naïvely pleased as a child with the important sound of it.)

Mrs. Foster stood breathing heavily, reluctant to go.

"Everyone's so unsociable. Venetia's shut in her room, Eliot's in his. Oliver has gone off out." Then she added inevitably, "Queer about that ring of your aunt's."

"Yes, very."

"Do you know what happened?"

"No, I'm afraid I don't."

"I don't either. They don't tell me anything. I expect it was that Rachel Massey. She was the only stranger here. Or it could have been Burgess Reid, though he's been here lots of times and nothing's ever gone missing before."

"I should think it was probably on the floor after all."

"Then why doesn't Oliver say so. No, he must be shielding that woman. These actresses. There'll be more trouble. Look what happened when Eliot was friendly with Lexie Adams. If Oliver takes a fancy to someone else I pity that poor spineless wife of his." Mrs. Foster chuckled richly, enjoying her flights of fancy. "And whatever you like to say to protect my sons—women always take the side of men—they are hiding something from me. Or why was Eliot saying this morning that he'd begun by telling Venetia."

"Telling her what?" Sarah asked involuntarily.

"You may well ask! It sounded like a dark secret from his voice. Oliver was joking with him light-heartedly, you know, but Eliot was in deadly earnest. Eliot never did see a joke. But whatever he was going to tell Venetia, Oliver wasn't worrying. He just said, 'Well, go ahead, old man, if it relieves your mind. Venetia will be entertained.'"

The old lady pouted. "I wish they'd entertain me with their secrets. They never tell me anything. Will you have a cup of tea with me, dear. I'll ring for it now."

Reluctantly Sarah was forced to accept the invitation. One had to be a little sorry for the lonely old woman.

But she tried not to linger too long in the cluttered room. Mrs. Foster had such a magpie collection of things that she could easily have been the culprit as far as Aunt Florence's ring was concerned. She might even suffer from lapses of memory and not know what she had done.

What Eliot had probably been going to tell Venetia was that he was in love with her.

Sarah said she would carry the tea-tray down herself to save Petunia coming up, and that was how she met Venetia coming down from the attic. Venetia heard her first and with a queer furtive movement backed against the wall. Then she realised she had been seen and came forward, her head averted. Sarah noticed at once that her face was curiously stiff, as if she were suffering from shock, and there were the damp marks of tears on her cheeks.

"I thought you'd gone with Tim and Jennie," she said in a breathless voice.

"No, I stayed in to do some work."

"I've been up with Eliot," she went on. Again her voice was too quick and glib. "He's been playing to me. I think he's lonely, always working by himself. He used to say he didn't want anyone up there, but now—"

She stopped, and Sarah saw that she was in a state of extreme tension. Had Eliot told her what he had threatened Oliver he would? If he had done so what was it? Something terrible, by Venetia's appearance now.

"He likes to have me," she finished flatly. "It's all right for him to have me."

Because he had found he loved her and her presence was not a deterrent but an inspiration? Or because he found it easier to share his secret with someone? Poor Eliot. Poor Venetia. But why poor Venetia? Why had that automatic thought come? Venetia surely did not need to be pitied. She was rich, pretty, Oliver's wife, mistress of a charming house. She was all that, and yet here she was running down the stairs in that furtive scared way, and there were tears on her cheeks.

Sarah couldn't let her go like that. She said, "You're worrying about something. Can't I help?"

But Venetia shook her head vehemently.

"There's nothing wrong. Really. It's just Eliot—I'm so sorry—no, no, you can't do anything!"

Oliver and Tim and Jennie arrived home together. They were all wet. Jennie's cheeks were scarlet with exercise and excitement. Tim was hunched in a raincoat, his face looking out with a kind of squirrel brightness from the high up-turned collar. Oliver had no hat and his hair was darkened with moisture. He shook his head vigorously, seeming to fill the hall.

"I've been walking in the park in the rain," he said in his hearty voice. "Just met these two off the bus. We're all as hungry as hunters. I'm going to have dinner put on half an hour because Rachel"s coming to discuss the play. She took the manuscript home to read last night."

"And if she doesn't like it?" Tim queried.

Oliver laughed.

"Then she won't take the part we're offering her, and that would be a blow to me. I wrote it with her in mind." But he was quite confident she would like it, his naïve pride showed that.

He went to the stairs and began bounding up them two at a time calling "Venetia! Where are you, darling? I'm home. I've finished work for the day."

Just as he was confident of his play he was confident of Venetia's welcome. But what would he say when he found her with tear-stained cheeks?

"Well, welcome us, Sarah darling," came Tim's voice. "Show us somebody likes us, too."

74

Sarah took off Jennie's wet coat and pinched her cheek gently. She didn't look at Tim. She didn't want to think how much fun it would be to welcome home a boisterous loving husband—someone like Oliver who deserved more than silly Venetia's tears.

"Miss Stacey, I wasn't frightened in the Chamber of Horrors. Uncle Tim said I would be, but I wasn't—very."

Tim held up a warning hand.

"Now, don't scold, Sarah. It wasn't my fault. I was quite content with cricketers and kings and queens, but she dragged me down the stairs. She's a one when she gets going."

Jennie wrinkled her brows.

"Why do some people kill other people, Miss Stacey?"

"That's hardly a question a demure little governess would know the answer to, Jennie," Tim answered. "A very common reason is because the person killed knows something the other person doesn't want told. The possession of dangerous knowledge is the reason. Not in every murder, mind you. But in a great many."

"Tim, stop that kind of talk at once," Sarah said sharply. "Jennie's likely enough already to have nightmares. Such a place to take her."

"You should have come with us," Tim said, unperturbed. "We had tea in a funny little restaurant underground in Baker Street. It was rather dirty and there was a cat sitting on one of the tables. Jennie thought him inferior to Hamlet. She ate three cakes and quite a lot of bread and butter. I shouldn't think she'll want any supper. If she has nightmares you can blame the cakes that were made out of synthetic sawdust."

"Come on up," Sarah said to Jennie. "You'll have to change your shoes and stockings."

"The bus conductor was Jimmy," Jennie said. "He said hullo and to give Petunia a kiss for him."

"Sarah, when are you coming out eating with me?" Tim called after them. "There's a place in Frith Street where the waiter knows me and produces pretty decent Chianti. Or we'll be classy and go somewhere in Piccadilly, if you like."

Coming after her queer gloomy afternoon the invitation sounded almost like fun. Sarah was on the point of saying,

"Some day, maybe," when it was all spoilt by Tim's impudence.

"Only Piccadilly doesn't lend itself so well to making love. So let's go to Soho, shall we?"

He got the last word, too, because at that moment Oliver appeared again and she had to refrain from making a scathing answer.

Rachel had Burgess Reid with her when she came after dinner. Oliver brought them into the lounge. He had a tenseness that he could not conceal. It was the first time Sarah had seen him anything but light-hearted.

"Have a drink," he said hospitably. "Nice of you to come along, too, Burgess."

"He had to," Rachel said. "I phoned him and insisted. He has to be in on this." Her black eyes on Oliver were glowing with admiration. She looked extremely handsome.

"What it amounts to," said Burgess, "is that Rachel has read the first two acts."

"And?" Oliver had one eyebrow raised. He was no actor. He couldn't assume an unconcern he didn't feel. "You can tell me here. Venetia's interested. Aren't you, darling?" He touched Venetia's shoulder in a light caress, but she did nothing more than nod slightly. "And Eliot, too." Then he took Rachel's arm. "Break it gently, for God's sake."

Rachel laughed softly.

"If the last act doesn't fall down—I'm keeping my fingers crossed—it's a masterpiece."

Oliver seemed a little breathless.

"Really! You really think so! Oh, I say, that's grand. We must drink to this. Venetia, Rachel likes it! She's going to play Alexandra. You are, aren't you?" he asked, turning to Rachel again.

"Try to stop me," she said.

"She's comparing you to Strindberg," Burgess put in.

"Without his madness," Rachel said. "You can be so bitter, but so exquisitely sane. That line where Alexandra says, 'If living is to live a lie, then I don't care to go on any longer.' That's the whole theme, isn't it?"

"What about the third act, Oliver?" Burgess asked. "When can we have it? I'd like to go into rehearsal right away."

"Not right away," Rachel demurred. "I want time for some business of my own first."

"I can let you have the last act in a couple of weeks," Oliver said. "That's a definite promise, and I keep my word. Come, we must all drink to this."

Tim went over to Oliver.

"This all sounds splendid. Congratulations."

"Thanks," said Oliver. "My luck these days is too good to be true. Isn't it, darling?" He looked again at Venetia, but again she failed to respond with anything but a blank gaze. Tonight, for the first time, she did look neurotic as Aunt Florence had said she was.

"She doesn't believe it either," Oliver went on pleasantly. "Well, a prophet in his own country, you know. Both Venetia and Eliot— Where is Eliot, by the way?"

But Eliot had gone out. Sarah thought she had been the only one to notice him go. In the uncomfortable silent way he entered a room he had gone out as Rachel was quoting Alexandra's line about living a lie.

Jennie did have a nightmare. Petunia came in a little later to say she was calling and Sarah went straight up. But by that time Jenny wasn't alone. Eliot was with her.

Jennie, gripping the bedclothes with clenched hands, wasn't taking much notice of her father. Her eyes were enormous in her gnomish face, and when she saw Sarah she burst into tears.

Sarah sat on the edge of the bed and took her in her arms. Her embrace mingled tenderness with satisfaction. At last she was getting the child's confidence and was being turned to in moments of crisis. Now she might make some progress.

"What is it, darling?" she asked.

"I dreamt about the Chamber of Horrors," she sobbed. "My family were there. Baby Robert and mother and father. Baby Robert was a real baby. He had no clothes on and he was dead. And there was the lady with the violets, too."

"Who was the lady with violets, dear?"

"The one Uncle Tim was asking me about. I couldn't see her face, but she was dead, too."

Eliot had leaned forward a little, his face curiously intent. But he said nothing, and Sarah gave her attention to Jennie.

"It was just a dream," she comforted. "Tim shouldn't have taken you there. I'll get you some hot milk. That'll chase the bogeys away."

Eliot came then and sat on the edge of the bed. His step had something uncertain about it as if he weren't sure he would be welcomed. His thin face looked haggard. Yet contrarily there was something gentle and shy about it. Sarah found herself suddenly feeling intensely sorry for him.

"I'll stay with Jennie while you get the milk." he said.

Sarah hurried down to the kitchen. When she came back Eliot was talking to Jennie, and Jennie was listening with interest.

"We never got trips to London," he was saying. "My father died when I was only eight and there wasn't much money. But we lived on the edge of the country and there was a river."

"Did you sail on it, father?"

"Yes, and swam in it, too. It was very cold except in mid-summer. Then I can remember the trees drooping with heat and the sun on the water. And the long warm twilights."

He was no longer talking to his child, he was back in those far-off days, a boy watching the sun on the river, happily knowing nothing of what was in the future.

"Here's your milk, Jennie," Sarah said softly.

Jennie took the glass and drank.

"I wish we had a river," she said.

Eliot stood up.

"You'll have other things, my dear." Then he added strangely, "You'll forget all this and begin to live in the future. Help her to do that, Sarah."

"Of course," Sarah said, bewildered.

Eliot stooped to kiss Jennie. For a moment he held her close as if he loved her.

"She isn't at all like her mother, Sarah. She's an individual. Sleep well, darling." He straightened himself and went to the door. There he paused to say, "Thank you, Sarah, for being

78

good to Jennie. She likes you. And she's a prickly little person with most people."

To Sarah's amazement and embarrassment she saw tears in his eyes. Then he went out.

Briskly she tucked Jennie up. The fool, she thought silently. He had loved and respected his wife, but had had to play around with an actress. What for? To bolster up his ego? But why worry about ego when one was happy with a wife and child?

Now the dangerous lonely state of his emotions led him to Venetia who was kind. And there could be nothing there for him. Poor Eliot, dreaming of his happy boyhood. . . .

"Father was nice to me tonight," Jennie observed sleepily.

"Yes, dear. And you must be specially nice to him, because he's lonely."

"He's got us. Me and you and Uncle Oliver and Aunt Venetia and Un—" but already she was asleep.

Sarah slept undisturbed that night because there was no sound from the attic. She awoke feeling refreshed and energetic, ready to cope with any odd happening that arose. It seemed necessary to be prepared for such an eventuality in this house.

But there was a different atmosphere this morning. She noticed that as soon as she went in to breakfast. Oliver was beaming with such infectious good spirits that even Venetia had lost most of her frightened look, as if she, too, were recovering from a nightmare. Tim had two eggs on his plate and was giving her his crooked teasing smile. It seemed as if the queer affair of Aunt Florence's ring and the tension that had been so apparent in the house were to be a thing of the past.

They discussed Jennie's nightmare, then, inevitably, Rachel's enthusiasm about Oliver's play.

"We're made," Oliver said blithely. "If we can't beat the record of 'Edward, my son' I'll give up play-writing and drive a bus. Eh, Petunia? You should be an authority on that."

Petunia, who had come in with toast, giggled.

"My Jimmy doesn't drive, sir, he's a conductor. He could

teach you that, sir. Your success is all in knowing what to say to your passengers. Have a joke with them, but be firm."

"Jimmy, the glamour bus conductor. I'll put him in my next play, Petunia."

"Oh, sir!"

Petunia went out, giggling happily.

The only two absent from the table were old Mrs. Foster, who frequently breakfasted in her room, and Eliot.

Petunia went upstairs to start the bedrooms before they had finished breakfast. Sarah heard her clattering up with her mops, singing as she went. Yesterday everyone had crept about. This morning they were carefree. What an unpredictable place it was.

Oliver wiped his mouth with his napkin, then folded the napkin meticulously. Sarah noticed how square and strong his hands were.

"Now to toil," he said cheerfully. "I've promised them that last act in a fortnight, but I may surprise them with it in a week. If I get no interruptions or worries—"

"*Mr. Oliver! Help!*" That was Petunia's shriek coming from upstairs. There was a clattering as she hurtled down. "*Mr. Oliver! Mr. Tim! Somebody—*"

Oliver sprang up, looking startled. Everyone looked at the door as Petunia, breathless, her mouth hanging open and her eyes protruding, gasped, "Mr. Eliot! Up there!" She pointed shakily to the ceiling, and then dramatically fainted.

Sarah was aware of Tim leaving the room and leaping up the stairs, Oliver following. She called to Mrs. Hopkins, who came running from the kitchen; between them they got Petunia on to a couch. Jennie had shrunk into a corner and Venetia was quite useless, sitting trembling, her face so white that in a moment she would follow Petunia's example.

Sarah got brandy and they were just forcing it between Petunia's lips when Tim came back.

"Not—murdered?" Sarah heard Venetia ask in the thin unnatural voice of extreme terror. Mrs. Hopkins gave a small scream instantly bitten back.

Tim shook his head briskly.

"Oliver is telephoning for the doctor. How's Petunia?"

"She's coming round." Sarah gave Mrs. Hopkins the brandy glass and pulled Tim away.

"What?" she whispered urgently.

"Hanged," said Tim with brutal clarity. "From the rafters."


# VIII

"I MUST get away from this house," Sarah thought wildly. "What's all this to do with me—Petunia unconscious, Venetia on the extreme edge of terror, Tim tight-lipped and grim. It's not my family trouble. I don't belong here."

Then she remembered Jennie. How much had the child heard and understood? She looked round quickly and saw Jennie standing with her back against the window. She looked very small, very calm, and at the same time very old. Sarah had a momentary illusion that she had been teaching an elderly midget. Petunia had recovered consciousness and was sitting up sobbing noisily. Venetia still in her chair at the breakfast-table looked quite dazed. But Jennie was the calmest of them all.

"Jennie, come here," Sarah said gently.

The child stood rigid.

Sarah went towards her. "Come here, darling. We forgot all about you."

Jennie turned on her a look of glittering enmity.

"Don't touch me!" she hissed.

"Jennie, darling—"

"Go away! Leave me alone!"

Tim looked round.

"Here, what's this? Sarah hasn't done anything to you."

"What's happened to my father?"

"He's ill—"

"He's not ill. He's dead. I know he's dead. The way it was in my dream."

"Oh, you poor kid." Sarah picked her up bodily and she began to scream, hard hysterical adult screams that were all the more terrifying because of the shocked silence in the room.

Oliver came in then and she stopped to look at him with her bright eyes searching for reassurance.

"She needs a shot of something," he said. "How did she find out? When Lionel comes— My God, why doesn't he hurry?"

"He has to come from Knightsbridge," Tim pointed out.

"I know. But shouldn't we—" he looked towards the stairs. He had completely lost his gay commanding manner. His face had a grey tinge. There was perspiration on his brow. Sarah had heard how people could age in a few minutes. Now she saw it happening before her eyes.

"No." Tim's voice was harsh. "It's too late. Better let the doctor see."

Venetia suddenly got up and went towards Oliver and Jennie began to scream again.

"Take her upstairs," Tim suggested.

Sarah turned a withering look on him.

"Where she can be alone to have nightmares. I'm taking her over to Aunt Florence."

When she reached Aunt Florence's Jennie had stopped screaming and was breathing in hard dry sobs, her body still rigid. Sarah opened the door and unceremoniously burst in.

Aunt Florence heard the disturbance and came hurrying into the hall, still in her dressing-gown, her hair pinned tightly on the top on her head. At the sight of Jennie her hand went to her mouth in alarm.

"Has she had an accident?"

"There's been an accident," Sarah said. "I've brought Jennie over for you to look after for a while. Will you, Aunt Florence? She could play with Hamlet, perhaps. She's had her breakfast."

"Of course," said Aunt Florence. "What—" She saw Sarah's face and was discreetly silent. Sarah set Jennie down and Aunt Florence took her hand. "Come along, dear. There's a fire in the kitchen and Jane's out there making cakes. There may be some dough and currants over."

Sarah waited for Jennie to protest, but she didn't. She allowed Aunt Florence to lead her into the kitchen. Her docility was almost more heart-breaking than her sobs. Sarah knew in that moment that she couldn't desert the child. This thing had to be seen through.

Aunt Florence came hurrying back.

"Sarah, what on earth has happened? That child is behaving as if she's seen a ghost."

Sarah told her briefly, hating herself as she did so for taking the gentle tranquillity from Aunt Florence's face.

"I must go back now. If you could keep Jennie for a few hours—she's over-strained, she imagines everyone is her enemy."

"And is it to be wondered at," Aunt Florence whispered. "Sarah, how dreadful! It's suicide, of course."

"Yes, I think so. He had it in his mind last night. He said goodbye to Jennie and I thought he was only saying good night."

Aunt Florence's eyes filled with tears of distress.

"Is it anything to do with my ring? Do you think he stole it and Oliver was hushing it up?"

Sarah considered that theory.

"It could have been one thing," she decided. "He might have had the crazy notion of getting money. He hasn't any, you know. But I'm sure it was much more than that. Much more. Last night—" She pressed her fingers to her eyes. "I mustn't start thinking of it. I must keep my wits. I'll come back for Jennie later."

When she got back Doctor Forsythe was in the hall talking to Oliver.

"I'm sorry," he said, "but the police will have to be notified. Had he anything on his mind?"

"God knows," Oliver said. "He always brooded. Particularly since his wife died. You know the way she died."

"But Mary's death was over a year ago. Has something happened more recently? Of course, it could be an accumulation of grief."

Oliver shook his head.

"This was ghastly, Lionel. Ghastly." He saw Sarah and exclaimed in relief, "Ah, Sarah! Would you stay with Venetia? Mrs. Hopkins is useless and Petunia worse. I've got telephoning to do, and there's my mother, too. She's in a state of collapse. Tim's had to go to her." For a moment he looked blank and tired. Beneath his shock Sarah could detect genuine grief.

"Oliver, I'm sorry—"

"I know you are, my dear." His voice was curiously grateful. "We shall need your help in the next few days. Go to Venetia now, will you? She's in her room lying down."

Sarah knocked at the door of Venetia's room but, getting no answer, went in. Venetia wasn't lying down after all. She was sitting on the extreme edge of the bed. Her figure had something of the same rigidity as Jennie's had had. Sarah sighed, seeing the pretty feminine room with the curtains looped with velvet bows, the rich carpet, the crystal and gold-topped bottles and jars on the dressing-table. It was a setting for a pampered woman, and Venetia sat in the midst of it utterly dejected.

"I've taken Jennie over to Aunt Florence's," Sarah said. "It's better for her to be out of the house. Can I get you anything?"

"No, thank you." Venetia's voice was quite clear, but flat, as if spoken by an automaton.

"Won't you lie down then? Oliver said you were lying down."

Venetia suddenly twisted her hands together.

"How can I?" she whispered. "How can I?"

Sarah's treacherous soft-heartedness was taking possession of her again. But she had to be firm. That was the only way to make Venetia pull herself together.

"Well, there's nothing can be gained by worrying," she said briskly. "I know it's a frightful thing, but it's nothing to do with you."

Venetia looked up then and Sarah had an unnerving shock at the terror in her eyes.

"You don't understand, Sarah. It is something to do with me."

"Aren't you perhaps imagining that?" Sarah said, but her voice was uneasy. Could that fear be caused by something imaginary?

Venetia shook her head violently.

If she could persuade her to talk, Sarah thought, it may relieve her mind.

"Eliot was in love with you, wasn't he?" she said. "Are you blaming yourself for that?"

"I know he was," she muttered. "He told me yesterday. I was in his room. But I don't think it was real love. I think he was lonely and I was kind, maybe, and he began to imagine—" She twisted her fingers together again. Her eyes were staring beyond Sarah as if she were seeing Eliot's dead body dangling from the rafters.

"But that's not why he killed himself," she said.

She spoke with such assurance that Sarah was startled.

"Why do you say that?"

Venetia's hands began their feverish twisting again. She would wear the skin off the knuckles, Sarah thought, the bones shone through like white paper already.

"Don't ask me!" she whispered, her frightened appealing eyes on Sarah. "Because I can't tell you. I can never never tell."

"But surely it would help everyone—"

"I can't tell you!" she cried. "I can't!" Then she began to give deep dry sobs and in between them her voice got higher and higher. "I can't! I can't! You mustn't ask!"

Sarah took her by the shoulders.

"What's in that glass?" she asked, pointing to a tumbler on the bedside table.

"Something—Lionel left—"

"Then you'd better drink it."

"No, I don't need it. I've got to keep my wits—"

Sarah picked up the glass. Three people with hysterics, she thought wearily—Petunia, Jennie and now Venetia. The next one would be herself. And who would look after her?

"Drink it," she ordered, holding the glass to Venetia's lips.

Venetia gulped and swallowed.

"That's right," Sarah said more gently. "Now lie down and I'll cover you up."

"I don't want—"

"Yes, you do. You'll rest and feel better and more able to cope with things. It's really quite necessary."

"Is it?" Her large eyes were on Sarah beseechingly. "Don't leave me, Sarah. Promise not to leave me."

"Of course I won't leave you. Lie down now. That's right. In a few moments you'll go to sleep. I believe I'd make a good nurse. Don't you agree?"

Venetia tried to smile. Her lips were quite stiff.

"Yes, I do. Sarah, don't leave me."

"And what's going to happen if I do?"

"I don't know. I—" The terror looked out of her eyes again.

"Well, don't think of it. Because I'll be here as long as you need me. Now close your eyes and go to sleep."

When Venetia finally settled down Sarah thought of Tim trying to cope with old Mrs. Foster, who probably was hysterical, too. Reluctantly she went upstairs, standing a moment on the second-floor landing and looking up the narrow stairway leading to the attics where yesterday Venetia had shrunk back against the wall as if she were guilty. What had Venetia learned yesterday besides the fact that Eliot was in love with her? What had changed her so suddenly from a normal happy person to a shrinking fear-filled creature?

A vivid picture of what Petunia had found that morning came to her, and she was filled with such revulsion and pity that she stood leaning against the wall, her face buried in her hands.

With a slight click the door of Mrs. Foster's room opened.

"Who's cracking up now?" came Tim's voice. It was hard, without pity or sympathy. "We can't have any more invalids."

Sarah bit her lip fiercely to stop its trembling. She wouldn't let Tim see her weakness. He apparently expected her to have neither imagination nor feelings. So she wouldn't let him see she had either.

"You don't need to worry about me," she said coldly. "I'm perfectly all right."

"Good girl."

But she didn't want his approval either. She looked resolutely at a spot above his head.

"Is Mrs. Foster all right?"

"She's wonderful. She's taken the news without a tremor. She says it was no more than was to be expected. Eliot was always weak and over-sensitive, and lately he'd been very jealous of Oliver's success. She's quite a character, that old lady. As far as she's concerned, the battle's to the strong."

How could he talk in that cold-blooded analytical way? Was Oliver the only one who showed grief at Eliot's death?

But all she said was, "Then she doesn't need me. I'll go down and see how things are in the kitchen."

"That's a good idea. They're taking the body away shortly. Then we can try to get the house back to normal."

Sarah stared at him blankly. He said, "How's Venetia?"

"Asleep. The doctor left a sedative and I made her drink it."

"Did she tell you anything?"

"Only a lot of hysterical nonsense."

"Nothing that would give you any clues?"

"What sort of clues? Good heavens, you're not suggesting that someone strung Eliot up there?"

"No, but there's more to it than meets the eye."

Suddenly Sarah remembered again Eliot's threat yesterday to tell Venetia the truth about something. So now she was the possessor of dangerous knowledge. And possessors of dangerous knowledge were liable to get murdered. . . .

Sarah saw Tim's keen stare and anger exploded in her.

"Isn't there enough trouble," she cried, "without your suspicions and shadows, your making things that don't exist? Your sister fell down the cellar stairs, your brother-in-law has just hanged himself. That's all there is to it. And I'm sick of the whole stupid senseless melodrama!"

Turning, she left him and ran down the stairs. She was behaving badly, of course, but she couldn't keep all her feelings inside her. She would burst and, as Tim said in his hard unsentimental way, they would have another invalid on their hands. But why should he expect all the self-control from her?

There was a crisis in the kitchen. Petunia was still weeping, hanging over the sink, her tears spilling helplessly on the unwashed breakfast dishes. Mrs. Hopkins was sitting at the table shelling peas, splitting the pods with the greatest deliberation and picking out the peas one by one. It was the slowest method of shelling peas Sarah had ever seen. It was a moment before she realised that obviously Mrs. Hopkins didn't know what she was doing; her hands were working automatically.

Sarah went over and took Petunia by the arm.

"Where do you live?" she asked.

"Earls Court."

"That's not far. Put on your coat and go home for the day."

Petunia stared at her, her face slack and stupid.

"If you're lucky," Sarah went on, "you might contrive to catch your Jimmy's bus. You can have a word with him."

A gleam of brightness shone through Petunia's misery. She sniffed.

"So I could. I could tell him—" A vast shudder shook her. "Coo, but he won't half believe it!"

Already the anticipation of telling her dramatic story was beginning to cheer her up.

"Then run along," said Sarah.

"I suppose you know—" Mrs. Hopkins began dimly.

"I'll give you a hand," Sarah interrupted briskly. "You can't expect Petunia to work in that condition, not after the shock she's had. Besides, I guess we won't be wanting much to eat today."

"Didn't I see it," Mrs. Hopkins declared, her eyes growing opaque as she gazed across the room. "Death!"

The police came later, and then the undertakers. After that the house was their own again with no strange presence in the shape of a dead and silent Eliot there.

Sarah found herself constantly listening for the sound of the piano. She wondered how she would sleep in the silence of that night.

Doctor Forsythe looked in again to see Venetia who was awake but flushed and torpid. The doctor told her to stay in bed and left sleeping tablets to be taken that evening. Old Mrs. Foster rambled about the house, stumping loudly with her stick almost as if to exorcise ghosts. Her eyes were glittering and she kept muttering "Spineless", but to whom she was referring, Eliot or Venetia, Sarah didn't know.

At four o'clock Sarah brought Jennie back. Aunt Florence said that at first she had refused to speak or do anything at all.

Later she had begun to play with Hamlet and had even eaten a little lunch. But she still refused to talk.

Sarah talked brightly all the time she gave her her tea and got her bath ready. Now and again Jennie made a non-committal answer. Mostly she sat quite quietly, her eyes enormous in her peaked face. Sarah noticed that she took no notice of her dolls and for the first time failed to take baby Robert to bed. She thought it wiser not to comment on this, but her heart twisted with pity as she saw the lonely little figure in bed, accepting her tragedy because she didn't know how to rebel against it.

"Good night, Jennie," she said, kissing her brow. Last night Eliot had said his unexpectedly gentle good night which had also been his goodbye. "Jennie," she said impulsively, "don't worry about anything. I'll always take care of you. I promise you that."

Jennie stared up with her dry glittering eyes.

"If you want me to, of course," Sarah added. "Maybe you don't want me to."

Jennie's lips moved.

"I—I guess I do want you."

"That's enough for me," Sarah said. She mustn't let her voice tremble. "That settles it. It's you and me now. If you can't sleep call out and I'll bring you some hot milk. I'll leave the door open and the light on in the passage. Good night, darling."

"'Night," came Jennie's faint answer.

Outside, Sarah felt as exhausted as if she had been working hard for twenty-four hours.

But there was still dinner downstairs and Venetia to look in on.

It seemed hours before everything was done, dinner over and Petunia back and much more cheerful, Venetia asleep, breathing heavily, Oliver shut in his study with Burgess Reid, who had come after dinner, and old Mrs. Foster in her room after a meal to which only she had done justice. Sarah looked in on Jennie and saw to her relief that the child slept soundly. There was nothing else at all to do, and now, suddenly, she was lost. She couldn't go to bed and try to sleep in silence. She couldn't be alone. All at once she was as bad as Venetia, as bad as Petunia who screamed and fainted. She couldn't bear to be alone.

She went down to the lounge to see if the fire was still alight, and there, to her relief, she saw blazing logs and in front of them Tim stretched out in an easy chair. Even Tim was better than entirely her own company.

She went and sat down in the opposite chair and he looked over and said in a surprisingly gentle voice,

"Had enough?"

She nodded briefly, sinking back into the chair.

"You've been grand."

"Grand! But this morning—"

"I'm sorry about that. I had to do it. You couldn't go to pieces at that stage. Now it's all over. You can relax."

To Sarah's amazement and utter disgust she felt tears running down her cheeks. She was helpless to control them. They just spilled over her eyelids and went on and on.

Tim disappeared. In a moment he came back with a glass in his hand.

"Have a drink," he said.

Sarah mopped her face. She took the glass and gulped the drink in an effort to get back her self-control. It embarrassed her extremely for Tim to see her in this childish state.

"That's Oliver's best brandy," he remarked. "It's not meant to be tossed off in that scientific manner."

Sarah tried to laugh but didn't quite succeed. Her lips were stiff. She was aware of Tim in his chair watching her. She should have been angry at his interest in her emotional condition, but she was too tired. Everything was beginning to seem a little remote, the dancing flames, Tim moving across the room with the empty glass, Jennie upstairs asleep, above her the room with the piano and no fingers left to play it. No fingers. . . .

"I'm sorry, Tim," she muttered. "I know you despise tears."

She felt something on her hair, his hand in a momentary caress.

"Cry if you want to," she heard him say offhandedly. "It will do you good."

And suddenly she felt relaxed, empty of all feeling.


## IX

WHEN Sarah awoke the next morning she could hear some-one talking in Jennie's room. It sounded like Aunt Florence's voice. Then she realised that Jennie was playing with her dolls. It was the first time she had done so since Sarah's first morning there.

"Of course Jennie must still have her party," she was saying. "She's set her mind on it, poor child."

Then in another tone,

"But you don't have parties when people are dead. You don't have parties and funerals together."

Then another voice still, "Jennie's an orphan now. Baby Robert's one, too. I expect he's glad he's dead."

Sarah went away quietly. One thing she knew now; Jennie had to have her party. Some way the ground lost had to be re-covered. Those morbid dolls to which she escaped in times of bewilderment and unhappiness had to be replaced by live play-mates. She would see Aunt Florence about the party and ar-range to have it held there. That way Venetia and Oliver wouldn't need to go if they preferred not to, and none of the children need know of Jennie's father's death.

There was no opportunity to speak to Oliver about it that day because the inquest took place in the morning and in the afternoon there was the funeral.

The inquest produced the inevitable result—suicide while the balance of the mind was disturbed. Oliver gave evidence as to how Eliot had tragically lost his wife as the result of an accident and then, the day before his death, had declared his love for Venetia, which she had had to tell him was hopeless. That impressed the coroner, and the verdict was at once pre-dictable. But Sarah had an odd feeling that the proceedings had an unreal and melodramatic note, as if they were part of a

Victorian novelette. Almost there was something melodramatic about Oliver standing there, big and handsome in his excellently cut dark suit, his voice sounding sad and beautiful.

Tim and Oliver went alone to the funeral. Venetia, who had pulled herself together today and attended the inquest, found she couldn't face any more and retired to her room. When Sarah went to see how she was, she found Venetia with a suitcase in the middle of the floor and a few things thrown haphazardly into it.

Sarah's entrance caused her to start violently, and she made an effort to push the suitcase under the bed. Realising she couldn't do that she gazed at Sarah with wide guilty eyes.

"I have to get away from here," she said breathlessly.

This was a development Sarah hadn't expected. Venetia gone a little haywire? One could scarcely blame her for that, poor thing.

"Where are you planning to go?" she asked.

"I have some friends in Bournemouth—at least, I think they're still there. Since I got married—well, one's interests change with marriage. I've rather neglected my friends."

Sarah wondered if the neglect had been intentional or forced on her. Was Aunt Florence's theory that Oliver had married her for her money true?

"And does Oliver think it's wise for you to go?" she asked.

Venetia clutched her arm. "Oh, don't tell him. He doesn't know."

"Aren't you going to tell him?"

"He wouldn't like me to go. He'd persuade me to stay. And then—"

"Then what?"

Venetia didn't answer. She put her hands over her face. Sarah thought she was going to weep again, but she didn't. She just stood there, her hair falling over the whitened knuckles of her hands.

"Venetia," she said, "what are you frightened of?"

Venetia shook her head violently as if to reject some thought. She made no answer.

"If you tell me," Sarah said, "I may be able to help you. If you don't I can only conclude you're imagining things."

She hesitated, then asked boldly, "What did Eliot tell you the other day?"

Venetia slowly took her hands away from her face. She didn't look even pretty now, but thin, white and dishevelled, with sulky eyes.

"He didn't tell me anything," she said. "Except that he was in love with me," she added.

"Then why do you want to go away?"

"Because I keep thinking of Eliot—up there—"

"We all have to live with that," Sarah said gently. "I know it's ghastly, but it's just as bad for Oliver as for you. Don't you think you should think of him more? And even if you go, knowing Oliver, I imagine he'd persuade you to come back."

Venetia sat suddenly on the side of the bed.

"Do you think he would?" she said breathlessly.

"I expect so."

Venetia twisted her hands together. "Yes," she whispered. "I expect he would."

And then all her energy left her and she sat slumped tiredly, not even speaking any more. Spineless, Sarah thought. She hadn't even the spirit to carry through one project.

"I'll go down and make you a cup of tea," she said cheerfully. "Then you can rest before dinner. You're not fit to travel, anyway. I'm sure Doctor Forsythe would never agree to it. In a day or two, when you're feeling better, why don't you do some shopping. Get a new hat or something. It's amazing what that does to one's morale."

There was a flicker of interest in Venetia's eyes.

"I like new things," she murmured. "We might go shopping together. Are you going now?"

"Yes, to get your tea."

"Sarah, don't tell Oliver—about this." She pointed to the open suitcase. "You're quite right, really. I wouldn't want to hurt him."

Oliver and Tim returned from the funeral together, but Tim said he was going out again and wouldn't be in to dinner. Sarah found herself missing him a little during that meal because at least he had a way of making light conversation. The atmosphere, with Venetia silent at one end of the table, Oliver toying with his food at the other, and old Mrs. Foster opposite eating heartily and reminiscing about Eliot, was not easy.

"The battle's to the strong," the old lady said repeatedly. Obviously she admired that statement. "Poor Eliot let himself get down to things. He hadn't much luck. Though as a child—you'll hardly believe this, Sarah—as a child it was the other way round. Oliver used to be the one who was jealous. Weren't you Oliver?"

"Was I?" Oliver said absently.

"Yes, indeed. You used to be jealous of his school reports. He was much brighter than you. Don't you remember? You must remember because you used to be quite angry. Right through school, that was, and even when you were grown-up. When you began to write, of course, it was different. Eliot couldn't do that. So the boot was on the other foot."

"Hidden talents, you see," Oliver observed, with something of his old jocosity. "It shows one never should despair of the dullest child."

Mrs. Foster took a chicken bone in her fingers and gnawed it with enjoyment. Eliot had been her son, but life to her now consisted of the elementals, eating and sleeping. Clearly she was not fully aware of his tragedy.

Venetia said suddenly, "I don't like this house any more. There have been two deaths in it." She looked up with her strained eyes. It was as if the statement had been forced out of her.

"Tush!" said Mrs. Foster. There was contempt in her voice. "Don't be superstitious."

Oliver said kindly, "I'm sorry about that, my love. But you'll have to put up with it a little longer. I've a play to finish, and that must come first. I must work."

Venetia gave a queer little laugh. Oliver looked at her and she explained a little breathlessly, "I just remembered Jennie's party. How can she have one in this house?"

"Yes, Jennie's party," said Oliver regretfully. "Will she be very disappointed, Sarah?"

"Very," said Sarah bluntly. "I think she should still have it.

Aunt Florence would be perfectly happy for her to have it there if you agree."

"Certainly I agree. It's an excellent idea. Mourning will do no good to Eliot. Jenny must be happy. I must finish my play. Things must go on. Yes, Sarah, by all means have Jennie's party."

Sarah excused herself early that night. She was tired and hoped to sleep. She would make her mind a blank, refusing to think of the silent piano in the attic. She was almost successful, but just on the verge of delicious unconsciousness she was aroused by a tap at the door. She snapped on the light and saw Tim's head poked inside the door.

"Asleep?" he hissed.

"I was," Sarah said crossly, too sleepy to be alarmed by whatever had brought him here. "What's the matter?"

"Can I come in?"

"Certainly not."

"Oh, come now. Don't be all prim. At the moment this is the only place where we can be sure of privacy. Put something round your shoulders so you won't get cold."

He came in, softly closing the door behind him. He picked up her dressing-gown and handed it to her. She pulled it round her shoulders, sitting up resentfully. He was dressed in evening dress and had a white carnation in his button-hole. Having been to a funeral that day she didn't think his air of festivity suitable. Besides which, the contrast in her own state of undress embarrassed her.

"Where have you been?" she asked coldly.

"Out to dinner with Rachel Massey."

"What!"

He grinned. "Does that surprise you?"

"I should think it does. Practically on top of your brother-in-law's funeral."

"Oh, there was no love lost between Eliot and me. You ought to have known that."

"But in common decency—"

"All right, I admit it looks bad, but I had a reason. How were things here? How's Venetia?"

Sarah's interest in Venetia's state of mind temporarily eclipsed her indignation with Tim.

"I don't know. She's behaving oddly, as if she's scared stiff."

Tim leaned forward.

"Listen, Sarah, I want you to watch what goes on here, the way people act, anything you overhear that seems significant. I'm not just inquisitive. This is deadly important."

"Why is it important?" Sarah asked, unwillingly impressed.

"Because I've a hunch we're only at the beginning. If we don't get to the bottom of what's going on something worse will happen."

"You mean something to do with why Venetia's frightened? She was going to run away today, but I stopped her."

"And she wouldn't tell you why?"

"It's something to do with Eliot. No, she won't tell me."

"Ah!" said Tim. His eyes were almost black, his face set in hard lines. The festive carnation looked as if it had got by accident into his buttonhole. "What else?"

Surprisingly enough Sarah found it a relief to talk. She told him of the quarrel old Mrs. Foster had overheard between Oliver and Eliot when Eliot had threatened to divulge some information to Venetia, and how she had met Venetia on the attic stairs yesterday looking scared and guilty, also Aunt Florence's theory that Eliot had something to do with the theft of her ring. She even went back to the conversation overheard in the garden when Jennie had been playing with her dolls, particularly Eliot's ironical remarks about their happy home. None of it made sense to her, but perhaps Tim could add it up to something.

Tim listened intently. He nodded once or twice. He made no comment until she stopped talking. Then he said, "I hate to ask you to do this, but go on observing. It may be important. It will certainly be helpful."

"And that reminds me," said Sarah, "who is this lady with violets whom Jennie talks about?"

"Someone Jennie remembers coming to the house in Pimlico. I questioned her the day I took her to the waxworks."

"Lexie Adams?" Sarah said sharply.

"It may be."

"Tim, what does this add up to?"

"I don't know," Tim answered. Then he added, "You might like to know that's why I dined with Rachel Massey tonight."

"I don't care why you dined with her."

"Well, I'm telling you. She was Lexie's closest friend. She's determined to find out where Lexie is. The girl had no close relatives, and no one else is taking any interest in her whereabouts."

"Is she going to the police?"

"No. They made an enquiry when Lexie was first missing but it seemed pretty obvious it was the usual thing. She'd gone off with a man of her own free will. So the enquiry was dropped."

"Is Rachel likely to find out anything different?"

"I don't know. For one thing she doesn't believe the porter's story about Lexie leading a double life. She's convinced he's lying."

"You mean he's been bribed to lie?"

"Possibly. The thing is to find him. He left his job almost immediately after the police enquiry, and no one seems to know where he is."

"So you and Rachel are setting out to find him?"

"Yes. We feel he has the key to this. Do you know you're a very observant and intelligent young woman. Didn't I tell you I'd grow to like you?"

"Like me tomorrow instead. I'm tired."

"So you are. When am I taking you to lunch?"

"Oh, some day, maybe."

"Not some day. Tomorrow?"

"It's not possible. I have to arrange Jennie's party with Aunt Florence, get the invitations out, and so on. Anyway, I can't leave Jennie at present."

"You're making excuses."

"Maybe I am. But they're genuine ones."

"Then the day after tomorrow. One o'clock underneath Eros in Piccadilly Circus."

"Why there?"

"Why not?" He grinned. Again his Jekyll-and-Hyde transformation bewildered her. "Good night, honey. I adore you with your hair rumpled and your nose shiny. Can I kiss you?"

"Get out," said Sarah.


# X

AUNT FLORENCE had a wonderful time arranging Jennie's party. She looked up the addresses of all her old friends and checked on information to see which of them had grandchildren or youthful nephews or nieces. She had always been a methodical chronicler, and it proved no trouble to issue invitations to a dozen or so children who would be sure to come, were their mothers able to bring or send them.

The date was fixed at ten days hence.

"I won't take down the garden swing," Aunt Florence decided. "We'll pray for fine weather. But if it's wet we'll shift the furniture out of the dining-room. You'll have to organise games, Sarah. I'm sure Tim would be very good at helping."

"What makes you think that?" Sarah asked. "He hasn't had anything to do with children for five years."

"One has only to see the way he manages Jennie. He has the knack. If his sister were anything like him then it's a wicked shame she had to die. But with that queer Eliot for a husband maybe it was best. Sarah, I'm still convinced Eliot took my ring that night and Oliver feels he must shield him."

"Perhaps you're right," Sarah agreed. Then she added, "Tim thinks there's more to it than that."

"More to Eliot's suicide?"

"Yes. And Venetia's acting as if there are ghosts in the house."

"Venetia," said Aunt Florence crisply, "is neurotic. I've always said so. But if Tim thinks there's more to it he's probably right. I admire that young man's intelligence. No one will fool him."

"Who would want to?" Sarah asked. But Aunt Florence couldn't answer that. She said a little impatiently,

"We haven't time to discuss intangibles now." She liked the

word and looked pleased with herself. "We're here to fix Jennie's party. And a grand one it has to be."

The thought of going shopping had cheered Venetia, but she had been through an intense emotional strain, and it wasn't until the next day that she had enough energy to go out. Then she came into the schoolroom dressed in a smart grey suit, with a jaunty little hat to match, and save for the slight hollows beneath her eyes looking back to normal.

"Pack your books, Jennie," she said. "I'm taking you shopping. We're going to buy your party dress."

Jennie, although self-controlled, had been almost completely silent for two days, neither hostile nor friendly. But she had showed an inclination for Sarah's company and dogged her footsteps, although she couldn't be induced to look lighthearted. Now, however, at Venetia's suggestion she came to life and slid excitedly off her chair. Then she looked at Sarah. Sarah nodded, thinking how, ever since Eliot's death, she had been attempting to get Jennie to do or say one spontaneous thing, and now the party with its thread of magic was doing it for her. How wrong she would have been to let Mrs. Hopkins's forebodings interfere with it when it was the only antidote for the shock that had made Jennie so quiet and unchildlike.

"Wash your face first," she said. "And you'll have to put on your good dress. See how quick you can be."

She was gone less than ten minutes, but in that time Venetia wasn't still a moment. She walked up and down the room, tapped her fingers on the window pane, picked up and put down things, looked at her face in her compact mirror, took off her gloves and then put them on again. Her eyes kept moving, never staying on one object. And she chattered all the time, about Jennie, about the weather, about how Oliver was absorbed in his play, about how much better all at once she was feeling.

Sarah realised that her gaiety was a reaction and might be only temporary. On the other hand, it might have been that she had allowed herself to be afraid of a bogey that didn't exist. Anyway, it was a relief to have her normal again, and, besides, by taking Jennie out it would allow Sarah to keep her appointment with Tim.

After Venetia and Jennie had gone Sarah looked for Tim in the house, but Petunia, dusting in the hall, said he had gone out an hour ago. The hall door was open and sunlight lay across the steps. Petunia was humming to herself as she worked, and from the direction of the kitchen Sarah could hear the cheerful clattering of dishes. The house was more normal than it had been for some days.

Sarah remarked on this and Petunia answered sagely,

"It's the sun. First bright day we've had since—well, you know. My Jimmy says I'm better not to talk about it. Forget it, he says. But I did wonder for a while there how I could go on staying in this house. You ought to be going out yourself, Miss Stacey," she went on. "Get a spell away from the house. There's only Mrs. Foster senior and Mr. Oliver in. Mr. Oliver's working—or he was until Mr. Reid came. They're both in the study now. I suppose he'll be here for lunch. But I'd go while the going's good, if I were you, Miss Stacey."

Sarah listened to the fat comfortable sound of the pigeons in the trees. The amber leaves seemed to colour the air, making it all golden. Petunia was right, she should go out and meet Tim and drink the Chianti he had promised her. It might even be fun.

She went to her room and dressed, taking special care about her appearance because somehow the day challenged her to look her best. In fifteen minutes she went downstairs again. She had to pass Oliver's study door to go to the kitchen to tell Mrs. Hopkins or Petunia that she would be home before Venetia and Jennie. The door of the study was open now, and as she passed she heard Oliver's voice, loud and angry. This was the more startling because she had never heard Oliver speak angrily before. He had been impatient with Venetia, scratching at times with Eliot, but this was different. It was a plain case of having lost his temper.

"For God's sake stop badgering me! Haven't you any understanding? How can I write at this stage?"

"My dear fellow," came Burgess's voice, placating, a little distressed, "I do understand. But you've only got the final scene to do. It's not more than a couple of thousand words. If you could do it—it's so important."

"Well, I can't," Oliver shouted. "I've sat here for two days and not done a line. You think I get words out of thin air! I grope for them and see nothing but Eliot's face. You didn't see that! If you had you'd have some idea of how I feel. God, it was awful!"

Burgess's voice came again. "You're letting it get you down. Come out for a drink."

"Oh, go away!" Oliver's voice was blurred now, as if he had his head in his hands. "Leave me alone. I've got to get over this in my own way."

"I'm sorry, old man. I do understand. I'll look in again when you're feeling better."

Burgess went out quickly, not noticing Sarah in the hall, and presently the front door banged. It was odd and uncomfortable the way people in this house seemed to force their noisy quarrels on her. She hadn't wanted to overhear that, but having done so now she couldn't go out with the thought of Oliver brooding alone in his study.

Impulsively she went to the door and looked in. Oliver was sitting at his desk with his head buried in his arms. Sarah crossed the room quickly and put her hand on his shoulder.

"You shouldn't let them worry you," she said.

He looked up, his eyes peculiarly lightless.

"They do," he said. "First Venetia, the state she got herself into, and now Burgess about this damned play. Why did Eliot have to be such a crazy young fool? Why, why, why!"

"I should make them wait for the play until you feel you can write," Sarah said.

"Should you?" He looked up at her. "I believe you would, too. You're a very self-possessed young woman."

"You can't be expected to write in this kind of emotional upheaval."

"No. You understand, don't you. Sometimes I wonder if I'll ever write again."

"That's ridiculous."

"No. The spark, the urge, whatever you like to call it, seems to have left me completely. Perhaps it is ridiculous. Writers get these fits of depression." He smiled at her with his gentle charm. "I'm being a great baby. You're all dressed up."

"Yes, I was going out to lunch."

"Important?"

"N-no." Why didn't she say it was with Tim? She hesitated, and then it was too late.

"What about skipping it and taking me somewhere? I need cheering up."

"But—"

"That's an order. We'll go to the Savoy."

After all, she decided later, she would tell Tim it was an order, and also an opportunity to find out something of the Fosters' past life. Because over liqueurs, which followed a very good white wine, Oliver became expansive.

"How was I to know," he said, "that both Mary and Eliot would die in my house? I thought I was doing them a kindness. They'd lived in that dark old house in Pimlico for long enough. I know how glad I was to get away from it. One couldn't work there, it was damp and depressing. Besides, I thought Mary would be company for Venetia."

"Was this just after your marriage?" Sarah asked.

"Yes, shortly after. I was tramping the West End trying to get someone to take my play. But Venetia had a little money. The house is hers, you know." He met Sarah's involuntary glance quizzically. "No, I didn't intend living on my wife. We had agreed I should have a year really to find out whether my plays were any good or not. If not, then I went back to the insurance company where I'd worked before. Fortunately I didn't have to do that." He began to smile reminiscently, his peculiarly naïve pleasure back in his face. "You've never heard the cry of 'Author' in a theatre and had to go on the stage and bow to hundreds of applauding people. It's something you can't understand unless you've experienced it. I still feel like a child staring at his first Christmas tree when I think about it. It's like a fanfare of trumpets. As my mother told you I was rather a duffer at other things. Eliot got all the plums at school. But this thing was mine, standing up there bowing, listening to all that applause, feeling one's power over a multitude. I tell you, it's like being God."

The glow in his eyes didn't come from the wine he had drunk, Sarah knew, but from reminiscent excitement. She wondered if all playwrights had this exaggerated sense of their greatness and power. She was sorry to destroy his exalted mood but there was something she wanted to ask him.

"So you left the house in Pimlico?"

"Yes. Mother shifted, too, and we found some reliable tenants."

(*God bless this happy home!* echoed in some far corner of Sarah's mind. Suddenly and irrationally she seemed to see Tim standing impatiently beneath Eros, tall above the crowd, watching with his keen narrowed eyes as the traffic went by.)

She knew that Oliver was lying, because she knew that no tenants had gone up and down the dark stairs or looked at the renovated air-raid shelter or listened to the doves. But why should Oliver lie about it? She was aware of his eyes on her, too closely.

"You're very attractive, Sarah."

She didn't know what to say. She wondered with apprehension if he were going to make love to her. But one didn't in the Savoy. This wasn't one of Tim's low haunts. (How long would Tim stand under Eros' mocking figure?)

"Let's have fun, Sarah. Don't let's go on being gloomy. Burgess came this morning to tell me *Meadowsweet* finishes next week. Let's make it go out with a bang. I'll arrange a party." Then he stopped uncertainly. "Would that be all right so soon?"

He looked too eager to be disappointed.

"I should think not too large a one would be perfectly all right. After all, it is an event."

"That's the spirit, Sarah. Come along, my dear. I feel a new man. You're good for me."


Venetia and Jennie weren't home when they returned, but they came soon after. Venetia looked a great deal better. There was colour in her cheeks and her face was full of excitement. Jennie on the other hand wore her most forbidding expression, her arched black brows drawn into a frown over the bridge of her nose. She was carrying a box obviously containing her new dress, and Sarah's first thought was that she must be disappointed with it.

As soon as she came in she left Venetia's side and came over to Sarah, putting her hand into Sarah's.

Venetia was carrying a mink scarf over her arm. Sarah hadn't noticed her with it when she went out. She must have picked it up as she left the house.

"We got Jennie's dress at Fortnum and Mason's," she said. "Don't scold, Oliver. It's the first party dress she's ever had and it's a honey. Isn't it, darling?"

Jennie said, "Yes," in a small voice, and Sarah felt her cold fingers grip tighter.

"It's white tulle with pink rosebuds," Venetia went on. "And we had to buy petticoats as well. Two, to make the skirt stand out. Open the box and show them to Sarah, Jennie."

Oliver touched the mink scarf on Venetia's arm.

"And what's this, darling?"

Venetia turned to him radiantly. Where, Sarah wondered, was the frightened girl of yesterday and the day before? She was acting as if she had been stimulated by some very potent drug.

"Oh, Oliver, I just had to buy that. It looks gorgeous on. See." She flung it round her shoulders and pivoted slowly. It was true that it looked well. She looked rich and pampered and luxurious. "And after all, you've never bought me a mink coat, so surely I can have one small scarf."

"Where did you get it?"

"In Oxford Street. I honestly don't remember the name of the shop. Jennie and I just wandered in. Didn't we, Jennie? But isn't it a darling fur?" She rubbed her cheek sensually against the fine skins. Sarah wondered, for a moment, when she had seen that bemused look in her eyes before, then remembered it was when she had put on the diamond ear-rings Oliver had given her.

Oliver, who had looked interested and benevolent all the time, put out his hand and lifted the fur from round her neck.

"Try to remember the name of the shop," he said. "If you can't you'll have to come with me and point it out."

Venetia looked at him questioningly. Already her eyes were dilating in swift alarm.

"Why, Oliver?"

He stooped and kissed her lightly on the forehead.

"Because, my dear extravagant wife, we can't afford mink scarves at the present time. I'm dreadfully sorry. But it was naughty of you to buy it without saying anything."

"You mean—I have to take it back?"

Oliver nodded.

"I'll come with you."

"But—" Her mouth was beginning to tremble. "Oliver, you don't mean that?"

"I'm afraid I do, my sweet."

"But you've bought me other extravagant things. How was I to know—"

"Of course you weren't to know. It just happens we've been a little careless. Money doesn't last for ever. Now, for a while, we must take care. Isn't that sensible, Sarah?"

Sarah hoped intensely not to be drawn into any domestic quarrel. But it was foolish of Venetia to buy a mink scarf as if it were no more than a new hat.

"But your plays, Oliver," Venetia said hesitatingly, "I thought—"

"One finishes next week and the other isn't completed. You know it isn't completed, don't you? And you know that the last scene can be much the most difficult to write."

And then, although his voice hadn't changed from its gentle blandness, Venetia's expression quite plainly showed fear. For a split second something significant passed between them, some thought or knowledge Sarah couldn't understand. Or had she imagined it? At least she didn't imagine Venetia twisting her hands in the old tortured way and making no protest at all when Oliver folded the scarf and put it carefully on the table.

Oddly enough it was Jennie who began to cry. She did so in a breathless half-hysterical way, her fingers clutching at Sarah's.

"What's the matter with her?" Oliver asked.

"She must be over-tired," Sarah said. "Too much excitement, I expect. I'll take her upstairs. Come along, Jennie. When you've had tea we'll try your new dress on. I'm sure it's perfectly lovely."

She was glad to escape herself from that uncomfortable

scene. How foolish and extravagant Venetia was, especially at this time when Oliver was worried about his inability to work. All the same, although her sympathies were with him, she retained a fleeting feeling of regret for the so final end to Venetia's excitement.

Jennie refused to eat any tea. She stopped crying, but she showed no desire to talk even when Sarah opened the box and shook out the lovely delicate dress with its fairy skirt and pattern of pale-pink rosebuds.

"Why, this might belong to a princess," she said. "It's the prettiest dress any little girl ever had. I'll do your hair in curls for the party and you won't know yourself."

"I don't want to be pretty," Jennie said in a prickly voice. "I'd rather be ugly. Bad things don't happen to ugly people."

"Why do you say that?" Sarah asked in surprise. "Has Aunt Venetia been telling you stories?"

But at that Jennie would say no more at all. She got baby Robert out of the cupboard and sat nursing him, his wooden head against her flat breast. Her eyes were expressionless. She looked like a small sphinx.

Tim didn't come home for dinner. Sarah was disappointed, because she wanted to tell him how Venetia, after having recovered, had got frightened of something again. She also meant to apologise for having missed her lunch appointment, but of course he would understand.

He came in at ten o'clock, just as old Mrs. Foster was folding her knitting and preparing, with noisy yawns, to go up to bed. Oliver had spent the evening playing short jerky tunes at the piano, with a determination to be light-hearted that was a little pathetic. Venetia gazed into the fire and did nothing at all except occasionally draw her hands across her breast as if she felt a cold draught.

Tim came over to Sarah.

"The next time we make an appointment to meet," he said pleasantly, "let's make it Trafalgar Square. Then at least I can while away time by feeding the pigeons."

"Oh, Tim, I'm so sorry. I did mean to come, but Oliver—"

Tim waved his hand.

"I don't want any excuses. You didn't come, that's all.

Let's put off this date now until you ask me. I know the chances of your doing that are improbable, but I prefer to leave it that way."

Sarah had a slight unreasonable feeling of chill. She had expected Tim to show indignation, reproach, anything but this cheerful inconsequence. Well, if that was as much as he cared about the matter they would never eat together.

"Let's forget it altogether," she said shortly.

"Ah, no, we won't do that. You may even enjoy my company more than Oliver's one day. If you live long enough!"

Any underlying grimness that may have been intended in his last sentence was discounted by his mocking smile.

Only one more thing happened that night. Jennie had a nightmare again and woke screaming, "Don't! Don't do it!" When Sarah went in to her her eyes were wide open and glazed with terror. It was quite five minutes before she could bring her back to consciousness and another half hour before she went back to sleep. But she would make no explanation about her dream.

"I don't remember. I don't know why I cried," was all she would say.

Cuddling the thin nervous little body in her arms Sarah had a feeling of desolation herself. It was the late hour, being woken suddenly from sleep, thinking how quiet the attic was. This house was getting on her nerves. And who was to comfort her if she cried?

## XI

SARAH observed Venetia closely the following week, but though inclined to be jumpy and nervous she seemed to have a hold on herself, as if she were determined not to let things get her down, or, more significantly, not to *believe* something. Then Petunia came out with the announcement that she had begun locking her door at nights and that Oliver was sleeping in the dressing-room

"I know, because when I take up the tea in the mornings I

can't get in, and it isn't till she knows it's me that she comes and opens the door. Then she looks kind of nervous, as if it might be burglars."

"And Oliver?" Sarah couldn't help asking.

"He don't take morning tea so I don't see him till he comes down to breakfast. I must say he looks all right then."

Sarah could confirm that. In fact, for the last two or three days Oliver had seemed to slough his low spirits and become his old genial happy self. She couldn't decide whether he were of a naturally resilient nature or whether something had happened to cheer him up. But he certainly didn't seem to be worrying because his wife had locked the bedroom door against him.

"My Jimmy says I shouldn't work here," Petunia said suddenly. "He says there's too many queer goings on. He says next thing we'll all be dead in our beds."

Mrs. Hopkins turned on her angrily.

"Now isn't that just the sort of nonsense your Jimmy would talk. Just because poor Mrs. Eliot died having her baby and Mr. Eliot couldn't stand the loneliness no longer."

"Well, you've said yourself about what you've seen in your teacup," Petunia protested.

"That was Mr. Eliot's death. It was there quite clear and it happened."

"But there was something about Jennie's party."

Mrs. Hopkins scowled irritatedly.

"Oh, that was just fancy. Now the party isn't here it will be all right. Won't it, Miss Stacey?"

Sarah didn't like the slight beseeching note in Mrs. Hopkins's voice. It made her uneasy, because it showed Mrs. Hopkins, for all her bravado, was not happy about the party.

"Of course it will," she said reassuringly. "What could happen at Aunt Florence's place?"

"Indeed, yes. Your aunt is a fine woman. You're both being wonderful to that poor little orphaned child. To tell the truth I only stay here myself because of her. Someone has to keep the place going for Jennie's sake."

Petunia sighed deeply.

"Oh, I stay because of Mr. Oliver. He's such a dear, and

I'm ever so sorry for him. When I tell Jimmy that he gets the huff, but I say huff or no huff I'm not leaving while Mr. Oliver has troubles."

"Otherwise you'd both leave?" Sarah asked.

Mrs. Hopkins nodded.

"Now there's this party Mr. Oliver's planning. I don't mind the extra work, but the last one he had there was that queer business about your aunt's ring and the dinner was spoilt. I said to him when he mentioned this new party, Yes, I'll do the cooking, I don't mind, but not turkey. I can't look turkey in the face again."

"Mrs. Hopkins," said Petunia eagerly, "do read your cup about this party. Do!"

Mrs. Hopkins folded her hands in her lap. Her face was adamant.

"No, I've had my lesson. Not for the queen herself will I put my eyes in a teacup again."

"Oh, you shouldn't take it as seriously as all that," Sarah protested. She had to admit she was a little curious herself to know Mrs. Hopkins's forecast.

But Mrs. Hopkins shook her head.

"Plenty can happen at that party. There's going to be twenty sit down to dinner including stage folk from *Meadowsweet*. Oh yes, plenty can happen. But I'm not foretelling it."

"Oh, you're not a sport," grumbled Petunia. "All your readings haven't been about bad things."

Mrs. Hopkins twinkled.

"How about you with all those men I promised you? Wasn't that bad enough? And your young man, Miss Stacey? Haven't you met him yet? You with your bright eyes and all."

Sarah laughed good-naturedly. "A likely story, that."

Mrs. Hopkin's good humour was fairly representative of the changed atmosphere in the house due, Sarah thought, mostly to Oliver's cheerfulness. It was a happy relief after the gloom of the previous week. Jennie was still quiet and a little difficult, but there had been no more nightmares and she was slowly becoming more responsive. The party hung before her like a light on a Christmas tree. Certainly there was Venetia's odd behaviour about locking her bedroom door at nights, but that was probably due to a purely private quarrel with Oliver. Perhaps she was still sulking about the mink scarf.

But apart from Venetia things had returned to normal. Oliver resumed his habitual working hours as if he had never had that brief emotional breakdown; Tim went in and out without any explanation. Particularly in the evenings he disappeared, and when once Sarah was goaded into asking him where he went he answered, twinkling, "Pub crawling. Like to come one night?" But she was so indignant at this sudden apparent aimlessness, as if all his previous anxiety had been a pose, that she didn't even answer. Old Mrs. Foster ate enormously, scarcely having time to make conversation between mouthfuls, and as all the day apart from mealtimes was a dead loss she spent that time dozing.

It seemed as if Eliot's uneasy presence had left the house at last.

It was the day before the dinner party and two days before Jennie's party that Sarah took Jennie to the café in the Gardens again. She had no thought of Oliver in mind this time, but only that the fine weather might not last much longer and the sunshine was better for Jennie than the atmosphere of the house. They called to see Hamlet on the way, and he condescended to be stroked and petted by Jennie, while Aunt Florence had Jane bring out the cake especially made for the party.

It was a large cake iced in pink and white, and Jennie, round-eyed, spelled out "Happy birthday" and counted the eight candles.

"But it's not my birthday," she gasped.

Aunt Florence smiled with gentle benevolence.

"No, dear. We're just pretending. This is really because of the cake you didn't have on your birthday. See, you have to blow those candles all out in one blow. So you'd better start practising."

Jennie picked up Hamlet and he squawked in her tight clutch. Her fierce eyes looked over his furry body.

"But it's a lie being my birthday," she declared.

"I know, dear," Aunt Florence admitted. "But I did so want there to be a cake with candles. Don't disappoint me."

Jennie said, "I don't usually tell lies," gruffly. Then she

added, "I suppose the other children won't know any different. I guess it will be all right."

Apart from the tell-tale fierceness of her eyes she looked quite unconcerned. It was Aunt Florence's lip that was trembling.

"Your Aunt Florence isn't very old for her age," Jennie observed with her disconcerting maturity as she and Sarah walked along the edge of the Serpentine.

"How do you mean?" Sarah asked.

"She truly likes candles on a cake, doesn't she?"

"So do you, don't you?"

Jennie scuffed at the worn path. Her hands were tight in her pockets.

"It isn't good to like things too much because that makes you lose them."

"Why Jennie, whoever told you that?"

"My father did, but I know it's true, too. I don't like anything. Or anybody," she added with finality.

The adult cynicism was a little shocking. Sarah had to treat it with humour.

"Not even me, darling?"

Jennie flicked her an upward glance. Then she scuffed harder than ever.

"Don't say those things," she ordered. "They're silly. They're lies."

Sarah tweaked one of Jennie's braids gently.

"It's perfectly safe to like me, darling. Because you couldn't lose me even if you tried. What do you say we find some chestnuts and take them home to roast? Look, we can fill our pockets."

As a result it was with pockets bulging that they arrived at the café for tea. And there was Oliver sitting at a table with a dark-haired young man.

"Well, well, look who's here!" he exclaimed. "Come along, kitten. Come, Sarah, join us. This is my friend, Brian Page. Miss Sarah Stacey and my niece, Jennie."

Oliver, clearly, was in an excellent humour. His face was beaming.

"I've asked Brian to come along to our party on Wednesday

evening, Sarah. He's interested in the theatre. I thought he'd like to meet a few of the gang."

Sarah looked at the dark young man. He seemed very youthful, not more than twenty-one. He also seemed overcome by Oliver's friendliness. Oliver himself was getting a tremendous kick out of being pleasantly patronising to the young man.

"This little affair on Wednesday will introduce you to a few people," he went on. "Sonia Helm and Jack Lye will be there. And Rachel Massey. She's over from the States. You've heard of her?"

"I should say so."

"She's accepted the lead in my new play," Oliver observed. "Sarah, are you going to have tea or coffee? Milk for Jennie, of course. Jennie's having a party, too. Aren't you, kitten?"

"Yes, Uncle Oliver."

"She's got the grandest dress. This is a very precious child, Brian. She's the only Foster descendant."

Afterwards, when the dark young man had gone, Oliver walked home with Sarah. He swung Jennie on to his shoulder and gave his jolly laugh.

"There, you're higher than houses. Well, Sarah, it's going to be quite a good party, I think."

Sarah said tentatively, "I don't want to interfere, but do you think Venetia is fit to have such a big party?"

"Oh, you mean she's still sulking about that mink scarf," Oliver said. "Hey, kitten, don't hang on so tight. You won't fall."

"Not exactly that," Sarah said. She couldn't approach the subject of the locked bedroom door. "She seems rather nervy, not herself."

"Her throat's worrying her again," Oliver said. "She's sleeping badly. I want Lionel to have another look at her, but she's being a bit stubborn. I think the party will do her good. And she'll be fine when I let her in on a secret. I may decide to buy her that mink scarf after all."

"But you said you couldn't afford it."

"I know. I was very despondent about my play then. I thought I'd never write again, as you know. But now I feel quite different. A writer has these moods."

That night Sarah heard Tim telling Oliver that he would be leaving shortly. He stooped in front of the fire to knock out his pipe, then stood erect and said casually,

"I've just got a short research job to finish here, then I'm going off into the country to write my book."

So he was planning to write a book! Sarah hadn't known that. Somehow she had thought he never had two serious ideas. She tried to think that it would be a relief not to have him about the house, getting in her hair and deliberately annoying her. But hadn't he come to solve what he considered a mystery? Had his little bit of detective work been just for amusement, and now, making no progress, he was abandoning it?

"Are you, indeed?" Oliver said. "We'll be sorry to lose you. I will, anyway. What with Eliot gone and Venetia not too fit—well, of course you know best. What's this research you're doing? I thought you'd done it all down in the Antarctic."

"Not quite. There are authorities I have to check up on. Have to be absolutely accurate, you know. And I like to know what the other fellow knows."

"Exactly. How long do you think it will take to complete?"

"Oh, a week or ten days."

"Well, at least I'm glad you're not walking out on my dinner party." Oliver's voice was genuinely regretful, though how he could ever have considered Tim a successful guest was hard to imagine. He turned to look across the room at Sarah.

"Sarah, do you hear Tim's leaving us?"

"Yes, I heard," Sarah answered calmly. She was aware of Tim's bright inquisitive gaze on her. Did he expect her to say she was sorry? Did he think she would miss him bursting into her bedroom on the flimsiest of pretexts? Him investigating a mystery indeed! He had invented it to while away the time.

But there was a mystery. She knew that herself. How would she fare when even Tim, her very unstable prop, had gone?

"Where do you plan to write your book?" she asked.

"In Cornwall. Fellow's sold me a cottage in a place called Ruan Minor near Land's End." He paused and added with apparent irrelevance, "I hear the wild flowers there are particularly lovely."

If he thought that by the mention of wild flowers he would

make her homesick for the country he was absolutely right. She had a moment of intense longing for windy skies and the fragrance of wet earth and green hedgerows.

"The roof will probably leak," she said.

"I haven't a doubt. And there'll be an ancient Cornish curse combined with no plumbing."

"The latter could easily be the curse," Oliver observed, giving his hearty laugh. "Well, we'll be a quiet house, won't we, Sarah?"

(With Venetia's door locked at night and the piano in the attic silent, and no one but herself to heed Jennie's nightmares?)

"Cheer up," came Tim's exasperating voice. "I'm not going for a few days. I've this job to finish and an important luncheon date to keep. Then let the wild storms do their worst."

Sarah didn't make any attempt to see him alone later to find out the real reason for his leaving. If he wanted to walk out that was his business. She wasn't going to show she was sorry.

Oliver must have told Venetia about the possibility of her getting the mink scarf after all, for she became a little brighter towards the end of the week. She walked about more briskly and didn't start if she met anyone unexpectedly in a passage. She even began to discuss what she would wear to the dinner party. But she still locked her door at nights, Petunia reported. Sarah tried to tell herself that this was her method of getting the mink scarf, but she couldn't forget the furtive nervousness in Venetia's eyes that had nothing to do with possessions.

But with two parties on her hands Sarah hadn't very much time to worry about Venetia or Tim. She was helping both Aunt Florence and Mrs. Hopkins. The day of the dinner party she gave Jennie a holiday from lessons and spent the entire morning in the kitchen, to the great delight of Petunia who liked, she said, a different face to talk to.

"We're all strung up about this do tonight," she said. "Mrs. Oliver won't have no candles on the table. Mr. Oliver wanted them, but she says no, let's have plenty of light. She said candles would always remind her of that last dinner when your aunt's ring disappeared. So she's put them away herself where no one will find them. I wonder what did happen about that ring."

"It's none of your business," Mrs. Hopkins said sharply. "Get on with your work and don't gossip. What are you wearing tonight, Miss Stacey, if it's not impertinent to ask?"

"Of course it's not impertinent, Mrs. Hopkins. I was going to wear my grey chiffon again, but Aunt Florence says I must get a new dress, she's ashamed of me. So I'm going to slip into town this afternoon if I can manage it."

Mrs. Hopkins smiled affectionately.

"Get a green dress, love. Mr. Tim would like you in green."

"Mrs. Hopkins, what a lot of nonsense you do talk!"

At half-past six that evening Sarah heard old Mrs. Foster calling her. She had just put on her new dress. She hadn't had time to go farther than Harrods for it, but there she had got exactly what, no doubt, Mrs Hopkins had had in mind—a dull-green velvet cut on classical lines. She wore it with a fine gold necklet and ear-rings Aunt Florence had given her for her last birthday, and she thought ironically that she looked the way Joan of Arc might have looked in a formal dinner dress.

But there was no time to worry over her own appearance because Mrs. Foster was rapping at her door now and calling impatiently,

"Miss Stacey, didn't you hear me calling?"

"I'm coming, Mrs. Foster," Sarah answered.

Out in the passage Mrs. Foster was waddling back to her own room. Her black lace dress gaped open all the way down the back.

"I must have put on weight," she complained. "I can't do up my dress. Help me with it, will you, Sarah? And you might pin up my back hair, too. It's getting so difficult for me to reach."

She sat on the stool in front of the mirror and dabbed powder over her purplish face until her skin looked like the bloom on a grape. Sarah struggled with the fastenings and got them secured. But what would happen if Mrs. Foster over-ate as usual was a conjecture of interest.

"It's exciting having a party," the old lady was saying complacently. "Of course a lot of people will think we shouldn't have one so soon after Eliot's death, but I'm entirely on Oliver's side in this. Eat, drink and be merry! What a motto! You're looking very grand, Sarah. Is that a new dress?"

"Yes. I bought it today."

"Ah—ha! Nothing of the governess about you, my dear. Not that you don't seem to make a very good one. By the way, have you noticed that young man Oliver's had to the house?"

"Brian Page?"

"Yes. Don't you think he's extraordinarily like Eliot?"

Small, dark, introverted—yes, there was a similarity to Eliot. But Brian Page hadn't Eliot's look of utter disillusionment.

"I only hope Oliver's not unkind to him," Mrs. Foster went on.

"Unkind?"

"Yes. He was to Eliot, you know. He was always so big and unafraid of anything, and he knew that Eliot was nervous and sensitive. He used to play on it, the scamp; and when Eliot was so much ahead of him at school he bullied him."

"But didn't you stop him?" Sarah exclaimed.

Mrs. Foster gave a fatuous smile.

"Oh, I tried to, of course. But then I thought if Eliot's ever going to have guts this will develop them. A boy has to stand up for himself. Eliot never did learn to, though."

"He had his spirit broken," Sarah said in a shocked voice.

"Nonsense! He had none to break. Oliver grew out of his naughty ways, and look at the good friend he was to Eliot. But Eliot remained the same, the scared little boy keeping out of sight. Pah!" Mrs. Foster made a disgusted sound. "He was my son, but I've no time for weakness."

"I realise that," Sarah murmured. She had a sudden desire to take a hairpin and stick it hard into the heartless old creature's head. Had she always been such an unnatural mother, or was this a symptom of senility?

"I can't help wondering," Mrs. Foster was saying, "whether Oliver sees a likeness to Eliot in this young man, too. Oliver misses his brother, you know. Ah well, it's an unkind world. The battle's to the strong." She tugged with her thick white fingers at the waistband of her dress. Her face was peevish.

"This dress is much too tight. I shan't be able to do justice to my dinner."

The clock struck a quarter to seven as Sarah left her and went downstairs. Oliver met her in the hall. He looked startlingly handsome in evening dress, with a white camellia in his buttonhole, but he had an anxious air.

"Sarah, you look charming. Would you be so good, my dear, as to run up and see how Venetia is getting on. She has some idea of not letting me into her room until she's dressed. To surprise me, I suppose. But tell her not to be late down, will you?"

Did he really think she didn't know Venetia had locked her door against him for a week? He wanted to keep up appearances, of course.

When Sarah knocked at the door there was a complete silence, then Venetia's voice came sharply, "Who's there?"

"It's me. Sarah. Can I come in and help you?"

"I don't need any help," Venetia called back. But she came and unlocked the door and Sarah saw that she had nearly finished dressing. She had on a rose-coloured tulle dress over a stiff taffeta petticoat. She would have looked angelic had her expression not been so wan and dispirited.

"What a lovely dress," Sarah said. "Oliver thought you must have wanted to surprise him."

"Oh no, he's seen it before," she answered uninterestedly. Then she added quite spontaneously, "That isn't why I keep my door locked."

"Then why do you?" Sarah asked.

"I feel safer that way."

"Safer!"

Venetia nodded. Her cheeks had slight hollows in them that Sarah had never noticed before. She must have lost weight in this last week.

"Yes. This house isn't safe, you know. You do know that, don't you?"

"Oh, come now, you're imagining things."

"No, I'm not. You'll find out some time, perhaps before very long, that I'm right."

She was getting a little queer, Sarah thought uneasily. What ought to be done? Perhaps she could have a word with Doctor Forsythe during the evening.

"Well, cheer up now," she said briskly. "You're very pale tonight. How about a little rouge to match that pretty dress?"

"You don't believe what I say, do you?"

"Well, not altogether. I think you're encouraging yourself to be morbid. Make up your mind to forget things and enjoy the party tonight."

Venetia nodded seriously.

"Yes. I don't mind this party because there will be plenty of people about. That makes it safer." She sat on the stool in front of her dressing-table, her skirt frothing about her like a full-blown rose, her fair hair curling softly on her shoulders. From the back she was a picture of a beautiful girl going to a party.

"I know you don't believe me," she said. "You think I'm just silly and scared and neurotic. But I know the truth. There's someone in this house wants to kill me."

## XII

OLIVER was at the piano singing "*I love sixpence, pretty little sixpence, I love sixpence better than my life . . .*" as they went down. He turned and saw them come into the room and with his eyes on Venetia in her glowing dress he skipped the rest and sang with absorbed tenderness, "*I spent nothing, I lent nothing, I love nothing better than my wife. . . .*"

Then he got up and went to her, taking her hand.

"My sweet, you're delicious. You look like pink candy. Or a sunset. Or a rose in winter time."

He stooped to kiss her, and Venetia made no protest. But neither did she return the kiss. She said in an agitated voice, "Why aren't all the lights on?"

"Don't you think it's rather pleasant with not too many?"

"No, put them all on. In the dining-room, too. We must have plenty of light. We can't have people groping about in the dark."

"I thought it looked artistic. But as you say," Oliver agreed good-humouredly. He snapped on the ceiling light and at the same time the front doorbell rang.

"Here they are," he said. He kissed Venetia swiftly on the forehead. "Buck up, darling. We're going to have fun."

Half an hour later they were all seated round the dinner table. Sarah had Brian Page on her right and Doctor Forsythe on her left. Rachel Massey was next to Tim, and Oliver, at the head of the table, had the leading lady of *Meadowsweet*, Sonia Helm, on one side, and Burgess Reid on the other. Venetia, looking fragile and remote at the other end of the table, was apparently listening intently as Jack Lye told her a story with gesticulations.

It had all the makings of a very successful evening. The company was animated, there were enough diverse interests to provide good conversation, the ducklings were done to perfection and the vintage champagne following an excellent sherry was calculated to do all it was meant to.

But Sarah couldn't relax. She kept remembering Venetia's odd desperate remark that someone was going to kill her. She kept looking at Tim, who seemed to have a lot to say to Rachel Massey, and wondering indignantly how he would feel if he heard, down in his Cornish cottage, that Venetia had been murdered.

But of course she wasn't going to be murdered.

"What a mind he has," she realised Brian Page was saying.

"Who? Oh, you mean Oliver? Yes, indeed. He's becoming very successful."

"That scene in *Meadowsweet* . . ." Sarah tried to pay attention, but she was hearing scraps of conversation all round the table. Burgess Reid was saying to Oliver, "You old devil, you would keep the good news from me," and Oliver answering with his deep jolly laugh, "I'm still not entirely out of the wood. But I'm making appreciable progress."

From across the table she heard Rachel Massey saying to Tim, as if she were making an assignment, "The Rose and Crown at Hammersmith? It's a very small place along the tow path on the right of Hammersmith Bridge."

"Good. I'll be there."

So Rachel shared Tim's recently developed enthusiasm for pub crawling. Or were they up to something more important.

"And then," Jack Lye said to Venetia, "thank God the curtain came down."

"Have you noticed, Miss Stacey," said Doctor Forsythe in a low voice, "whether Venetia is constantly in that nervous condition? Or is it only being a little keyed up about this party?"

Here was her opportunity to tell him about Venetia's odd fancies. Her words, "There's someone in this house who wants to kill me," were going to sound very bald and unconvincing when repeated, but the doctor ought to be told about them.

"I'd like to have a talk to you afterwards, doctor," Sarah said. "Venetia has been behaving a little oddly."

"Certainly, my dear. At the first opportunity."

It was a pleasant meal and was carried to its conclusion of coffee and liqueurs in the lounge without any upset. Sarah at last began to relax. When Tim came over to her to say, "Sarah, love, you're ravishing. Marry me tomorrow and be damned to 'em all," she smiled in complete friendliness.

"What a shock you'd get if—"

And there her words were cut off as, without warning, all the lights went out. Except for the firelight the room was in darkness.

There were some gasps and excited chattering, and then Oliver's unperturbed voice came out of the darkness, "It must be a temporary power failure. Don't move, anybody. The lights will come on again in a minute."

"A good thing it didn't happen at dinner," old Mrs. Foster said.

"The firelight's rather pleasant," said Rachel Massey.

Petunia came fumbling her way to the door and then over to Venetia. She said in a rather scared voice, "Ma'am, we've no lights in the kitchen. Mrs. Hopkins wants to know where you put the candles."

"Just wait a minute or two, Petunia," called Oliver. "The power's bound to come on."

But Venetia pushed back her chair and stood up. Sarah could hear the edge of terror in her voice.

"Oliver, we can't sit in the dark. It's ridiculous. The failure may last half an hour. I'll get the candles, Petunia."

"I'll go if you'll say where, ma'am."

"No. They're in a special place for an emergency. I didn't know we'd have one so soon." Her voice was breathless. She hated the dark. Sarah remembered how she had wanted all the lights on. Her panic was even driving her to grope her way to the place where, in her recent suspicious way, she had hidden the candles, rather than sit in the dark.

"Let me strike a match for you," said Jack Lye.

Everyone began getting up. Sarah saw Venetia go to the door, then her glimmering dress disappeared in the darkness of the hall. A match flared and went out. Jack Lye's voice said, "Sorry. I got jostled."

"Hasn't someone got an electric torch?" demanded Tim. Suddenly his voice was sharp with apprehension. "Venetia, don't go down to the cellar in the dark. Wait till I get my torch." He was thinking of what had happened to Mary, of course. That must be the only reason for his sharp warning.

But his injunction was unheeded, or too late. For scarcely had he said the words than there was a scream. Then a dreadful clatter. Then, after a petrified moment, another scream this time from Petunia. Then pandemonium.

"Get a light," shouted Oliver. "Petunia's fallen. For God's sake, hasn't someone got a light!"

Everyone was crowding into the hall, but no sound at all came from the cellar. Venetia obviously was unconscious—or dead.

Two or three people struck matches, and Oliver scrambled down the steep stairs into the pitch blackness below. Then the white beam of Tim's torch shone down. He stood at the doorway and said authoritatively, "Stand back, everyone. Let Doctor Forsythe come down."

Doctor Forsythe went briskly down and Tim followed him with the light. Sarah had a glimpse of Oliver's fair head bending over the crumpled form that was Venetia. Petunia began sobbing noisily. Then Tim called, "Sarah, come and help me find these damn candles," and she herself went down the treacherous stairs into the cold dark cellar.

"Is she alive?" she heard Oliver asking hoarsely. "I couldn't feel her heart."

"Yes, thank God," Doctor Forsythe answered. "She seems to be suffering from concussion. She's fallen on her head. I can't make a complete examination until we get her upstairs. Aren't there any lights yet?"

Sarah struck matches frantically while Tim searched on the shelves for the candles. He found them at last where Venetia had carefully secreted them because she was afraid of a dim light. She was so afraid of darkness that she had unthinkingly rushed to the cellar, not realising that to fall might be worse than sitting in the dark.

"Get upstairs and light them," Tim said. "We'll bring Venetia up."

They brought Venetia right up to her bedroom, Tim and Oliver carrying her. Sarah had thrust some of the candles into Mrs. Hopkins's trembling hand, but she had kept four for the bedroom and their wavering eerie light flung huge shadows about the pretty room as Venetia was laid on the bed.

"Bring the light here," Doctor Forsythe said curtly, and Sarah held the flickering candle, her hand trembling so that she had difficulty in not spilling grease on the silk bed coverings or the pale-blue carpet.

Beyond the circle of light Oliver stood watching. She could sense rather than see the tenseness of his figure. She thought of the tenderness and pride in his face as Venetia had come into the room before dinner. And now she lay here unconscious, scarcely breathing.

"No bones broken," Doctor Forsythe said, his voice all at once more cheerful. "I was afraid at first she'd broken her neck."

"What is it?" Oliver asked.

"Concussion and multiple bruises."

"How long will she be unconscious?"

"It's hard to say. A few hours, perhaps. She must be kept absolutely quiet."

"Is there any danger?" That was Oliver again. In the uncertain light Sarah could see perspiration shining on his brow.

"A certain amount, of course. Quiet is the essential thing.

We'll have to arrange for a nurse. If you don't mind my saying so, Oliver, you ought to have something done about those stairs."

"Yes," came Tim's voice from the doorway. Sarah could see him standing there, tall and thin, his brown flesh making his face scarcely discernible. "When Venetia recovers consciousness she'll tell us how it happened."

Oliver turned to face him.

"There's only one thing that could have happened, surely. She tripped in the dark."

"Yes. I suppose so. Even if you know the stairs well they're so steep you could trip. Mary did, didn't she? And she must have known them." Tim's voice was reflective. It wasn't even bitter the way it usually was when he talked of Mary's accident. "Yet Venetia may be able to throw some interesting light on the subject."

There were other people crowding to the door. Mrs. Hopkins, pushing in front of everyone, whispered sibilantly,

"How is she, Mr. Oliver?"

Oliver said heavily, "She's still unconscious. But Lionel hopes for the best. I blame myself. I should have had something done about those rotten stairs. They're a deathtrap."

"Now don't you take on, sir," Mrs. Hopkins said soothingly. "Who was going to know she'd run down there in the dark. By the way, sir, the street lights are still on so the power failure's only in this house. It must be a fuse. What should I do?"

"I'll telephone for an electrician," Oliver said. He was pulling himself together with an effort. "Is there anything more I can do, Lionel?"

"Nothing at all, old boy," Doctor Forsythe said reassuringly. "Don't worry. She'll come out of this all right."

Oliver stood a moment at the bedside. His head was bent. His thick fair hair was almost as yellow as the candlelight. He looked desperately anxious, his gaze fixed on Venetia's unconscious face. But all he said was, "Shouldn't she be undressed?"

"Mrs. Hopkins will help me do that," Sarah said. She wanted to reassure him, too. This shock was too much so soon after Eliot's death.

"Yes, there's really nothing you can do here, old chap,"

Doctor Forsythe repeated. "Go and do something about the lights. That'll be the most helpful at the moment."

Oliver agreed reluctantly and went out.

Mrs. Hopkins shut the door and between them they got Venetia undressed, cutting the elegant dress in a way that made Mrs. Hopkins "Tch, tch!" remorsefully.

"The least possible movement," Doctor Forsythe cautioned. "Miss Stacey, you've had nursing experience, I take it?"

"Yes, I nursed my father."

"Then I can leave her in your care until I get a nurse? Just see that she keeps absolutely quiet. If she recovers consciousness let me know at once. I'll come no matter what time it is."

"Thank you, doctor," Sarah said. At the moment she was too concerned for Venetia to worry about the long vigil ahead.

"Seems like parties in this house are fated," Mrs. Hopkins said grimly. "It's just as well Jennie is at your aunt's, Miss Stacey. Well, she looks more comfortable in bed, poor lamb. What a head she's going to have tomorrow. It's a miracle she wasn't killed outright. Just fancy her tripping on those stairs. I mean, she's lived in this house long enough. Not like Mary, just finding her way around."

"It was an unlucky accident," Sarah said firmly. "I'll let you know if I want you again, Mrs. Hopkins."

"Very well, miss," Mrs. Hopkins answered, withdrawing rather reluctantly. "Are you going to sit up all night?"

"If it's necessary."

"Then you must let me know if you want me to take a turn. I'll get cleared up in the kitchen now. I expect everyone will go home. I should think after this they'll be nervous of having parties in this house."

She finally got out of the room and almost as soon as she had gone Tim came in, carefully closing the door behind him. He crossed over to the bed and stood a moment looking at Venetia. His face was lean and sharp, the uncertain light making hollows in his cheeks and exaggerating the protuberance of his skull bones so that he looked strange and a little frightening.

"Sarah," he said in a low voice across the bed, "there's something I want to say quickly before anyone else comes in. Can I trust you not to leave this room before I come back?"

"Where are you going?" she asked sharply.

"I have an important appointment. I'll be back before midnight."

"Tim, you can't keep an appointment tonight. Not after this."

"Sorry, but I have to."

"Where is it?"

"At Hammersmith."

Sarah remembered the fragment of conversation she had heard at dinner, Rachel Massey saying in her confidential voice, "The Rose and Crown? It's just along the tow path. . . ." She hadn't heard any more because Brian Page had spoken to her.

"If it weren't really urgent—" Tim was going on, but Sarah interrupted him with a scathing,

"Oh yes, I understand its urgency. It would be an awful pity to miss it, and she'd be so disappointed."

"Sarah, what are you talking about?"

"Well, aren't you going to the Rose and Crown?"

He looked surprised.

"Are you learning Mrs. Hopkins's art? As it happens, I am going there. We think Haley, the porter of Camelot Flats, may be there. But I should be back well before midnight. Why I want you to be here is in case Venetia recovers consciousness. That's where the danger lies."

"Danger?"

"Yes, it's possible she'll remember what happened."

"I suppose she will. She'll know she fell down the stairs."

"She may even know more than that."

'Tim, what are you suggesting? That—" (*There's someone in this house wants to kill me!*) Uncomfortably Sarah remembered the deep conviction in Venetia's words. They were mad words, of course, spoken as the result of a strained mind. But now this had happened, this wasn't imagination. Oh, nonsense! she told herself firmly. Venetia had simply fallen down a dangerous flight of stairs in the dark.

"Two similar accidents could be too much of a coincidence," Tim said. "The lights going out may have provided an opportunity too good to be missed."

"You stand there suggesting"—Sarah's voice wasn't entirely steady—"that this wasn't an accident, that it was—no, it couldn't have been premeditated. If it happened at all it must have been on the spur of the moment because opportunity—Oh, what am I talking about?" She pressed her fingers to her eyes, saying angrily, "You make these—these incredible suggestions, yet you calmly go out to trace an old mystery. Nothing more's going to happen to Lexie Adams if you don't trace the porter tonight."

"Whether you think it or not," Tim said patiently, "its extremely important. The whole thing's going to tie-up or I miss my guess. Now look, honey, do as I say. Dont leave this room under any circumstances whatever. Understand?'

"And what would happen if I did?" she asked coldly.

"Nothing may happen at all. But it may happen someone will find it very important not to let Venetia recover consciousness—and talk."

"But who?" Sarah demanded. "It isn't possible—Oh, get out of here with your melodramatic notions. One moment you're talking like this and the next you're going off to live in Cornwall, as if nothing whatever was happening here. You're not consistent."

"Everything in its turn," Tim said. "Cornwall isn't for another week. Look, I've got to fly. I'll be back as soon as I possibly can, within an hour, I hope. Then I'll share this with you. But you're the only one to hold the fort in the meantime."

And suddenly Sarah realised that he wasn't being either melodramatic or facetious. Quite frankly he meant her to stay there because if danger existed for Venetia it existed most intensely before she could recover consciousness and tell what she knew.

But how was she alone to hold off a murderer?

The room, with its dancing candlelight and the deep breathing of Venetia on the bed that was like another person there invisible was suddenly frightening and menacing. Why should Tim go and leave her to face this danger alone?

"Tim, I can't stay here. I'm scared."

Then he had come round to her and his fingers were biting deeply into the bare flesh of her shoulder.

"It's something you have to do, scared or not. And I won't

be long, I promise. No one will even know I've gone. They'll think there's two of us in here and that will make it doubly safe. But if anything happens and you're really afraid, ring for the police."

Then he went to the door and opened it, hesitating a moment and looking into the darkness in both directions before going swiftly and softly away.

Sarah began to realise that she was cold. Tim had said she wasn't to leave Venetia, no matter who came into the room, but he might have thought to ask her if she wanted anything first. He might have realised she wouldn't keep very warm in a dinner dress on a chilly autumn night. She opened Venetia's wardrobe and found a woollen jacket and slipped that on. Then she looked at her watch and saw that it was only eleven o'clock and there were eight more hours to daylight.

If only the lights would come on! Even Venetia's unfamiliar breathing that was like a stranger in the room would seem less frightening in a normal light. What had happened to everybody? Had all the guests gone home? Poor Oliver's parties were doomed. He would never want to have another in this house.

It was impossible to sit in the flickering light imagining things. Sarah began to walk about on tiptoe, though no noise at present would disturb Venetia. She tiptoed to the door, opened it and looked down the dark passage. Downstairs, so far off that it seemed like a dream, she could hear voices. So everyone hadn't gone yet. She longed to go down and hear what they were saying and surmising. Did any of them think, as Tim did, that Venetia's fall may not have been an accident? But Tim was behaving oddly enough himself with his cottage in Cornwall, his urgent appointments at Hammersmith inns and his fantasy about accidents that were not accidents.

But Tim hadn't said those words, "There's someone in this house who wants to kill me!"

Sarah listened to Venetia's heavy breathing and clenched her hands, repressing a desire to scream or cry, she didn't know which.

Then all at once, like a conjuring trick, the lights came on. She gave a small gasp of relief. She hurried to turn off the main switch and leave only the bedside light burning in case too much glare disturbed Venetia even in her dark unconsciousness.

At the same time footsteps came up the stairs. The door opened and Doctor Forsythe came in. He crossed to the bedside and examined Venetia again, feeling her pulse and lifting her eyelid.

"Is there any change?" Sarah asked.

He shook his head. "This is going to last for some hours, I'm afraid. Don't let people come in and out of here. And be sure to call me if you're alarmed about anything."

"Thank goodness at least the lights are fixed," Sarah said.

"Yes. It was a blown fuse. Everyone's going home. You'll have the house to yourselves in a few minutes. Good night, Miss Stacey. I'll be round first thing in the morning."

When he had gone Sarah expected Oliver to come up. She heard the banging of the front door and a few far-off good nights. Then old Mrs. Foster came lumbering up the stairs. It was too much to hope that she wouldn't stop at the door. She tapped with her stick, and when Sarah opened the door she stood wheezing and gasping on the threshold.

"I knew this dress was too tight," she said peevishly. "I couldn't do justice to my dinner—what Venetia didn't spoil by her stupidity. Falling downstairs indeed! Why, I've gone up and down those stairs a hundred times and never fallen. For Mary there was some excuse. She was heavy with child. But for Venetia none whatever, unless she had been drinking. How is she?"

Sarah had a desire to shut the door in the face of the callous old woman. Could it be by any chance she, who despised Venetia so entirely, who certainly would not grieve at her death. . . .

"She's still unconscious," Sarah answered.

"H'm. Well, Lionel ought to send a nurse. You can't sit up all night."

"It won't hurt me in the least, Mrs. Foster. A nurse will be coming tomorrow."

Mrs. Foster gave a cracking yawn that displayed all her teeth.

"Well, I'm going to get some sleep, anyway. Good night."

"Good night, Mrs. Foster."

She trundled away with the grace, Sarah thought, of a sea elephant. Sarah left the door open because it was reassuring to see the lighted passage. No one could come along there unexpectedly. Yet a little later Oliver came so quietly that Sarah didn't hear him until he was in the room.

He went and stood at the bedside, gazing at Venetia silently. His hair was tousled and had a dampish look. His eyes looked curiously dark and smudged in his pale face. Sarah noticed that although his arms hung loosely at his sides his big hands were clenched.

"I'm glad you got the lights fixed," Sarah said.

"Yes. It was a fuse," Oliver answered absently. He continued to gaze at Venetia. His absent words hadn't touched his thoughts. What were his thoughts? Sarah watched silently while he stooped and kissed Venetia gently on the forehead.

"Poor darling," he murmured. Then, without another word, he went out.

Sarah knew his words and action had been complete forgiveness to Venetia for her behaviour. They must have been. Yet why had she been unable to ask him if he thought Venetia's fall an accident? It had been on the tip of her tongue, then suddenly she had been unable to say it. Surely, surely, Oliver! No, that was impossible. It must have been an accident. Venetia's previous fear amounted to nothing more than the development of a persecution mania. Nothing more, she told herself firmly.

Yet supposing it were highly important to complete a half-done task and silence Venetia before she could talk. . . .

Sarah looked at the clock. It was a quarter to twelve. Soon Tim would be home. He had said he would be back by midnight. Then she would not be alone any longer, even if Tim, with his alarmist theories, were disturbing company.

She switched on the electric heater because she was still cold, and sat in an easychair. Venetia's breathing like a third person sounded above the tick of the clock. Outside the room the house was utterly silent. Had Oliver gone to bed? He hadn't said what he was going to do. He had just wandered in and out like someone lost.

It couldn't have been Oliver who had pushed her, because if it had been he would have sent Sarah out of the room and stayed with Venetia himself. To finish a bungled job? No, no! Sarah found herself shaking with horror. It was nothing to do with Oliver or anyone; it was entirely an accident.

But to send her away would not have been subtle. Rather, whoever was guilty would attempt to get her out of the room on some pretext so that she would not see who entered and left.

Someone knocked softly at the door. Sarah almost leaped out of her chair in a panic. Who was there?

The door began to open slowly.

"Who is it?" Sarah demanded, and her voice, because she had been so concerned that it shouldn't tremble, was sharp. A tray appeared, followed by Mrs. Hopkins's round pink face poked enquiringly round the door.

"Thought you'd like a cup of tea," she whispered.

"Oh, come in," Sarah whispered back in relief. "I didn't know who it was. One gets a little edgy alone in a sick-room."

"I should say so," Mrs. Hopkins said sympathetically. "Especially the way it is."

"What way?"

"Well, you must admit too many things are happening in this house for our comfort." Mrs. Hopkins set the tray down on Venetia's dressing-table stool and took the cosy off the teapot. "I think it's time Mr. Oliver sent for the police."

"Why? Because of an accident?"

"Two accidents and a suicide. There's something behind all this, Miss Stacey. I can't stand much more of it, and I fancy Petunia will give in her notice tomorrow." She nodded towards the bed. "Does she show any signs of coming round?"

"None at all."

"Poor thing. Might have broken her neck. I don't want to cast aspersions, Miss Stacey, but it was mighty queer the lights going out and this happening."

"Now, come, Mrs. Hopkins, who could arrange to have the lights go out?"

"Well, I don't say that that was arranged so much as it provided a heaven-sent opportunity."

"You're as bad as Tim."

"Does he think the same? I'm not surprised. However, don't let us get it on our minds now. I thought you'd like a cup of tea to keep you awake."

"That's very kind of you, Mrs. Hopkins."

"Are you sure you wouldn't like me to take a turn sitting up?"

"No, Tim will be back any time. He asked me to stay here until he came."

"Ah yes, now he's reliable. I'd trust him. Then there's nothing more I can do?"

"No, thank you. I'd get away to bed if I were you."

"Very well, Miss Stacey. If you say so. Everyone else has gone. The house is quiet as a grave." She tiptoed to the door, then turned to whisper, "You'll have to yell loud if you want help. Petunia and I are right down in the basement."

"I won't need help, Mrs. Hopkins," Sarah answered firmly.

But when Mrs. Hopkins's comfortable little figure had vanished Sarah had an unreasonable desire to call her back. She was going down into the basement far away. The house was so silent. Supposing . . .

"Now, stop that, Sarah my girl," she admonished herself severely. "Nothing's going to happen. Tim will be home presently and all will be well."

She drank a cup of hot tea, blessing Mrs. Hopkins for her thoughtfulness. The clock on the mantelpiece struck twelve in a tinkling bell-like voice that took her back to her childhood and the beautiful safety of her nursery where both her mother and nurse were within call. Comforted, she settled back in her chair to rest and await Tim's return.

Another half-hour went by. Sarah felt drowsiness creeping over her. She stretched and walked softly about the room. It was odd that Tim was so long. He must have missed the last bus by this time. She lifted a corner of the blind to look out at the window, and saw that it had begun to rain. The street light opposite was obscured in a halo of mist and the raindrops, scarcely more than a webby fog, tickled the windowpane with a faint monotone. The street was deserted. It looked dark and a little sinister save for that one haloed light. There would be no help there if she had to call.

Suddenly, as she dropped the blind, the telephone downstairs began to ring. Sarah's first impulse was to rush eagerly to answer it. It would be Tim saying he was on his way. But, no, he wouldn't do that because he would realise she would be the only one up and he had insisted on her not leaving Venetia's room.

Then if it were not Tim who was it? Why didn't someone answer it? They couldn't be all sleeping so soundly. Mrs. Hopkins and Petunia in the basement might not hear it, but Oliver would wake up. Surely he would hear it.

Then, as the bell went on shrilling, another thought came to Sarah and she felt prickles of gooseflesh up her arms and down her back. Was someone waiting for her to answer the telephone, so that for five minutes Venetia would be alone? Had this call, perhaps, been arranged? If she were to rush downstairs and pick up the receiver what strange voice would sound in her ear? The imperious ringing was suddenly sinister. Sarah pressed her hand tightly over her mouth, afraid she would scream. Surely the sound must rouse even Venetia.

Then, with an impatient *ping* it stopped, and the silence was even more terrifying. For now whoever had laid the trap and failed would be angry. And find some more devious method to deal with her.

Sarah gave an impatient exclamation. Was she losing her reason, having these fantastic ideas?

Venetia lay motionless on the bed and the little hand of the clock went on. The rain was growing harder and there were brief gusts of wind that would be blowing out the last flame of the leaves in Kensington Gardens. Tim must be getting wet now, wherever he was. Sarah lifted the blind to look out at the window again, and saw the light shining on the spears of rain and the wet black pavements. She felt more alone than she had ever done in her life before. Her father had died and she had been left alone in a cottage in Sussex with his familiar things all about her. But that nostalgic loneliness was far different from this feeling of complete desertion with its element of suspicion and fear.

Where *was* Tim? Why didn't he come?

The clock struck one with its tinkling fairy-tale chime.

A little after that Sarah became conscious of another sound of breathing besides that made by Venetia in the bed. It was coming from the passage. It was accompanied by the furtive but rather clumsy tiptoeing of someone heavy. Sarah stood petrified.

The sound came nearer the door, which was slightly ajar. Did whoever it was think she may have fallen asleep and so was coming to reconnoitre? Sarah looked round and picked up Venetia's silver hair brush. It was the first weapon she could see. If she had been near the telephone she could have picked it up and begun dialling 999. But it was down in the hall and she couldn't leave Venetia alone.

With slow stealth the footsteps reached the door and without pausing went past. For a moment Sarah felt too weak to move. Then she pulled herself together and going swiftly to the door opened it just in time to see old Mrs. Foster's broad figure disappearing down the stairs.

The old lady hadn't enjoyed her dinner. Her dress had been too tight and the lights had gone out. She was going down to the kitchen to forage. That undoubtedly would be her destination. She couldn't have any other motive in her devious old head.

Sarah sighed with relief. Nevertheless she couldn't relax until fifteen minutes later the shuffling footsteps came up the stairs and passed the door again.

It was queer what could have happened to Tim. Had he had too many drinks at the Rose and Crown? Was he following up another clue? Sarah was beginning to feel distinctly uneasy about him. Angry, too, that he had left her in this kind of a situation. She was sure his failure to return wasn't intentional, but the only alternative was that he had become involved in something, perhaps something dangerous.

The strain of the evening was now making her feel extremely tired. She felt drawn tight, the muscles of her face rigid, her eyes staring with weariness. She sat down again and drank a little more of Mrs. Hopkins's tea, cold now but still retaining a shadow of its cheering element. Venetia's breathing, she thought, had grown a little quieter and more normal, but she still lay locked in her unconsciousness.

In five more hours it would be daylight, Doctor Forsythe would arrive with the nurse and she could go to bed. Bed! What a paradise that would be. She shouldn't have refused Mrs. Hopkins's offer to share the sitting up. But then she had expected Tim back. What could have happened to him?

The rain was now falling quite steadily, and its rhythmic sound on the window was beginning to make her feel over-poweringly sleepy. She sat up straight, but automatically her head drooped, her body slid back in the chair. Was this what the attacker was patiently waiting for? She mustn't sleep, she had to keep awake. No matter how enticing sleep was she had to fight it off. Tim had said . . .

A scream cut through the silence. Sarah stiffened, all sleep vanished. Where had the scream come from? The second floor? Jennie?

"Sarah! Sarah, where are you? Sarah!"

Yes, it was Jennie. She was screaming in an access of terror. Automatically Sarah sprang to her feet and ran to the door.

Then she remembered: she mustn't leave this room. Like the telephone, Jennie's scream might be a trap.

"Sarah!" wailed Jennie heart-rendingly.

How could a little girl crying in the night be a trap? It might not be a premeditated one but, like the lights going out, it might provide an opportunity. . . .

Sarah stood at the half-open door grinding her nails into her palms. Jennie was having one of her nightmares, that was all. She could hear the child sobbing now, each deep indrawn breath a gasp of terror. It was the first time she had failed Jennie in one of her nightmares. But she had to fail her this time. She would somehow recover from it alone, but Venetia, left for a few moments, might never recover.

The desolate sobs tore at her heart. Tomorrow Jennie would look at her with reproach and suspicion. All the ground she had gained would be once more lost. And it was Tim's fault for being away so long. If he had been here she could have left Venetia. When she saw him again she would kill him.

No, no, what an awful expression to use! Even metaphorically speaking it was awful. She was getting too agitated, standing here as if she were chained, longing to go to Jennie who was suffering.

But Jennie was quieter now. Her sobs were scarcely audible. It could be that she had her head under the blankets, of course. But at least she was recovering. Sarah could go back to her chair without having to fight sleep for a while, at least. That much she had to thank the poor child for.

As she turned to go she thought she saw something move in the darkness of the stairway above her. She couldn't be sure. The stairs went round a curve and it could be that her tiredness was making her eyes play tricks on her. At any rate, there was no more movement, although she stared until her eyes pricked with strain. At last her jumping heart quietened and she went back into the room.

## XIII

IT WAS still raining when, in the first grey light of dawn, Mrs. Hopkins came bustling up the stairs with another tray of tea. She stared at Sarah in the chair by the bedside, and Sarah stared back at her from under heavy eyelids.

"Mercy, Miss Stacey, are you still there? You must be dead on your feet."

"All over me," Sarah said ruefully. "Is it really morning? Don't tell me I'm imagining it."

"It's half-past six and I thought whoever was here would like early tea. I did think it would be Mr. Tim. How's the patient? Any change?"

"I think she's not so deeply unconscious," Sarah said. "She's a little restless. Mrs. Hopkins, have you heard Tim come in?"

"I haven't heard a sound. You don't mean to say he isn't in?"

"He can't be. I haven't heard him and you haven't."

"And you've sat up here all night by yourself?"

"There was nothing else to do. He said I mustn't leave Venetia under any circumstances. And the telephone rang and Jennie had a nightmare and—oh, God, it's been awful!"

Mrs. Hopkins put down the tray and poured a cup of tea.

"Here, drink this! You're all to pieces, and no wonder. Why didn't you come for me?"

"I told you, I couldn't leave Venetia. I thought I saw—" She shuddered all over, her body prickly with cold. "Never mind, I was seeing things that weren't there by that time."

"But who answered the telephone?" Mrs. Hopkins asked.

"Nobody. I don't know who was ringing. I imagined all kinds of things. And poor Jennie cried and cried and I couldn't go to her."

Mrs. Hopkins patted her shoulder.

"Drink your tea, love. It's all over now."

Sarah gave a deep sigh of exhaustion and relief.

"I know. It's morning. Isn't it wonderful. Doctor Forsythe will soon be here with a nurse. I can go and get out of this bloody dress. Don't you ever tell me to wear green again." She sipped the hot tea, feeling optimism as a reaction from that awful strain flowing through her like wine.

"I know all that," said Mrs. Hopkins worriedly. "But whatever can have happened to Mr. Tim?"

Oliver, dressed but unshaved, and with circles round his eyes as if he hadn't slept, came in while Mrs. Hopkins was still there.

"How is she?" he asked briefly.

Sarah gave him the answer she had given Mrs. Hopkins. He listened, looking all the time at Venetia's unconscious face. Then he turned and said,

"Can I have that cup of tea?"

"Of course, sir. I'll just get another cup."

Mrs. Hopkins hurried away and Oliver looked at Sarah with concern.

"You look worn out, my dear."

Sarah tried to speak evenly.

"It's been quite a night."

"You should have had help. You shouldn't have done this alone."

"I was expecting Tim all the time. He doesn't seem to be home yet. I can't imagine where he is."

"Oh, he'll turn up. I shouldn't worry about him. He's a little irresponsible."

Mrs. Hopkins came back with a cup and saucer and poured tea for Oliver.

"There you are, sir. Nice and hot. You don't look as if you had slept, either. Didn't you hear the telephone ringing and Jennie crying, like Miss Stacey was telling me?"

"No." Oliver looked at Sarah enquiringly. "Who was ringing?"

"I don't know. No one answered the phone."

"But you said—oh, I see, you thought you shouldn't leave Venetia. No, I didn't hear a sound. But I don't when my door's shut."

"That explains it," Mrs. Hopkins said cheerfully. "But I wish that Mr. Tim would come home. Never takes anything seriously, he don't. Ah, that's the doorbell now."

"It will be Lionel," Oliver said. "Tim never rings the bell."

It was Doctor Forsythe. He came up at once, his manner brisk and businesslike. "I have a nurse waiting downstairs," he said. "You people will be wanting some sleep." He went across to the bed. "Any change?" he asked Sarah.

For the third time Sarah gave her report. Doctor Forsythe nodded.

"Good. She's coming out of it. She'll probably be conscious in an hour or so. That's the critical time. But Miss Benson understands concussion cases. You don't need to worry. I'll get her up at once and she can take charge."

"That's fine," said Oliver. "Thanks, Lionel. What would I do without you and Sarah? But I can't start telling you now. You're busy and Sarah has to get some sleep. Come along, Sarah."

But Sarah, her tired mind remembering nothing but Tim's injunction, wouldn't leave the room until she saw the nurse come in. Miss Benson was a fair pretty girl with baby blue eyes, but in rather odd contrast a chin that gave Sarah complete reassurance. Sarah was quite happy to go then, knowing that neither Venetia nor anyone else would get the better of that determined little jaw.

When she had slept and was clearer in the head and when Tim had come home she would decide how much to tell Miss Benson. In the meantime it was safe to leave her with Venetia for a few hours.

She didn't know how much to worry about Tim's absence, but before she went to bed she had to see that Jennie was all right.

She went straight up to Jennie's room and opening the door quietly looked in. At first in the dim light she could see only the bed with its blankets tossed and rumpled. Then, going nearer, she could distinguish Jennie's shape curled up in a knot beneath the blankets. None of her showed, not even the top of her head, poor little creature, she had apparently hidden beneath the blankets in fright after her nightmare, and had gone to sleep in that position.

Sarah gently lifted the sheet to see that she could breathe, and at the movement Jennie shot up convulsively. She crouched away to the other side of the bed and sat like a little frightened animal.

"It's only me, darling," Sarah said. "Did you have a bad dream in the night? I heard you calling, but I couldn't come because Aunt Venetia was ill."

Jennie said nothing at all. She crouched there, wrapped in her hostility.

"Really I couldn't Jennie. I wanted to badly."

"You said you'd always be there"—Jennie's voice choked—"if I called. You promised."

"I know, but this time I couldn't help it. I've been up all night with Aunt Venetia." She realised how overpoweringly weary she was. It was almost too much even to talk. But for Jennie's sake she had to make an effort. "Anyway, it's morning now and everything's all right. You can get dressed and run down to Mrs. Hopkins for your breakfast." She straightened the bed and went on talking briskly. "And of course you know what day it is."

"My party day." Jennie's voice was small, but a little more normal.

"Yes, so it is. And it's going to be fine, too. The rain stopped an hour ago. How'd you like to ring up Aunt Florence and say good morning?"

"I might," Jennie said cautiously.

"Of course. She'll want to know if you're excited. And another thing, I'm afraid you'll get no lessons this morning because really I must get some sleep. Can you amuse yourself?"

"Yes."

"That's fine." Sarah stooped over her. "How about a kiss to show I'm forgiven."

Jennie drew back, then suddenly, as if against her more cautious judgment, she flung her arms round Sarah's neck. She was shivering violently and Sarah's neck was in a vice.

"Come, darling," Sarah said soothingly. "It's all over now. It's morning. No more bad dreams."

"It wasn't a dream."

"Then what was it?"

Jennie's trembling increased. Her voice grew more and more breathless.

"It was someone in here in the night. They touched my face. I felt them. On my cheek. They were cold."

"Jennie, are you sure—"

"I did! I did, I tell you! I screamed and then—then I didn't feel any more. But I had my head under the blankets."

"Jennie, are you sure—"

Jennie pummelled her with her fists.

"It wasn't a dream! I heard breathing! Like this!" She breathed in a loud exaggerated way. "And you wouldn't come."

Sarah hesitated to show the child how shaken she was. She spoke calmly, "I'm sorry, pet. We'll find out about it. Until we have you can sleep in my room with me. Will that be better?"

Jennie clutched her fiercely.

"Promise!"

"Of course I promise. Now let me go. I'll pull the blinds up and you can dress."

Jennie's arms untwined from round her neck and Sarah stepped back. As she did so her foot slipped on something. She stooped to investigate and picked up from the carpet a small rubber frog.

"Where did you get this, Jennie?" she asked.

Jennie looked at it in surprise.

"That's mine. But I haven't had it for ages. It's a baby thing. How did it get there?"

Sarah thoughtfully laid it against her cheek. It felt cold and clammy. She didn't answer Jennie because the thought going through her mind was no thing to tell a child.

Now, at last, when she was free to sleep she found she could not. If she were going to worry at all it should be about the significance of Jennie's disturbance in the night. But at the moment she had something else taking precedence in her mind. She found she was missing Tim quite astonishingly.

She had taken off her dinner dress and she lay in the comfort of her old woollen dressing-gown. But although she ached all over with weariness and reaction from strain she didn't sleep. It would be unwise to take a pill for then she might not wake up when she was needed. If she couldn't sleep she would at least rest here for a couple of hours and then go downstairs.

Actually she did doze a little, for her clock showed the time to be nine o'clock when she was roused by an urgent knocking on her door.

"Miss Stacey!" came Petunia's voice. "Miss Stacey, Mrs. Hopkins says for you to wake up and come down."

Sarah was off her bed and at the door in a flash. She opened the door and confronted an excited Petunia whose mouth fell open even more loosely than would have seemed possible.

"What is it, Petunia? Venetia—"

"No, not her. Mr. Tim."

"What's happened?" Sarah asked sharply.

"He's home. Mrs. Hopkins says you had better come down."

Sarah brushed past Petunia and rushed down the stairs.

Tim was in the hall sitting in one of the carved antique chairs that hitherto had been used for ornament only. His head was bent and Sarah's first thought was that he was drunk.

"Tim!" she said angrily. "I must say—" Then she stopped, for she saw that he wasn't drunk at all. There was a large bruise on his right temple and his right arm was inside his coat in a sling.

"Tim, you're hurt!"

"Hullo, honey," he said. He gave his tilted smile. His face was very pale. "Sorry I let you down last night. But you managed, Mrs. Hopkins told me. Great work. She says Venetia hasn't come round yet."

"Tim, how did you get hurt?"

He lifted an eyebrow.

"Well, it wasn't in a fight. I got knocked down."

"By a car?"

He nodded.

"Bad show, wasn't it? But this car—well, I guess the driver was drunk or suicidal or just nuts. I've spent the night in a damned hospital. Mrs. Hopkins says you didn't know. I got them to telephone, but they said they couldn't raise anyone."

So that was the explanation for the telephone last night. It was unfortunate for Tim, but not sinister after all.

"The telephone did ring, Tim. I couldn't leave Venetia to answer it and no one else heard it."

"No one at all?"

"Well, no one answered it." She lowered her voice. "I thought it might be a trap. But it wasn't after all. My goodness, the night I've had."

"Me, too. Trying to get out of that hospital."

"Tim, do you mean you're not supposed to be out?"

He grinned again.

"It isn't exactly official. But I don't think they'll pursue the case."

Mrs. Hopkins came bustling into the hall with a glass in her hand.

"There he is, Miss Stacey. Isn't he the limit! A hit-and-run driver and him not killed. Well, you couldn't kill him that easily. Here you are, my lad. Drink this."

"What is it?" Tim asked suspiciously.

"And if it was cod-liver oil it would be no more than you

141

deserve. If you must know, it's milk with brandy out of Mr. Oliver's cabinet."

"Shame on you, Mrs. Hopkins. You'll go to heaven, sure as fate!"

Mrs. Hopkins laughed happily.

"I must say it's good to have you back. Miss Stacey and I were getting quite worried. But that potion will fix you. I'll leave you to take care of him, Miss Stacey. I've got Jennie in the kitchen and I don't want to leave her. She seems nervous as a kitten today. Excitement over her party, I expect."

"What's wrong with your wrist?" Sarah asked Tim as Mrs. Hopkins left them.

"It's broken, I'm afraid."

"And you didn't see this car at all?"

"It was raining and I was in a hurry. I probably jay-walked, but not enough to warrant the driver not seeing me. He just appeared from nowhere."

"Where did it happen?"

"A couple of blocks from here. He was swerving to turn on to the Kensington Road and collected me in his path."

"And didn't stop?"

"I guess not. By the time I came round the ambulance was the only vehicle in sight."

"Would you know the car again?"

"In London!"

Sarah sighed. "No, I suppose not. It's just—" Then she said impatiently, "Tim, how *awkward* of you to get knocked down at a time like this."

"I know," he said humbly.

"There was I waiting for you all night."

"A worse thing is that I didn't keep my own appointment."

"Your appointment at a pub!" Sarah's voice rang with scorn. "And I here alone facing heaven knows what."

Tim stroked her hand.

"Honey, you look horrible in that dressing-gown."

"And Jennie had a nightmare, at least I thought it was a nightmare until I found the frog."

"Frog?"

"Yes. Someone frightened her with it and she screamed.

And I couldn't go to her as no doubt I was meant to. Tim, do you realise what I'm saying?"

"Yes, of course." He spoke with an effort. She looked at him sharply.

"Drink that brandy quickly."

"Yes, honey."

He began to lift the glass but she had to grasp his hand and steady it. His head rested against her breast as she held the glass to his lips.

"Good stuff," he murmured. "Sorry—I can't—enjoy—"

Sarah took the glass from him.

"Put your head between your legs."

She supported him as he did so, feeling the hard line of his shoulders between her fingers. When a little colour had drained back in his face she helped him upright and said, "You're going to bed."

"Not on your life. I've just escaped from bed."

"You're going to bed or I telephone the hospital and have you sent right back."

Tim said wearily, "I don't like your voice or that colour you're wearing. Neither suits you. They make me feel ill."

Sarah eyed him reflectively.

"I may be able to," she muttered.

"What?"

"Carry you."

Tim struggled to his feet.

"Good Lord, you mean that, don't you? All right, I'll go to bed. For one hour."

Sarah took his arm and helped him up the stairs. She didn't ask him any more questions because he was in no condition to answer them. She got him into his bedroom, which was at the opposite end of the passage from Venetia's, and helped him out of his coat. Then he tumbled on to the bed and without bothering about further undressing she covered him with the eiderdown. She thought he had fainted, but when she moved he said,

"Don't go."

"I wasn't going. I was wondering what I could do for you."

"Nothing. I've just got one whale of a headache. But it will improve. It'll have to. Because today is important."

"If Venetia recovers consciousness?"

"Exactly. I've got to have a talk with the nurse. And there's this frog business of Jennie's. Nasty, that."

"Don't worry about it now."

"To think of wasting all last night in a damned hospital."

"Tim, don't worry now."

She sat on the edge of the bed and touched his head with the cool ends of her fingers. He opened his eyes to look at her thoughtfully. Apart from the scowl of pain on his forehead he might have been his old mocking self.

"How tall are you, Sarah?"

"Five feet ten."

"You'll have to stoop, then."

"What on earth for?"

"To get through the doors of my cottage."

"And when am I going to be stooping through the doors of your cottage?"

"Sooner than you think, my sweet. Much sooner than you think."

"I don't intend to run away, even if you do."

"So that's what you think. That I'm running away."

Before Sarah could answer, however, there was a tap on the door. The next moment the door burst open and Petunia appeared. She was still in her breathless state of excitement.

"Oh, Miss Stacey, I thought you'd like to know. I was in Mrs. Oliver's room taking a tray out just now, just a minute ago, when all at once she opened her eyes and said 'The rope! The rope!' just like that."

Tim started up in bed. "Nothing else?"

"No, sir. The nurse said she was wandering and gave her an injection. She said it was only semi-consciousness. I heard her telling Mr. Oliver. But lor, if you'd heard the way she said it, as if she was scared stiff."

"All right, Petunia," Sarah said calmly. "Thank you for telling us."

"You're making a damp squib out of that information, Sarah," Tim said.

"You can't encourage Petunia in her love for melodrama. And what else is it? Obviously Venetia is having nightmares about Eliot."

Tim lay back. His eyes were reflective.

"I wonder," he said.


# XIV

IT WAS as Sarah was leaving Tim's room that she met Oliver. She expected him to remark on Venetia's return to consciousness, but instead he looked Sarah up and down and his usually amiable blue eyes were flinty.

"What have you been doing in that room?" he asked with ominous brevity.

Sarah, taken unawares by his manner, answered, "Why, Tim's had an accident. Didn't you know?"

"Is he unable to help himself?"

"Not exactly. But he shouldn't be out of hospital."

"I imagine Mrs. Hopkins can attend to his requirements."

"I daresay she can." Sarah was still bewildered by his apparent hostility.

"Then oblige me by letting her do so. You have enough of your own duties. Jennie can't run wild, and you'll probably be needed to take a turn in Venetia's room again, besides getting some necessary sleep."

Before Sarah could make any answer to that he had gone past her into Tim's room.

"Mrs. Hopkins has just been telling me about this," he said. "I must say you chose a damned inconvenient time to get knocked down."

"Maybe the motorist thought differently," came Tim's lazy answer. "Maybe he was looking for a little sport."

"Don't talk balderdash. Do you want Lionel to look at that arm?"

"No, don't bother him. It's fine. And he must be awfully tired of accident cases." Tim's words sounded innocent, even airy. "How's Venetia?"

"She's a little better, but wandering. Talking nonsense." Oliver's voice was beginning to grow more friendly, as if he were ashamed of his outburst. "Lionel says her mind may be a little vague for some time. I'm sorry you've been knocked about, old chap. It's damned bad luck. But don't monopolise Sarah, will you? She's got her hands full."

"Sarah, my girl, you're developing into a first-class eavesdropper. Aren't you ashamed of yourself?" Sarah admonished herself as she slipped away to her room. But she was smiling a little, too. Poor Oliver, now she knew why he had been so unnaturally bad-tempered. He was jealous. He didn't like Tim to have attention.

All at once Sarah stopped smiling, because it wasn't amusing after all to be the object of Oliver's interest. Not after last night, after the vague doubts assailing her, the frog in Jennie's bedroom, the unidentified movement on the stairs. . . .

"And what you need," Sarah added firmly, "is a good sleep to get those cobwebs off your brain."

Oliver must be all right. It must only be Tim who was the untrustworthy one, with his slick sweet words and his appointments with other women. He was the sly one to talk about her in his house in Cornwall and at the same time to be wondering when next he could meet Rachel Massey, giving as his excuse the search for the mysterious Lexie.

But Tim had nothing to do with Venetia's fall, or any of the other things that had happened. His crime was to be nothing but a honey-tongued philanderer. Him with his head resting against her breast. . . .

Sarah sniffed angrily. She took off her dressing-gown and put on a sweater and skirt. It was useless to think of sleeping, for she had no time even had she been able to sleep. She must go over to Aunt Florence and help with preparations for Jennie's party. Venetia would be all right with the nurse, Mrs. Hopkins had Jennie in the kitchen, and as for Tim, he was perfectly well able to look after himself.

She took the trouble, however, to tell Oliver what she was doing. He was now his usual courteous self, and stood listening with his gentle smile. He had shaved and his skin looked firm and smooth. Sarah found it curiously revolting to her that he should be looking so splendidly healthy when Eliot had died with a rope round his neck, when Venetia lay wandering in the dim halls of semi-consciousness, when Jennie screamed in the night and even Tim by an odd mischance had suffered injuries.

"That's right, Sarah," he said in reply to her statement. "I'm sorry I was a little sharp just now, but I won't have people imposing on you. Jennie's your job here. Go ahead and make this party a good one for her. Now Venetia's out of danger there's nothing to worry about."

"Is she out of danger?"

"Lionel says so. But her mind's cloudy. It'll recover, of course." (If she lives long enough, came Sarah's involuntary thought.)

"I've got a man coming to look at those stairs," Oliver went on. "I suppose that's locking the stable door after the horse has gone."

"Has it ever occurred to you," Sarah heard herself saying in a cool analytical voice, "that Venetia's fall may not have been an accident?"

Oliver was staring at her with wide-open eyes. They had an unfocused look, as if he were pursuing some picture inwardly. It was almost as if shock had rendered him expressionless.

"You mean she may have been tripped," he said.

Tripped! The rope! Venetia's first words on returning to consciousness. The rope!

"I've got to go," Sarah said unevenly. "That was just a theory. I should think it was most unlikely. I guess I'm going haywire after not enough sleep. Don't worry about it."

"I do worry about it. A thought like that is extremely disturbing."

Why had she mentioned her suspicion to Oliver? Tim wouldn't have approved of that. She knew why she had done it. It was to surprise him into some kind of a statement. And she had obtained that, disturbing as it could be if her first involuntary interpretation were right.

"I've got to go," she said again, almost desperately, and without waiting for him to answer she hurried out of the house.

It was like a refuge to go into Aunt Florence's house and smell the fragrant odour of fresh scones and spicy cakes coming from the kitchen, to see Aunt Florence bustling down the hall, and to relax in the blessed normality.

"Bertha's just finishing the last batch of cakes," Aunt Florence said. "I know Oliver said Mrs. Hopkins would do all the cooking, but I doubt if anyone knows the real capacity of children. They're bottomless wells. I don't know about Jennie, she's a peaky one, but I expect she'll be the same as the others. Aren't we lucky to have such a lovely day after the rain last night?"

Sarah remembered the rain, she had lifted the blind to look out at the window and had seen it sparkling on the pane and shining in black pools under the street light. And all the time above it there had been the sound of Venetia's breathing in the room. . . .

"I'm going to put chairs and tables in the garden," Aunt Florence went on busily. "They'll be able to play hide-and-seek and drop the handkerchief, that is if children still play those games. We want plenty of lemonade, I told Jane. I'm really enjoying this, you know. Sometimes I like children so much better than adults. Dear, you're very quiet, you haven't said a word."

"Give me a chance," Sarah said, trying to smile. In this warm normal atmosphere she found the happenings in the house next door so far from reality that surely they couldn't be more than a nightmare.

Aunt Florence gripped her arm. Her little mild face was suddenly tense with interest.

"Sarah, has something else happened? Wasn't the party last night a success? Tell me, did someone else lose some jewellery? Oh, that would be too awful! Poor Oliver, do you know he still sends me flowers every day."

Compared with last night the strange loss of Aunt Florence's ring seemed a trifle. It all came back to Sarah like a dark stifling cloud enveloping her—the lonely sound of the rain, Venetia's breathing, the fairy-tale chime of the clock, the telephone ringing and ringing, Jennie's screams, the unidentified movement on the stairs; then this morning Tim collapsing in the hall, Petunia's excited announcement of Venetia's return to consciousness, Oliver's hand on her arm and the queer creeping of her flesh. . . .

It all came out in a breathless account as if it were something she had to eject from her mind. She saw Aunt Florence's soft face expressing varied emotions, astonishment, horror, incredulity and then pity accompanied by a mild "Tch! Tch!" when she was told of Tim's accident.

"Oh dear, I am sorry about that. How could he come to get knocked down? Have the police been notified?"

"I don't know. I expect they'd be there when he was picked up."

"Then they'll be round asking questions. So there'll be no more funny business, if it is funny business, going on while they're about. Fancy that frog! Well, all I can say is it's a good thing Jennie's having her party today. It'll take her mind off things, too. Now, dear, you look absolutely worn out. You go upstairs to your own room and have a couple of hours' sleep."

"Thank you, darling, but I can't sleep. I mustn't. I've got to see what Jennie's doing and how Tim is."

"I don't think that house is good for you," Aunt Florence said severely. "You're getting thin."

"Thin!" Sarah said humorously. If that were all!

"I don't think it's good for any one, but I've got to stay for Jennie's sake."

"Until you're pushed out of an upstairs window or knocked down by a car."

"Tim's accident has nothing to do with the house."

"Hasn't it?" said Aunt Florence suspiciously. "I wouldn't be too sure. And all the lights going out. We didn't have any trouble with our lights last night. Well, if you won't rest come and have a good hot cup of coffee. Then you can help me with the chairs in the garden before you go."

There were yellow oak leaves draggled like wet silk on the grass in the garden. The swing, Aunt Florence said, must come down after today. The garden was getting the dishevelled look of approaching winter and it, too, had to be shut away till the spring. In the spring, Sarah thought, carrying chairs and setting them about the shorn grass, she would go back to the country and spend the days in the open air with her sketch-book. It seemed impossible now that such a simple life existed. Suddenly it had the charm of the unattainable. Because it was impossible to see what was going to come out of this present situation. She felt she was involved to the extent of never being free again. She was beginning to be more than a little frightened.

But the calm sunny day was reassuring. It would be fun to see Jennie being light-hearted at a party. The chrysanthemums along the wall, just bursting into their shaggy blooms, were like children at a party themselves. There were pale-pink ones the colour of shells. Sarah decided to pick some to take back for Venetia. Their pastel colour would look well in her pale-blue room. She went over to the dividing wall to pluck them, but in the act of doing so she was stopped by the sound of Jennie's voice from the other side of the wall.

"Now, Jennie," she was saying in Venetia's light sharp voice, "if you don't behave, I'm sorry but we'll have to take that dress right back to the shop."

She had her dolls out in the garden and was playing with them. Well, perhaps it was a good thing for this morning while everyone was busy. Evidently she was playing going shopping with Venetia to buy her party dress. But why was Venetia threatening her? She was not likely to have been as naughty as all that.

"You wouldn't like to lose the dress, would you, Jennie?" the precocious Jennie-Venetia voice went on. "I promise you you will if you say anything about this crazy idea of yours at home. Of course I paid for the scarf. Didn't you see me talking to the shop-girl? Why, if I hadn't paid for it it would be stealing, wouldn't it?"

"Sarah," came Aunt Florence's high voice from the house, "What are you doing down there?"

Sarah motioned violently for her to be quiet. She listened again to the voice next door.

"You know what happens to people who steal, don't you, Jennie? I knew a girl who stole things and went to gaol for three months. She didn't like it a bit. It was cold and uncomfortable and people were unkind. So I wouldn't be risking that happening by taking a mink scarf, would I?"

There was a short silence. Jennie, apparently, was rearranging her dolls. Then the voice went on, "I paid for the scarf, Jennie, as you very well know, and if you say anything to anybody, *anything* at all, I'll take your party dress away from you, and of course there'll be no party."

Now Sarah knew all she wanted to. With half a dozen chrysanthemums in her hands she hurried up the garden. Aunt Florence caught a glimpse of her face and said anxiously,

"What's wrong, dear? Are there spiders, or something?"

"I've got to go, Aunt Florence. I must talk to Jennie and see if anyone else has heard what she's just been saying."

"You mean she's playing make-believe with her dolls again?"

"Yes, and this time it's serious. To think that child knew all the time—"

Aunt Florence snatched at her sleeve.

"Sarah, keep out of this now. It was listening to Jennie over the fence sent you there the first time, and I encouraged you, more shame on me. But you've had enough of it. Stay here now."

"And leave Jennie in possession of dangerous knowledge?"

"Dangerous!" Aunt Florence faltered.

"Definitely. And that's where your ring went, too, of course."

"My ring! Darling, are you quite in your senses?"

"Venetia's a kleptomaniac," Sarah said shortly. "I always thought there was something unhealthy about her love for clothes."

"Well!" Aunt Florence gasped. "So that's it. And Oliver's been shielding her. How tragic for him. I wonder how long he has known."

"Since the event of the ring, I should think. That's when Venetia started to be frightened."

"Of course he couldn't tell the police. He would have to protect his wife."

But Sarah had another thought which she didn't impart to

151

Aunt Florence. Was it for a reason quite different from protection and chivalry that Oliver shielded Venetia?

"Don't worry about it, Aunt Florence," she said quickly, "I must go now. If I can't come back before this afternoon can you manage?"

"Yes, indeed. Bertha and I have everything under control. Send Jennie over early. She can come on her own if you get tied up with things." Aunt Florence reached up to give Sarah a kiss. "Now be careful, dear. Be discreet."

"Oh, don't worry about me. I'm only the onlooker. Nothing will happen to me."

"I hope not." Aunt Florence watched her to the door. Then she called in a bewildered voice, "But, Sarah, what about Eliot? If he didn't steal the ring what made him take his life?"

There was no one in sight in the house when Sarah went in. She hurried to the kitchen, and Mrs. Hopkins, seeing her face, said hastily, "It's all right, love. Jennie's safe in the garden playing with her dolls. I know you don't care for her to have them, but she wanted them this morning, poor mite."

Sarah went to the back door and looked out. At the other end of the cobbled path Jennie was sitting on a cushion on the grass with her dolls like a macabre family arranged about her. There was no one else in the garden.

"You see, she's all right," Mrs. Hopkins said.

"Who's been digging over there?" Sarah asked pointing to a mound of earth and a narrow trench.

"Oh, that's Mr. Oliver. He's so agitated about things he can't settle to write so he said he would do some physical work for a spell. It's a trench for sweet peas he's making. But I had to call him in just now because that young Mr. Page came. They're in the study together."

"Just now?" Sarah queried.

"Well, five minutes ago. I don't know exactly. Petunia answered the door."

"Oh," said Sarah slowly. Then she asked, "Can you hear what Jennie's saying?"

"No, she's mumbling away down there but she's always

talking to herself. Everyone's too busy to listen to her play-acting."

"Go on watching her, will you," Sarah said. "I have to see Tim."

But on her way back through the hall she ran into Oliver coming out of his study. She noticed that his hair was rumpled and his shirt open from the exertion of his digging. He smiled amiably.

"Ah, back already, Sarah? That's grand. I'm doing a little gardening for a change. By the way, I'm letting Brian work in my study this morning. He's finishing a thing he wants me to see. Don't let anyone interrupt him if you can help it."

"Very well," Sarah answered stiffly.

"Are those flowers for Venetia? That's very sweet of you. I hope she'll be well enough by this afternoon to enjoy them."

Sarah had forgotten she was still carrying the pink chrysanthemums. She was thankful for them because it gave her an excuse to get away.

"Yes. I'll take them up now."

"Fine. I've told Mrs. Hopkins to have lunch half an hour earlier today so there'll be plenty of time to get Jennie ready. Oh, and my mother wants to go to the party. That's all right with your aunt, I take it?"

"Of course," said Sarah, wondering if Aunt Florence's preparations for a dozen hungry children would stretch to satisfy one greedy old woman.

"Then back to my toil," Oliver said cheerfully. "There's something very satisfying about preparing the earth for seeds. One almost has the sense of a creator."

Sarah had a flash-back to the day she had lunched with Oliver when he had talked of the triumphs of swaying a theatre full of people to laughter or tears. Then there was his knowledge of Venetia's weakness and his apparent wish to hold her in a state of fear. Was he a little obsessed with the sense of power?

Sarah left him and went rather breathlessly upstairs to Tim's bedroom. But when she opened the door the bed was empty.

After all, that was to be expected. Tim wouldn't stay in bed a moment longer than he could help. Where was he, though? He couldn't have gone out of the house in his condition. She went along to Venetia's room and tapped gently at the door. Nurse Benson came out in answer. She looked very pretty and competent in her crisp white uniform.

"Oh, Miss Stacey," she whispered, "did you want to see the patient? She's a little better, but not conscious yet. She's only said those two words, you know. The rope! Poor thing, she's had her brother-in-law's suicide on her mind, hasn't she?"

"I was really looking for Tim," Sarah said. "Has he been in here?"

"You mean that thin young man with his arm in a sling?"

Sarah nodded.

"Oh, he was here ten minutes ago. Miss Stacey, who is the boss in this house?"

Sarah hesitated. She even had time to reflect ironically that a week ago she wouldn't have hesitated an instant. But now she wasn't sure.

"Mr. Foster is, of course," she said carefully. "But he's been terribly shocked by his wife's accident and his brother's death, too. So Tim and I are trying to keep all the decisions off his shoulders."

Nurse Benson looked alarmed.

"Do you really mean that? Because Tim's been in here more or less scaring six months' growth out of me, and I've been telling myself he's a little delirious, too. You don't mean he's serious, do you?"

"What's he been telling you?" Sarah asked. "Things like never leaving Mrs. Foster alone for an instant?"

"Yes."

"I'm afraid it's true."

"But Mr. Foster says so long as I'm in the house on call——"

"We prefer it the other way," Sarah said. "Don't ever leave her alone. If you want help call either Tim or me, or even Mrs. Hopkins, the housekeeper. She's perfectly trustworthy."

"But Doctor Forsythe didn't tell me this."

Sarah patted her arm.

"Maybe Tim and I are alarmists. But it has to be like this until Mrs. Foster is normal again. Doctor Forsythe doesn't know everything." She saw the apprehension on the girl's face and added reassuringly, "Nothing's likely to happen. We're just taking special care. We know you're perfectly capable of a job like this. All right?"

Nurse Benson nodded reluctantly.

"I suppose so. I must say—well, Mr. Foster doesn't seem that frightfully upset about his wife's condition, does he? Doesn't he know concussion can be serious?"

"Maybe he doesn't show his feelings," Sarah said. "Now I must run along and find Tim."

"Oh, he went up to the second floor," Nurse Benson said. "To the old lady's room, I think."

That was where Sarah found Tim, sitting at the table in old Mrs. Foster's room having a leisurely game of chess.

Sarah could have struck him. Last night in the midst of a crisis he went light-heartedly off to keep an appointment with Rachel Massey, and today, when there were all kinds of important things to do, he chose to while away the time playing chess.

"Hullo, Sarah," he said cheerfully. "I'm recovering, as you can see."

"Go away, Sarah," Mrs. Foster said impatiently. "We're busy, can't you see."

"I can see both things," Sarah said coldly. "Tim, I'm sorry to interrupt your game, but I have something urgent to tell you about."

"Well, tell him," said Mrs. Foster, "and let us get on. We started this game yesterday and couldn't get it finished."

"I'm sorry, but—"

"Oh, it's not meant for my ears." The old lady wagged her head with angry petulance. "No one ever tells me anything. Except Tim here, and he did have the good manners to come and tell me about his accident. There are too many accidents around here. You'll be the next, Sarah."

Tim grinned up at Sarah.

"Won't that be fun. Then I can resuscitate you."

"Tim—"

"All right, my dear. Wait two minutes." He made a move across the chessboard with his bishop. "Check," he said gleefully.

Old Mrs. Foster stared in incredulity. Then her face crumpled up and grew scarlet. With a movement like a spoilt child she tilted the board and spilled the men to the floor.

"You cheated!" she shouted. "You must have cheated."

"No, honey, you were outmanoeuvred,"

"I couldn't have been. It wasn't a fair game." She pounded her fist on the table. "He cheated. Sarah, didn't you see him cheat?"

"I'm afraid I didn't see anything."

"I hate to be beaten," the old lady sobbed childishly. "I can't bear it. I'm just like Oliver. He hates to be beaten, too. Oh, go away, both of you, and talk your secrets. I'll play solitaire and cheat as much as I please."

Sarah led the way out.

"Come along to the schoolroom," she said briefly.

Tim followed with deliberate slowness.

"I'm still pretty shaky, Sarah," he said wistfully.

"Then why aren't you in bed? Why are you wasting time playing games with that cheating old woman?"

"Chess is a pleasant game," he answered. "One chats between moves. We've exchanged a lot of gossip, the old lady and I."

"Gossip!" said Sarah scornfully, shutting the door of the schoolroom behind them. "What I have to tell you isn't gossip."

She related Jennie's conversation briefly, and had the satisfaction of seeing the mocking levity leave Tim's face.

"So that's what it is," he said. "I had suspicions."

"Of course, it's awfully hard for Oliver to find out a thing like this about his wife," Sarah said fairly. "He has to protect her."

Tim looked at her with his narrowed gaze.

"Are you still the wide-eyed admirer? One doesn't protect a woman by putting the fear of death into her. Nor does one use her rather pathetic weakness for reasons of one's own."

"But what reasons?"

"That's what we find out. And pretty damn quick."

"Tim, you can't interfere with Jennie's party this afternoon. That has to go on."

"I suppose so."

"But it has. The child would break her heart. Besides, it will be perfectly all right. Nurse Benson will be with Venetia, and the rest of us will be over there. Unless you prefer to stay in the house here."

"I do," said Tim. "All right, I'll leave the party to you. And you leave me to my games of chess or whatever means of diversion I see fit to pursue."

"You have peculiar means of diversion."

"Yes. So has the old lady. Look at this." He drew from his pocket a length of strong black thread. "Take that end and pull it," he said. "Feel its strength."

"Tim, what has this got to do with anything?"

"The old lady has sharp eyes. She didn't go to the larder last night, as you thought. She went to the cellar stairs."

"Yes?" Sarah demanded sharply.

"She found this. Broken, of course, by then. But enough when tied to a couple of nails to trip anyone. Don't you agree?"

For a moment Sarah felt the room whirling. "Tripped," Oliver had said. "The rope," Venetia had said. "I hate to be beaten," old Mrs. Foster had sobbed.

"Don't take it to heart, honey," she heard Tim saying from what seemed a long way off. "This time next week we'll be in Cornwall away from it all."

That brought Sarah to her senses.

"Tim, it's time to get the police."

He shook his head. "Not yet."

"But with things like this happening, with someone in the house—"

"There isn't enough proof," Tim said patiently. "What have we got—a suicide, a girl fallen down what is a very dangerous flight of stairs anyway, a piece of broken thread that may have hung there for months."

"Then we wait until someone actually dies," Sarah said scathingly.

"You forget. Someone may have died. And I don't mean Mary."

Sarah was conscious of prickles of horror along her scalp.

"Lexie Adams," she whispered.

Tim nodded. "The lady with violets. Haley, the porter, has the key to that mystery, I'm quite sure. We might have got him last night if that damned car hadn't got in my way. We'll try again tonight."

"Tim, you're not fit enough to go out tonight."

He looked at her with his gaunt earnest face.

"Much fitter than someone may be if we don't find out what's going on."


# XV

JENNIE'S cheeks were pink with excitement. With as much patience as she could muster she stood letting Sarah curl her dark soft hair into ringlets.

"I didn't believe it would come true," she said. "I never thought the party would really happen. When can I put my dress on, Sarah?"

"In a few minutes. Do you like your dress?"

"Oh, I love it. It's like a princess's, isn't it?"

"Definitely it is. Would you have minded very much if Aunt Venetia hadn't let you have it?"

Jennie twisted her head sharply. Her face was suddenly distraught.

"I didn't tell!" she cried. "Truly I didn't tell."

Sarah was sorry then that she had said anything. She had only wanted to confirm that Jennie's conversation with her dolls hadn't been purely make-believe.

"I know you didn't, darling," she said soothingly. "And you can forget it now because it's all over."

"Do you know about it?" Jennie asked.

"Yes, I know."

"Aunt Venetia said bad things happened to people who steal. Is that why she fell down the cellar stairs?"

"That was an accident, dear. She tripped." (Tripped! That horrible suggestive word again. She had to keep back the horror. She had to be gay and light-hearted for Jennie's sake. Sarah put a pink ribbon round Jennie's head, tying it in a festive bow. "There you are. Now you can put your dress on."

Jennie's fingers were impatient with excitement. She got the dress over her head and Sarah pulled it straight and buttoned it. Then Jennie stood in front of the mirror and gazed at herself wordlessly. At last she whispered,

"It's not really me, Sarah."

"Oh yes, indeed it is. It's Jennie Foster, aged eight years, going to a party."

Jennie touched the skirt standing out stiffly over the taffeta petticoats with reverent fingers.

"I'd like to wear it always," she said.

"And that would be like having chocolate for every meal. You'd soon get sick. But you're going to have lots of fun in it today. And don't forget, you have to blow eight candles out in one blow."

Jennie began to smile with shy joy.

"It's not really my birthday, but I feel more as if it were than on a real birthday. Oh, I'm so happy, Sarah."

Old Mrs. Foster, wearing black silk and a hat with bobbing plumes which was safely guaranteed to frighten every nervous child at the party came in just then and announced regally,

"I shall take Jennie over, Sarah. You, no doubt, have other things to do before you leave and I'm ready now." She looked at Jennie critically. "How is she going to play rough games in that dress?"

"She can do what she likes," said Sarah emphatically. "The dress is for today." She was not going to have any pessimistic old woman spoiling Jennie's joy.

"I was taught to have more respect for my clothes," the old lady said disapprovingly. "What with Venetia's extravagance and now you and Jennie aiding and abetting, all you women will bankrupt my son. He's too generous. Well, come along, then, Jennie, if you're ready. What sort of a cook has your aunt, Sarah?"

"Very good."

"I'm glad to hear it. I'm feeling peckish."

Jennie, her small hand swallowed in the large plump one of her grandmother's, looked back at Sarah.

"When are you coming, Sarah?"

"Almost at once, darling. I just have to change. You go and have fun."

When they had gone out Sarah found she had to sit down abruptly. The strength seemed to have gone out of her legs. Of course she had had no rest for what seemed a very long time. But it wasn't only tiredness making her weak at the knees now. She suddenly felt that she couldn't go on any longer. It was all very well for Tim to say blithely that the case had to be cut and dried before the police were called, he could go out into the good cheer of public houses searching for the mythical Haley, and with Rachel Massey's attractive company, too. She had to remain here in this unhappy haunted house, wondering what shadow or sound would materialise into acute danger.

She looked at herself in the mirror, dragging her hands over her wan weary face. She looked haggard. Her hair hadn't been properly brushed for twenty-four hours, her make-up was sketchy to say the least. The freckles stood out on her cheekbones as if she had just had a summer at the seaside.

Well, what did it matter? She had come here gaily thinking of herself in the role of Rebecca or Jane Eyre, and what had happened? The eligible widower dead by his own hand and the husband unhappily married to a neurotic and a thief. . . . But her mind shied violently away from the thought of Oliver. She couldn't begin to comprehend what might be the truth about him. It was incredible and fantastic, but who else was there? Who else?

Sarah picked up the hairbrush, and brushing fiercely at her short bright hair resolutely thought of other things. Tim—was he serious about his Cornish cottage? It sounded like a haven. She would like to go there, but probably everyone else, including Rachel with her dark dramatic good looks, had been airily invited also. She wasn't going all the way to Cornwall to join in a noisy party. Tim, with his hard narrow hands touching some other woman with meaningless caresses. Tim with his head on someone else's breast. . . . Sarah flung down the hairbrush and began applying lipstick extravagantly to her grim lips. What she needed was a sound sleep. Her thoughts were distorted and out of control.

Through the open window she could hear the sound of children's voices from Aunt Florence's garden. The party had started. That was grand. She would put on another dress and go over at once. The change was almost as necessary for her as as it was for Jennie. It would prepare her for the long night.

When she was ready she intended to tiptoe past Venetia's room, but Nurse Benson was lying in wait for her.

"Oh, Miss Stacey," she whispered urgently, pulling the door closed behind her and standing in the passage, "I wish you'd come in. Mrs. Foster is crying and I can't get her to stop."

"You'd better get the doctor to give her something," Sarah said.

"It's more than that, Miss Stacey. It's reassurance she needs. She's got something on her mind. When she came to half an hour ago she couldn't remember anything. Then her husband came in and spoke to her and straight away she got excited and sort of frightened. Since he went out she's just cried and cried. Do come in and see if you can help."

If she had let Venetia go that day she was packing her bag, Sarah thought irrelevantly, none of this would have happened. Or it wouldn't have happened in this house.

"I'll come in for a minute," she said to Nurse Benson.

It was true that Venetia was crying. She lay with her mouth slack and the tears trickling down her cheeks into the pillow. She made no sound and she seemed incapable of speech. Only her dilated eyes sought Sarah's in desperate pleading, and as Sarah leaned over her she felt her hand clutched weakly.

"It's all right," she said gently. "It's all right, Venetia."

Venetia gave a quivering sigh and seemed to relax.

"You see," Nurse Benson whispered. "It's reassurance she wants."

Sarah sat on the edge of the bed.

"You have to rest," she said to Venetia. "You have to sleep. When you're stronger you have to tell Tim and me about it." The swift alarm came back into Venetia's eyes. "Not now, but later. Because we're making everything all right. Do you understand?"

Venetia's eyelids flickered.

"Stay here, Sarah," she said in a thready voice.

"I think you'd better stay until she drops off," Nurse Benson whispered. "She has to be kept calm."

Sarah nodded resignedly. Jennie's party would have to go on without her. But Aunt Florence was capable of managing everything and would understand.

"All right," she said. "Just so long as I don't fall asleep, too."

The voices of the children sounded only faintly in this room. They had a drowsy quality, like bees on a summer day. Sarah watched Venetia drift into a restless sleep, and sitting in a chair by the bed fought sleep herself. It seemed as if she had spent half her entire lifetime in this room. There were so many things she should think out and assemble in her mind like a jigsaw puzzle; they must all fit—the words Eliot had spoken to Oliver in anger, Oliver's grief and then his abrupt recovery from the shock of Eliot's death, Venetia's perpetual state of fear for some reason bigger than having her kleptomaniac habits discovered, the convenient way the lights had gone out last night. . . . And another thing that niggled at her, why the house in Pimlico had been allowed to remain empty for so long.

But all she could think of was old Mrs. Foster tipping the chessmen on the floor and crying childishly, "I can't bear to be beaten. . . ."

An hour must have gone by before the telephone rang downstairs. This time, unlike last night, it was answered immediately, and a little later there was a discreet tap at the door.

Sarah crossed to open the door.

"It's your aunt, Miss Stacey," said Petunia in a loud whisper. "Will you speak to her? She says it's urgent."

Venetia was still dozing and so was Nurse Benson in a chair by the window. Sarah roused Nurse Benson and said she would be back presently. Then she went downstairs and spoke into the telephone,

"Hullo, darling, are you waiting for me?"

Without any preamble whatever Aunt Florence's voice came back,

"Sarah, has Jennie gone home?"

"Why, no, not that I know of. Isn't she with you?"

"She was. But just lately—"

Sarah abruptly became completely awake.

"Aunt Florence, are you telling me she's disappeared?"

"Now, don't get alarmed, Sarah. She's probably hiding the way children do. The others were teasing Hamlet and she rescued him and took him into the kitchen. But when Bertha went in ten minutes ago she found Hamlet there, but no Jennie. Haven't you heard us calling her?"

"I've been with Venetia. Her room's on the other side of the house. Have you looked everywhere for her? All over the house?"

"Jennie isn't one to pry about the house. And we've certainly looked under every bush in the garden. All the children have been looking." Aunt Florence's voice gave a sudden tremble, indicating for the first time how anxious she was. "They think it's fun."

"Don't worry, darling," Sarah said quickly. "She's probably slipped in without my hearing her. Looking for me, perhaps. Or wasn't she having a good time?"

"She was having a lovely time. So gay. I've never seen her like that before. Sarah, if anything's happened—"

"Nothing can have happened. I'll call you back in a few minutes."

She knew before she went upstairs that Jennie wouldn't be in her room. All the way she could hear Mrs. Hopkins's words, "There's a sort of darkness. Don't let Jennie have that party." She tried to shake the thought away. Mrs. Hopkins had a certain flair for clairvoyance and she loved the sensation she created.

But hadn't all her other predictions come true?

Jennie's room and the schoolroom were empty and the house was very quiet. Sarah could still hear the shouting and laughter of the children over at Aunt Florence's. Surely, if they were all so carefree, Jennie must be there. But Aunt Florence would immediately telephone.

She went downstairs again and to the kitchen. There the blind was drawn against the afternoon sun and Mrs. Hopkins was dozing in the rocking chair. She started up at Sarah's entrance.

"What is it, love? Do you want Petunia? She's gone out marketing."

It was clear that Jennie was not here. Sarah hesitated about disturbing Mrs. Hopkins who was much too easily upset.

"Jennie hasn't come in here during the last half-hour, has she, Mrs. Hopkins?"

"No, indeed. She's at her party, isn't she? I just dropped into a doze sitting here. The house is so quiet." Then she seemed to realise Sarah's tenseness. "Is there something wrong, Miss Stacey?"

"We're just looking for Jennie," Sarah said. "She's hiding somewhere."

"Ah, hide-and-seek, is it? She'd be a shrewd one at that. But she wouldn't come over here, would she? Her in that grand dress and all." Suddenly Mrs. Hopkins sprang up. "Miss Stacey, are you telling me the truth? Is everything all right?"

"Why shouldn't it be, Mrs. Hopkins?"

"I was thinking of what I saw in my cup," Mrs. Hopkins muttered. "But you convinced me I was wrong. I was wrong, wasn't I?"

"I hope so," said Sarah, still keeping her voice natural, though now panic was rising in her. "Let me know if Jennie does come in, Mrs. Hopkins."

From the kitchen she went out into the garden. Sunlight, growing cool and yellow, lay over the leaf-spattered grass and on the zinnias and dahlias, drooping and top-heavy from the night's rain. There was a small heap of freshly dug earth from Oliver's half-finished trench in the corner. Here the sound of the children next door was quite shattering. Surely Jennie's voice was among those shrill lively sounds.

The garden here seemed to be ringed in by an invisible wall of quiet. There was no movement anywhere. Sarah stood narrowing her eyes against the sun, thinking. From next door there was a brief silence, then Aunt Florence's voice, then abruptly a full-throated roar, "Jennie! Jennie! Where are you? Jennie!"

The panic Sarah had been trying to control rose overwhelmingly. All the nightmare was back. The sun was shining, the children were playing, but one little girl in a party frock was missing. Missing. Where?

Impelled by no comprehensible thought Sarah ran inside, down the hall and into Oliver's study. She didn't know what she had expected to find there. When she saw Oliver sitting at his desk, his thick hair ruffled in its familiar way, his face lifted enquiringly, her relief was so overwhelming that she couldn't speak.

"Well, Sarah," said Oliver, "is there any special reason for this very unceremonious intrusion? Not that I'm not always glad to see you, but at the moment you look as if the devil's after you."

Sarah, fighting to regain her breath, took a couple of steps across the room. She saw Oliver make a quick, almost guilty movement, then he got up, smiling with naïve charm.

"Well, you've caught me this time, Sarah." He turned and indicated the solitaire board on his desk. "I'm afraid I'm not always working in here. I get bored with writing and out comes the solitaire. But it's very hush-hush. One has to build oneself up a little, doesn't one?"

What was he talking about, Sarah wondered impatiently. She had got her breath back now.

"Oliver, have you seen Jennie?"

"Not since mother took her to the party. Why, what has happened?"

"She's disappeared."

"Is that all? She's probably got herself shut in somewhere. I'm sure there's no need to get in a panic about it."

"No, of course not." Sarah's reassurance was rapidly coming back. She almost felt she should apologise to Oliver for her half-formed horrible suspicion. Instead she said, "I'm sorry for bursting in in this way."

"That's all right," Oliver said pleasantly. "I really thought I was going to work this afternoon, but after all I couldn't. Let me know if Jennie isn't found. I'll come and help search."

Sarah's relief at having found Oliver in his study turned then to resentment against Tim. Why wasn't he about? Why wasn't he at Jennie's party, for that matter? There was nothing to keep him away from it. He left everything to her. Well, perhaps she was paid for it, but Jennie was his sister's child and he should be taking an interest in her affairs.

On enquiry from Petunia who was just coming in laden with a large shopping basket she heard that Rachel Massey and Tim had gone into the garage not long ago.

"I saw them as I was going out," Petunia said. "He must be taking her somewhere, though you wouldn't think he'd be fit to drive with that arm of his. Oh, I must tell Mrs. Hopkins. There was a new man in the corner shop, and the look he gave me. You could read it plain as plain. Won't Mrs. Hopkins have a laugh, all those men she saw for me in her cup."

"Go and get on with your work and don't talk nonsense," Sarah said sharply, to Petunia's obvious mortification.

She was too worried at the moment to care about Petunia's feelings. If Tim had taken Rachel somewhere in Oliver's car she would have to manage on her own once more. She was getting used to it, but it wasn't fair!

When she opened the garage door, however, the car was still there and Rachel and Tim were just coming out. It looked as if they had been sitting in the car, and now Rachel was holding Tim's arm in a proprietary way. Tim saw her first and said,

"Hullo, Sarah. Thought you were enjoying the party with Jennie. Don't think it's odd us being here, we just wanted a place where we could be private."

"I don't want to intrude on your privacy," Sarah snapped, "but you ought to know that Jennie isn't enjoying her party. She's lost."

"Jennie!" exclaimed Rachel, lifting her curved black brows. "Lost!"

"How long has she been missing?" Tim demanded.

"I'm not very sure. Aunt Florence has just discovered. She's rather upset."

"Where's Oliver?"

"Oliver's in his study. I've just come from him."

"Tim," said Rachel, "now surely you'll call the police."

Tim shook off her arm. His nostrils were pinched, his face all hollows. But he spoke quite pleasantly.

"First we'll make a thorough search. The police wouldn't

166

appreciate having to give their assistance in finding a child playing hide-and-seek."

"But with all the evidence, and now this—"

"All circumstantial, my sweet. There's still the missing piece. Come along, Sarah, you ought to know all the cubby holes at your aunt's place where a child could hide."


# XVI

An hour later Tim called the police. By that time they had searched every nook and cranny in both houses without finding so much as a hair ribbon. The sun was going down and the trees in Kensington Gardens were throwing shadows twice as long as themselves. The Gardens were strangely empty this afternoon. Sarah knew because she had been in them herself, going over to the familiar café and casting quick glances at every low-foliaged shrub. Anywhere a child might hide—or be hidden. She had stood a few minutes on the banks of the Serpentine watching a scattering of boats coming up the stream. But no one would throw a small girl into the water by daylight, with boats on the river and people walking about. Even the Round Pond drew her by a peculiar fascination and she stared at its bright shallow water, innocent of secrets. Then all at once she was hurrying back, unable to bear being away from the house any longer in case something had happened in her absence.

Now it was growing dusk and Sergeant Jackson had the matter of Jennie's disappearance written down in his little notebook. At first he had been inclined to be not too serious about it. It was a child's prank, probably. Maybe in a fit of pique over something that had happened at the party she had decided to give everyone a fright by running away. She would be picked up down the Bayswater Road or perhaps over towards Earls Court.

But Aunt Florence said she hadn't noticed anything untoward happen at the party beyond the children teasing Hamlet and Jennie carrying him away. That was the last anyone remembered seeing of her, a little girl struggling into the house with a large sulky cat in her arms. Hamlet was still there safely enough but he, unfortunately, couldn't speak.

Then Tim talked to the sergeant alone, and after that he seemed to catch Tim's urgency for he had a couple of constables sent out and the search began.

It was then that Sarah lost her temper, because Tim said she must not go out any more. The women, he said, must stay at the house. They could do nothing outside that the police were not doing, and it was unwise for them to wander about in the dusk.

"But Jennie will be crying for me," Sarah insisted angrily. "Like last night. I couldn't go to her then and you won't let me go to her now. Tim, for God's sake, can't you understand? It's so *awful*!"

Tim patted her shoulder briefly. He looked gaunt and tired, his eyes gleaming between their narrow lids, his mouth set in a straight grim line. He had taken his injured wrist out of the sling, for convenience, and had it tucked inside his coat. The bruise on his forehead showed like a wound.

"Hang on a bit longer, honey. I know you're almost out on your feet. But it's so important."

"Where are you going to look?"

"The police are combing the Gardens now and the bombed areas near here. Some of them have hoardings up, and—"

Sarah flinched, horror stopping her tears.

"There's one in Church Street—it has a big drop behind the hoarding. But Tim, in broad daylight—"

"Jennie's alive, Sarah," Tim said. "I'm quite sure she is. We'll come back with her, you'll see. You might have some hot tea ready. Keep the women busy, if you can. And get a little rest yourself." He added, apparently irrelevantly, "Oliver's coming with us."

Then he bent his head to kiss her on the cheek and when he had gone she stood rubbing her cheek slowly with her fingers and thinking that nothing was real, even Tim's impulse to kiss her.

So there they were in the house, a handful of helpless women. Aunt Florence had come over because, she said, she couldn't bear to stay in her own house. There was Jennie's cake in the kitchen with the still unlit candles on it and the "Happy Birthday" in pink icing mocking her every time she looked at it. Besides which Bertha was in the kitchen with her apron over her head in floods of tears, and that made you think there had been a death.

Aunt Florence clapped her hand over her mouth, instantly regretting her use of that word, but not before Petunia had burst into loud sobs and stood in her favourite position of misery, her head hanging over the sink.

Here Rachel took things in hand by filling the kettle.

"We'll all have a cup of tea," she said. "Isn't that a good idea?"

The stump of a stick at the door announced old Mrs. Foster's entrance, and she answered for everyone,

"An excellent idea. You're a young woman of sense. Where's my son? Has he gone out searching, too?"

Then Sarah remembered vividly how Oliver had acted when they had told him the police were coming. He had said in a loud excited voice,

"I won't have any more police in this house. Venetia's too ill and they'll likely disturb her as well as everyone else. What did they discover when Eliot died? Nothing at all."

"Did you expect them to discover something?" Tim had asked smoothly.

"Of course not, but they produce an unpleasant atmosphere of crime, and that's quite ridiculous in this house."

"Then you're not alarmed at Jennie's disappearance?" Tim said in the same quiet voice.

"Not at all. If all we adults can't find her we're pretty dumb. I'll come and help in the search at once."

"Jennie," said Tim, "has been missing nearly two hours. No child is going to hide voluntarily for that length of time."

Oliver looked at him with wide almost childish eyes.

"I say, old man, don't take that tone. One would almost think you're accusing me of hiding her. Why should I do that? She's a precious child. I see more than anyone that she's well cared for."

"Nevertheless," said Tim, "the police are coming."

For the barest instant Sarah thought she caught again that flicker in Oliver's face, the suggestion that another person lived behind the smooth genial exterior. Then he said resignedly, "If you have, you have. But I'm afraid they won't be particularly amused at this sort of wild-goose chase. And I do think, old chap, you might allow me to make decisions in my own house."

But when the police had come he had been perfectly affable, and now had gone out to join them in their systematic search.

It was quite fantastic of her to have a suspicion that Oliver knew of Jennie's whereabouts because he had been in his study at the time she had gone missing. It was more likely old Mrs. Foster knew something about it. She sat there, her pouchy old eyes bright with anticipation of an extra meal. She hadn't expressed any kind of concern for Jennie, neither had she explained why she had wanted to go to a children's party or to take Jennie herself. On the other hand, what possible motive could she have for hiding the child?

Hiding her! If Jennie were hidden near here she would be calling out, screaming with fear—if she were alive. . . .

"Come along, Sarah, help me to get the cups out," Rachel said. "Petunia's quite useless."

Sarah had always admired Rachel's good looks, but her poise and confidence had made her a little nervous. Now she had nothing but admiration for her altogether. She was a grand person in a crisis and that seemed to be the most necessary attribute to have in this house.

Mrs. Hopkins's face was crumpled like a faded rose petal. She sat at the table, her hands lying empty and palms upwards on it.

"Don't give me any tea, Miss Massey," she said heavily. "Heaven forbid, but I'd be looking at the leaves. I remember how Jennie was always at me to do that. Then she'd mimic me, the minx. She hasn't done so much mimicking since Sarah came, though I did hear her at it this morning in the garden. She was that clever you had to hear it to believe it."

"Stop that, Mrs. Hopkins," said Aunt Florence sharply. "You're talking as if she's dead."

Dead! Again the word seemed to remain in the room as

everyone fell silent. *I'm so happy,* Jennie in her party dress had said. Never before, thought Sarah, had she ever heard Jennie say she was happy. And now she was out somewhere in the darkening twilight, cold, lonely, afraid.

Mrs. Hopkins moved her empty hands.

"Where's that tea?" she asked in a high thin voice.

"O-ooh!" sobbed Petunia shudderingly.

"Can't that girl be quiet!" grumbled old Mrs. Foster. "She sounds like a funeral."

Sarah could stand it no longer.

"I must go and see how Venetia is," she said.

"Don't be long," Rachel called after her. "I'll keep your tea hot."

Venetia, Nurse Benson said, had been asking for Sarah. She had taken some hot milk, but she seemed to be wandering again. Sarah went across to the bed. When Venetia was out of danger, she thought, she would never willingly come into this room again. Indeed, she would never be able to see any bedroom with pale-blue carpet and tasselled velvet cushions without having this aura of fear and menace come back to her.

Venetia was watching her with feverish eyes.

"Sarah, where have you been?"

"Oh, doing a lot of things," Sarah answered.

"Why is the house so quiet? Why does no one come to see me?"

"Doctor Forsythe says you mustn't have visitors."

"I feel forgotten." Tears welled into her eyes again. She lay a moment, silent, then she said in a rapid excited voice, "Sarah, there's something I want to tell you. I have to tell somebody and I can trust you." She turned her head on the pillow, looking at Nurse Benson. "Send her out."

Sarah nodded to the girl and she went to the door.

"All right, Venetia," she said gently. "You can tell me."

"It's about—something—that mink scarf and your aunt's ring—Oliver found out. He said he wouldn't tell if I agreed—to something. . . ."

"Yes," Sarah encouraged. "What did you agree to?"

This was bad for Venetia. Perspiration was standing out on her brow and her lips had a blue tinge. Sarah knew she had to cut short the explanations and get to the essential information at once.

But her abrupt question seemed to frighten Venetia and her coherence began to leave her. She moved restlessly.

"I don't know! I don't know!"

"But it was something important."

"I don't know. My head, I can't think. . . . Tell Lionel to give me something to make me sleep."

"In a moment, dear. Try to tell me first."

"Tell you what?" Venetia asked, with a feverish blank gaze.

Sarah tried again. "Why is Oliver threatening you?"

"You mean he's threatening Eliot. That girl—Lexie. . . . It was Eliot's. He told me." She rolled her head on the pillow. "But, Oliver, I didn't take the scarf. I paid for it. Jennie will tell you."

Sarah went to the door to call the nurse back.

"She's wandering again," she said. "Can you carry on for a few more hours?"

Nurse Benson nodded resignedly.

"Of course I can. I couldn't sleep anyway, with that child lost in the dark or maybe strangled on a rubbish dump."

Sarah winced at the girl's brutal imagination.

"Thank you, nurse," she said wanly. "You're doing a good job. I'll have some supper sent up to you."

When she went down again she found Rachel lighting a fire in the lounge. There was a tray set with tea things on the table.

"I've brought your tea in here, Sarah," she said. "You've got to relax."

"Relax!" echoed Sarah. What an odd sense of humour actresses had.

"Yes. Because Jennie will need you when they bring her home."

Sarah clenched her hands until she felt the skin break on her palms.

"Rachel," she said pleadingly, "will they bring her home?"

"I'm sure they will."

"You don't know what I do."

"I think I do. I've been helping, you know. Tim and I have

done quite a bit of investigation. When I came here it wasn't because I was interested in Oliver's play. Certainly it's a damn good one, as I guessed it would be. But it wasn't that that brought me. And it's only secondary now."

"Lexie," Sarah said.

"Yes. She was my best friend. I've been breaking my neck for months to get back to London and find out what really happened to her."

"You came here because you knew she was Eliot's friend?"

"Because I knew she had some connection with him."

"Venetia knows what it was," Sarah said wearily. "First she was too scared to talk and now she can't. She just says 'It was Eliot's', as if she were talking about the ownership of something. What does she mean?"

"I haven't any idea. And by the time she can talk it might be too late. The porter, Haley, knows something vital, too. Obviously he was bribed. He's supposed to be an incurable pubgoer, so Tim and I have been visiting all the pubs in the vicinity of where we think he lives. Haley isn't a common name and he's sure to be known at his local pub. It's been fun, too, when we've forgotten the grim side of it. We should have employed a private detective, but Tim thought we had plenty of time to do it ourselves."

Because he liked pub crawling in Rachel's company, Sarah thought wearily. She was aware of Rachel regarding her with her intelligent eyes.

"You're in love with Tim, aren't you, Sarah?"

"In love! Me!" Sarah began to laugh in sheer astonishment, then found she was too tired. It wasn't very funny, anyway, it was probably Rachel's method of warning her off the grass. Well, there was no need. She had never stepped on it. She had no desire to.

"He's a grand person," said Rachel caressingly.

"Who are you talking about?" came old Mrs. Foster's strident voice from the door. "Oliver? Of course all you women fall for him. And then he marries a poor spineless creature. Haven't those men come home yet? Fancy one brat of a child causing all this trouble!"

She waddled across the room, and lifting the blind tried to peer out into the dark.

"Oliver will break his heart if anything's happened to that child," she said. "Besides being very fond of her she's the only descendant of the family, and likely to be the only one, considering the wife Oliver's got. He places a lot of importance on having heirs. It's a conceit, of course, but he always was an enormously conceited child."

Her voice was irritatingly smug as it always was when she talked of Oliver. Sarah felt her nerves stretched beyond endurance.

She had a sudden memory of Oliver in his study when she had burst in, looking up sharply, guilty because he had been caught playing solitaire instead of working. Or was that his reason for guilt? She had been so relieved because he was there before her eyes, but had he had time—Aunt Florence hadn't been sure how long Jennie had been missing—he could have just arrived back from wherever . . .

No, no, it couldn't be!

But it could because Mrs. Hopkins had said Oliver had been in the garden digging a trench for sweet peas when Jennie had been playing with her dolls. He could have heard Jennie's conversation about the mink scarf. Knowing that much he would wonder how much else she knew. She may even have said more before Sarah had come within hearing. Enough to make it imperative for Oliver to take action. The reasons for most murders is the possession of dangerous knowledge, she heard Tim's voice saying.

Sarah got up with elaborate caution. She had to go out into the back garden and she didn't want old Mrs. Foster poking an inquisitive nose after her.

"Sarah, you haven't had this tea after all," Rachel said. "Where are you going?"

"I'll be back in a minute," Sarah answered. She went out quickly, not even stopping to see how Aunt Florence and Mrs. Hopkins in the kitchen were.

There was a half-moon in the sky but it was still a pale unlighted colour. At first it was difficult to see even the brick path that led to the small arbour where Jennie usually sat with her dolls. What she had to find out was how far from there the trench Oliver had started to dig was. She stood half-way down the garden accustoming her eyes to the darkness.

Yes, there was the place where Oliver had been digging and several yards away under the dividing wall the arbour. It was possible from that distance he would not have heard Jennie's conversation, but Jennie's clear voice carried, particularly when she was mimicking someone else. That was proved by the ease with which Sarah herself heard it over a brick wall.

The chances, then, were that he had heard it and waited his opportunity. Sarah stood quite still, bothered at that moment not so much by the conclusion she had reached as by something different about the garden. What was it? The shrubs, in the grudging light of the moon, were in the same places, the leaves of the creepers hung like tattered rags just as they had that afternoon, the trench Oliver had begun. . . . Ah, that was it. The mound of soil had gone. It had stood piled up beside the trench, but now it was no longer there. It could mean only one thing. The trench had been filled in.

Sarah thought her trembling legs would never get her there. She tumbled on to the edge of the dug soil and began scrabbling with her hands, flinging up earth and dead leaves. Like a dog burying a bone, she thought. But this was for such a different purpose. She didn't dare to think of anything beyond the strangeness of Oliver digging a trench only to fill it in again. She didn't dare to let the horror seize her completely or her hands would become stiff and unable to work.

Then she saw the glimmer of white and for a moment it seemed as if a paralysis of horror would overcome her. Instead, she dug frantically, her breath coming in harsh gasps between her dry lips. But when she got the dress, Jennie's party dress, grimy and almost unrecognisable, into her hands, there was nothing else there. The innocent earth concealed no grimmer secret.

Sarah sat back on her heels holding the limp dress helplessly. She couldn't even think now, beyond the fact that someone had buried Jennie's dress here, probably because Jennie in it would have been to conspicuous and easily remembered by chance passers-by. But it brought one no nearer to finding the child. It only proved almost beyond doubt that Oliver—

A soundless scream escaped Sarah's lips as a hand touched her shoulder. She flung round to face a man. Not Oliver, thank God, not Oliver, but a stranger.

"Who are you?" she gasped.

"I just wondered what you was doing, miss," the man said. "Petunia said there was queer goings on in this house. Is there more trouble?"

"Oh yes," Sarah said. "It's Jennie. This is her party dress buried here. Buried!" She tried to pull herself together. "You're Petunia's Jimmy, aren't you?"

"Yes, miss. I came round because she didn't meet me where we arranged tonight. I thought maybe something had happened. Jennie's the kid, isn't she?"

"Yes, she's lost."

"Lost! But that's funny, miss. She got on my bus this afternoon, she and a tall blond sort of a gentleman. Big, he was. Mr. Oliver, I should think, from the way Petunia's described him. I recognised Jennie because Petunia's had her out once or twice."

Sarah gripped his arm.

"Where did they get off?"

"At Hammersmith Bridge. They turned down towards the towpath. I watched because I thought it was funny. The kid seemed sort of scared, and after the accidents that have happened here—hi, where are you going?"

Sarah didn't even stop to answer. She was running out of the garden on to the road and hailing a passing taxi.

Afterwards she knew she should have told someone where she was going. But Petunia's Jimmy would surely do that and Rachel would tell Tim and the police. There just wasn't a moment to waste. Jennie was the important thing. She knew now where she would be. At the man Haley's. And please God she was still alive.

## XVII

In the darkness of the taxi Sarah retained enough sense to try to clean up her earth-grimed hands, and also to feel thankful that earlier in the afternoon, from some meticulous sense of being prepared, she had changed into a suit and was carrying some money in her pocket. She asked the driver to let her out at Hammersmith Bridge and enquired from him how to get on to the tow path by the river.

He seemed surprised, but pointed out the way willingly enough.

"Follow the road between those buildings, then you cross a green, an old burying ground it used to be. Don't trip over a tombstone in the dark!" He gave a short guffaw at his morbid humour. "Then you come to the Rose and Crown and the tow path runs on from there."

Sarah found the track across the cemetery and hurried because although it wasn't very late there was no one about. A bomb had fallen in one end of the cemetery and there were slabs of ancient concrete torn up like the old whitened roots of trees, and one or two derelict buildings. Long seeded grass shook and rustled where the earth had been torn up. The thought crossed Sarah's mind that this would make a good place for a murder, if one brought one's victim at night. Oliver had brought his by daylight. He could not dispose of a body even as small as Jennie's in the light of a fine afternoon.

In contrast to the darkness of the green the isolated lights in the windows of shabby houses and then, a hundred yards further on, the swinging sign of the Rose and Crown were as comforting as a warm fire.

Sarah decided to try the Rose and Crown first, because that was what Tim would have been doing had he not been out on a different search tonight.

She tried to smooth her hair with her hands, but felt the curls spring up in disarray under her fingers. She would be stared at in the bar, and inevitably misjudged. That was a trifling matter at the present time. She went in boldly and saw the typical inn parlour with its polished counter, dartboard and piano. The patrons, a sprinkling of men and two women at a table in the corner all looked at her. Ignoring them she went to the bar and ordered a glass of ale.

As the barman served her she leaned across and said casually, "By the way, could you tell me if a man called Haley ever comes in here?"

"Haley?" said the barman. He was a young man with a pleasant face. He looked at Sarah curiously, no doubt puzzled by her wind-blown and haggard look. "Joe Haley?"

"I don't know his christian name," Sarah answered, controlling her excitement.

"If it's Joe he's usually here of a night. You'd better wait."

Somebody behind her spoke, "Joe Haley likely won't be in tonight. He's got visitors. I saw them arrive this afternoon."

Sarah swung round. But she remembered to keep the glass of ale in her hand and to look disinterested.

"Do you know where he lives, then?" she asked the man who was her informant.

"Yes. A dozen or so houses past here by the river. The last house before the boatsheds. If you go down there you're bound to find him."

"But he has visitors?"

"Yes. A tall gentleman and a little girl. The gentleman went away but the kid's still there, far as I know. He's not quite the kind of chap to leave a child with, if you ask me."

Sarah swallowed her ale. She had to remember to do that, she told herself meticulously, though when she had got out of here it didn't matter in the least what anyone had thought. Her luck in getting information at the first attempt was incredible.

As she went out someone began to play the piano. The melody followed her into the dark and for a while kept away the sound of the wind whistling in a lonely way round the sharp corners of houses. The street got narrower and finally came on to the river's side. Then she could smell the cool dark water and see it sliding past. Barges were anchored a little way out and scattered lights twinkled. Behind her, in the distance, the buses with twin rows of lights went over Hammersmith Bridge.

Before long she would be back on the safety of the main road, boarding a bus with Jennie clutching her hand. She had to tell herself that to make herself keep walking away from the lights along the empty path. The houses grew more isolated, then she saw the large dark shape of the boatshed jutting into the river.

Just beside it was a tall thin house with broken steps leading up to the front door. It had the look of possessing a tenant who grudged living in it and gave no attention to its appearance.

Sarah climbed the uneven steps, and feeling for the knocker found it and rapped loudly.

As she waited she could hear the slapping of water against the piles of the boatshed and again the faint weeping sound of the wind. She had a feeling of being completely in a nightmare, and had to force herself by a last effort of will to remain where she was. For in a moment the door would open and a figure out of her nightmare would appear, a man with no face, or a head supported by an invisible body.

If it were not possible that Jennie were there she would turn and run and never stop until she reached the lights and safety of Hammersmith Bridge.

Over there in the river, she told herself soothingly, is the island where the swans nest. They look like large white blossoms from the shore. This is just a house facing the river where the swans float up and down in the wake of the barges and schoolboys practise rowing on Saturday afternoons.

There was a faint sound on the other side of the door. Sarah tried to get her breath. If her heart thudded like this she wouldn't be able to speak, and how foolish it would be if she couldn't tell Joe Haley, ex-porter of Camelot Flats, that she had come to take Jennie home.

The door began to open. All at once a light flashed in her face. She was dazzled. She couldn't see who stood there, enemy or friend, headless man or angel.

"Why, Sarah!" came Oliver's voice, raised a little in surprise. "How ever did you find your way here?"

After all Sarah found herself speechless. Why had it never occurred to her that Oliver might be here. Ostensibly he was out searching with the police, but of course she might have guessed he would slip away and come down here. Tim had known the danger. Why, she thought in frantic anger, had he been so careless as to allow Oliver to get away? Oliver's big familiar figure standing there before her had the peculiar dual effect of both reassuring her and plunging her deeper into the nightmare. In that instant a vivid remembrance came to her of how she had first heard his voice over Aunt Florence's wall, deep and soothing as the doves in the trees, and in a queer way both past and present were one. The danger she had sensed then had now come to fruition.

"But come in," she heard Oliver saying hospitably. "Don't stand out there in the cold."

When she obeyed, her legs moving automatically, it was as if she were doing what she had known instinctively she must do some time—stepping into the mystery and danger that lay the other side of the wall.

He led the way down a narrow passage with an uneven floor to a living-room at the back of the house. Almost before she noticed the man on the couch Sarah was aware of the unkempt air of the place. There was dust thick on the table, except where damp rings showed where glasses had stood. Under the table and in the hearth there were empty bottles. The man on the couch, unshaven, small, with a face as sharp and pointed as a fox's, but with miserable apathetic eyes was too drunk to speak.

That, thought Sarah contemptuously, was Joe Haley. The Rose and Crown wouldn't be seeing him tonight. Oddly enough her contempt for his condition brought back her courage. Oliver, she told herself grimly, had got away with far too much, and he wasn't going to scare her!

Oliver had found a piece of cloth and was carefully dusting a chair.

"Sit down, Sarah," he said. "That's a fellow called Haley, but I'm afraid he's not in a condition to make conversation. Will you have a drink yourself?"

Sarah remained standing.

"I've come for Jennie, as you know," she said. "Just show me where she is and I'll take her home."

"Ah, don't be in a hurry, my dear. Jennie's asleep. She's perfectly all right."

"She can be woken."

"I'm afraid that would be difficult."

Sarah's new courage almost vanished. She looked at Oliver with her question unspoken.

Oliver gave his wide genial smile.

"You don't trust me now, do you, Sarah. That's a pity. But there's no need to be alarmed. I wouldn't have designs on Jennie's life. She's too precious."

So that was it. His enormous ego had saved Jennie. The solitary descendant of the family must not die.

"She was in such a state I've given her something to make her sleep," he announced blandly. "I was sorry I had to do this today, but it hadn't occurred to me that she knew more than she should. She's too sharp, the minx."

"And what were you going to do with her after she woke up?"

"I'm going to send her to the country out of harm's way. I know a woman who will take her." He turned his amiable smile on her. "Don't worry, Sarah. You won't know anything about it."

Sarah's relief that Jennie was all right turned to chilling horror. He still meant to go on with his intentions, her arrival was simply a trifling annoyance to be brushed aside—*how?*

He picked up a bottle and took the cork out.

"You ought to have a drink, Sarah. You look frozen. And tired, too. You had quite a night last night, didn't you? This is brandy. It will do you good."

Sarah said simply, "Take me to Jennie."

"But it's no use, my dear. She's dead to the world. Almost as dead as Haley over here."

The sound of his name stirred vague recognition in Haley.

"No party to this," he muttered. "This is different."

"Have another drink, old man," said Oliver, handing him a glass.

"Kidnapping!" Haley said, with a glassy stare. He took the glass and swallowed the brandy in one mouthful. "Christ!" he said feebly.

Oliver nodded towards him tolerantly.

"He's a useful fellow when he's sober. A little expensive. maybe, but it's been worth it."

His smugness and his profound pleasure in his cleverness suddenly made Sarah's fear and apprehension turn to pure contempt. So great was it that she became reckless. She would strip him of his conceit if it were the last thing she ever did.

"Not too expensive if it saves your life," she said.

He looked at her with interest. "What are you suggesting, my dear?"

"Why did you lie to me about the house in Pimlico?" she demanded. "Why have you deliberately left it empty? What's there that you're afraid someone will find out?"

It was a shot in the dark. But curiously his eyes seemed to darken with a queer kind of excitement as if her words had released something in him.

"You're too inquisitive, Sarah. And you're jumping to conclusions. You're thinking about Lexie Adams, aren't you? Don't worry, she's where no one will ever find her."

"*No!*" Sarah whispered. The suspicion as to what he meant was like a blow, taking her breath away, choking her with horror.

"And he knows—where she is, too?" she got out, indicating Haley.

"By no means. He's merely been useful in inventing a double life for her. There was no other man, of course."

Sarah remembered Jennie's story about the lady with violets coming to the house in Pimlico, and Oliver being there alone to receive her. Now she couldn't speak at all.

"It saved a lot of awkward enquiries," Oliver went on. "I always had much more forethought than Eliot." He shook his head with genuine sadness. "Eliot had brains, poor fellow, but what he wouldn't admit was that I had the ingenuity and organising ability. He should have worked in with me better."

He poured some more brandy into a glass and leaned across the table.

"This is grand, you know, having someone to talk to at last. I've had to keep this particular piece of cleverness to myself for so long that I must admit I enjoy boasting about it. As a boy I was always told I was so dull."

"But you enjoy power."

"Yes. That was a compensation I discovered. It's the most intoxicating thing in the world. Manipulating people at one's will—"

"Venetia—too?"

He nodded. "Venetia knew too much. That was Eliot's fault. He told her our secret, told her deliberately as a sort of legacy to me, and then hanged himself." Oliver pouted, obviously amazed and indignant at Eliot's failure to play the game. "He thought that would make things just too difficult for me. But I found a way out even then. Only Venetia had to be kept quiet."

He stopped to have a drink, savouring the brandy with enjoyment. Then he went on,

"Venetia's unfortunate tendency which I only discovered the night your aunt indiscreetly left her ring lying about gave me a lever, but I found later it wasn't enough. Do you know, she'd been doing that kind of thing since she was a schoolgirl. No wonder her family was anxious to get her married off, with a good slice of money as compensation for the unlucky husband, I suppose. But as you can see I was able to turn the whole thing to my own advantage. You might think I meant to kill her last night. I didn't really, you know. I just meant to give her a good fright. I don't particularly want her dead. I'm very fond of her."

"Fond!" Sarah gasped.

"Indeed, yes. I'm fond of you, too, Sarah. I respect your intelligence. And you're a fine-looking woman. I wish you'd had the sense to keep out of this."

"And Jennie?" Sarah said, little above a whisper.

"Ah, Jennie." His face became soft and affectionate. "She's a sharp one. She was even wary when I suggested this afternoon that we should slip down to Kensington High Street for ten minutes and buy a present that she could take back to the party. I'd been wondering how I could get her alone, and then I found her carrying that cat of your aunt's into the house. The opportunity couldn't have been better. I made good time over that little errand, too, because I was back before she was found to be missing. It was really quite amusing."

"I think you're mad," Sarah breathed.

"No, not really," he answered seriously. "Just a little more of a superman than most people."

"You can't possibly hope to get away with all this."

"Why not?" His large naïve eyes were on her. "You're the only person who knows anything. And even you don't know where Lexie Adams is."

"Isn't one person enough?"

"Not when she no longer exists. You're looking very white, my dear. I told you I was sorry about this. But you would poke your nose in."

"Mine won't be the only one poked in," Sarah said, succeeding with a tremendous effort in keeping her voice calm. Why, *why* had she been so foolhardy as to come down here alone. But surely by now Jimmy would have told someone else and there would be help on the way.

"Yes," said Oliver thoughtfully, "I realise now it wasn't a wise thing to take Jennie away. I should merely have talked to her and held her by the power of fear as I did Eliot and Venetia. I shall probably have to take her home saying I found her sleeping in an empty allotment. But you, my dear, have unfortunately slipped into the river during your search." He sighed, spreading his chest. "Too bad, isn't it? I'm damned sorry, but there it is."

Sarah turned her head jerkily towards Haley who was staring rigidly at the wall. Oliver followed her glance.

"Oh, don't depend on him. He's unconscious when he gets to that stage. I know of old." Oliver crossed over and touched the man on the shoulder and he subsided slowly, like a puppet, on to the couch.

"You see?" he said. "There's really no escape for you. The doors are locked and the windows are too small for you to get through quickly. I'd be bound to catch you, and I'm very much stronger than you are. But don't be afraid, my dear. I'll make it as painless as possible. All you have to do is drink a sleeping draught I'm going to give you. It's Lionel's prescription for Venetia; you've been pouring it into her often enough."

"You are mad," Sarah said between dry lips.

Oliver smiled.

"Have it your own way." He was dissolving some tablets in water. When they were sufficiently dissolved he poured a little brandy into the mixture.

"Just to make it tasty," he said. "That's really a very fine drink and it will have an effect quite quickly because I've used a generous amount. Is there anything else you want to say while your mind's clear?"

Sarah held out her hand for the glass.

"Oh no, my dear, don't be so anxious. You might spill it, mightn't you? I shall hold the glass myself while you drink."

With the glass in his hand he advanced towards her.

"I'd rather you didn't scream, Sarah, it's distressing, but if you must it will be quite all right. The house next door is empty and there's a boatshed on the other side. Nobody's around there at this time of night."

His hand, Sarah thought in a fascination of horror, was very large and white like a toadstool, or one of those poisonous puff-balls she had trodden on as a child and which had oozed a dark brown evil substance. He was still smiling in a kind gentle manner, but now his eyes glittered in a way that reduced her all at once to complete panic. The nightmare she had been fighting assumed gigantic proportions and swept over her like a dark wave.

"No!" she screamed, leaping away from him. "No! You can't make me drink that! You can't!"

When the window behind her was thrown up with such a jerk that the glass shattered she hardly heard it. Glass tinkled in staccato sounds on the floor, the blind was wrenched aside and Sergeant Jackson's face appeared in the aperture.

"All right, that's enough," he said. "Don't drink that little mixture, miss. I'll just be keeping it for a curiosity."

After that Sarah's mind couldn't take in very much. She was aware of Oliver drawing himself up haughtily and saying with devastating confidence,

"And on what charges do you arrest me?"

"Well, there's a little matter of a hit-and-run-driver charge, to begin with. Your car answers to the description of the one that knocked Mr. Tim Royle down last night in Kensington Walk."

Sarah, in a peculiar blurred way, saw Tim come in at the door. She noticed that his face was taut with anxiety and that when he saw her it went blank with relief.

She stumbled towards him and felt his arm, his one good arm, so tightly round her that she couldn't possibly fall no matter how much the floor tilted.

"Is that all?" she heard Oliver saying contemptuously.

"By no means. If you want the rest you can have it. We'll be asking you to explain how the body of a woman came to be buried in an air-raid shelter at 57 Birchell Street, Pimlico, a shelter that is now converted into a toolshed with a fine new concrete floor."

And then at last the jigsaw puzzle was complete, and Sarah, watching Oliver's eyes becoming curiously blank and unfocused, knew why Eliot had hated the sound of doves. Because they had been crooning in the old pear tree the afternoon he had helped Oliver to dig the grave in the disused air-raid shelter, and they had become mixed for ever in his mind with the bland compelling voice of his brother.


# XVIII

WHEN Sarah awoke it was daylight. Instinctively she looked at her bedroom clock and saw that it was a quarter-past ten. She started up, half dazed, not knowing whether the blurred memory of the previous night was real or part of a disordered sleep. Then she heard Tim's voice,

"And high time, too, my pet. You've slept the clock round."

Sarah sank back on the pillow with an exquisite sensation of relief.

"You're here," she murmured. "Rachel said I was in love with you. What nonsense!"

"What nonsense, indeed," Tim agreed cheerfully. "You'd sweep the floor with me, wouldn't you, honey?"

"And don't call me names when I'm half asleep."

"Then wake up. You've got a lot to hear."

At that Sarah began to come completely back to reality.

"Tim, your arm. How is it?"

"It's fine. I can tie my own shoelaces now. I believe I've clipped several seconds off the record for a one-armed man."

"Where's Jennie?"

"She's downstairs with Mrs. Hopkins and she's none the worse for her experience. She was fortunately put to sleep yesterday before she had time to get really frightened, so she doesn't remember much now. Mrs. Hopkins is spoiling her shamefully, and Petunia's very smugly flashing a diamond ring. The element of danger seemed to bring Jimmy up to scratch."

"Yes, Jimmy," said Sarah, repressing a shudder. "If it hadn't been for him—"

"If you hadn't rushed off like a mad thing, my sweet. You might have known we had Oliver covered. The only reason we let him come out was because we guessed he'd eventually lead us to his hide-out."

"You mean you were there all the time!"

"No, not all the time. He gave us the slip for a while. By the time we got on his trail again you were there." Tim reached out to touch her hand. "It was horrible. As much as we heard and what you must have gone through."

"It wasn't real," Sarah said. "It was a nightmare. But, Tim, in telling me everything else he didn't tell me why he started all this—orgy of deaths and accidents."

"It's perfectly simple, of course," Tim answered. "I began to get it when the old lady said how jealous Oliver had always been of Eliot's ability."

"And he was also jealous of Eliot's lady-friends?"

"He would have been had Eliot had them. But Lexie Adams wasn't Eliot's friend in that sense. She was an actress. She was a very talented person and also very kind. She was helping him with his first play which she considered exceptionally promising. The play's name was *Meadowsweet*."

"Eliot's!" Sarah gasped. "Not Oliver's."

"Not Oliver's."

"But that was what Venetia was trying to tell me last night. I didn't understand."

"At first," Tim went on, "Lexie was the only person who knew that. When Oliver found she wasn't going to play in his little scheme there was only one thing to do according to his reasoning. That was to remove her. So he asked her to the house in Pimlico on an afternoon when he knew Mary and Eliot would be out, and strangled her. He had meant to shoot her, but after standing over her with a gun while she wrote that note he was afraid of the sound of the shot."

Sarah thought of Oliver's broad strong hands and shuddered deeply.

"And then he went on blackmailing Eliot into writing for him?"

"Yes. The shock of finding Lexie dead and her body hidden in the air-raid shelter, and then Oliver forcing him into assisting with the burial was more than Eliot could recover from. It sounds hard to believe that he would spinelessly let a thing like that happen, but as you know from their mother Oliver had browbeaten Eliot all his life. He was physically and mentally afraid of him. He was quite sure that if Oliver wanted it proved that Eliot had killed Lexie Adams it would be so. He couldn't risk that happening, not only for his own sake but for Mary's, who was expecting a child. He just simply, according to his unsound reasoning, had no alternative."

"And Mary?" Sarah asked involuntarily.

"I don't know," said Tim. "I can only guess. She'd hate coming to live here. I think she and Eliot were happy before. Then she wouldn't believe that Eliot had been having an affair with Lexie Adams because she knew he loved her. She was an intelligent girl. She would discover the truth. And that, as you know, was the first snag Oliver had to encounter in his pleasant little path of blackmail."

"Poor Mary!" Sarah whispered.

Tim was silent a moment. Then he went on,

"Oliver's first real difficulty arose, of course, when something he hadn't foreseen happened. Eliot's spirit, for a variety of reasons, broke. He committed suicide, and what I like to think deliberately before the second play was finished. It put Oliver on a spot."

Sarah remembered with distressing vividness the day Oliver had wept in his study after Burgess Reid had visited him. So his tears hadn't been from grief at all, but from fury and frustration at his inability to realise something so nearly in his grasp. Though she thought they might have been from grief, too, because torturing Eliot had become a lifelong habit with him, something he would miss.

"But he cheered up after that," she said. "He was confident the play would be finished."

"Ah yes. That was when Brian Page came on the scene. A promising young writer eager to earn a little money without talking about it. He was going to complete the play. I shouldn't be surprised if Oliver had much darker schemes afoot there. I'm quite sure he thought he had found a successor to Eliot."

Sarah thought of the study with the roses artistically in a silver vase on the writing-desk, and Oliver bending his fair head studiously over a solitaire board. What hours he had been condemned to solitaire!

She put her hands over her face in horror.

"Tim—at first I liked him."

"Why not? He was an attractive fellow. He went out of his way to make people like him. It was all right at the beginning when no one suspected anything, but when the pressure was on he got definitely panicky. His actions lost coherence and he did incredibly stupid things, like taking that fuse out of the switch-board because he knew Venetia would be the one to go down for candles. He knew she was more likely to be frightened than killed, the power of fear was his biggest weapon, but he over-looked the investigation that must follow, with a household that wasn't completely dumb as it had been when Mary fell. The same with Jennie's abduction, the drama of the moment appealed to him without working out the consequences. And you last night—he was living completely in the moment, not think-ing of what would happen when the young woman's body fished out of the Thames had been identified. Sorry, honey, I don't mean to be brutal."

"I can take it now," Sarah answered. Then she said, "What's going to happen?"

"He'll be tried for murder, but it's almost certain insanity will be proved. At the moment he doesn't mind, you know. He's enjoying having headlines in the newspapers. He's read them all. He's saying that now everyone will have to admit the greatness and ingenuity of his brain. He's not in the least down-trodden like that poor little specimen, Haley, who's scared to death of a perjury charge."

"He's like his mother," Sarah said, remembering the chess game yesterday, "vociferously turning his defeat to a sham victory." After a moment she asked, "What about Venetia?"

"She's much better now she knows it's all over. Poor thing, she's had a ghastly time since Eliot's death. She's going home to her people. They've agreed to be responsible for her. The old lady will have to go into some sort of institution, I'm afraid."

"And Jennie?"

Sarah was surprised to see Tim suddenly look self-conscious and almost shy.

"Well, that cottage of mine in Cornwall has quite a lot of room."

"Are you taking her there, Tim? She'll be head over heels with delight."

But even while she spoke whole-heartedly, Sarah had a feeling of sadness. She had grown very fond of Jennie. Besides, she would be jobless again. Her cosy position for the winter had ended before the winter had begun.

"She won't want to say goodbye to you, Sarah."

"Oh, she'll get over that. When are you leaving?"

"In a day or so. I just have a lunch appointment to keep."

"The important one you talked about? You knew almost to the day when this mystery would clear up, didn't you?"

"Yes, I calculated rather nicely. I'm not so sure about the lunch calculations, though."

"Why? Is it Rachel, Tim?" Sarah was proud of the nonchalance of her voice.

"Rachel! Good lord, no. She's decided to go right back to the States now this thing's been cleared up."

"Has she? I didn't know. I thought—"

"Honey, for a person of your intelligence you think the greatest amount of distorted nonsense. Just what goes on in that charming head of yours—"

Before he could finish he was interrupted by the door opening sufficiently for Jennie to insert her neat dark head. Her cheeks were pink, her eyes sparkling with excitement.

"Sarah, Mrs. Hopkins is reading her cup again," she announced excitedly. "Just for me, she said. And she's seen a bride's veil."

"Fancy!" said Sarah. "Tim, please go. I want to get dressed."

Tim stood up. His expression was both self-conscious and impatient.

"Dash it all, honey, do I have to go back on my word after all? I swore I'd never ask you to lunch with me again."

Sarah stared at him. She saw the mocking twinkle in his eyes, but beneath it the tenderness, the longing, the sincerity that was not to be doubted. Colour began to rise in her cheeks. All at once she felt soft, limp, peaceful, and deeply happy.

"Oh, Tim, you ass," she said gruffly. "All right, I suppose I must come. I'll meet you in Trafalgar Square under Nelson's Column at a quarter to one. And don't be late."

"Me late!" Tim ejaculated indignantly. "Me!"

"But, Sarah, listen!" Jennie implored. "The bride's veil is for you!"

# CORONET'S GARDEN OF 'EDEN'

| | | | |
|---|---|---|---|
| ☐ | 12800 3 | THE VINES OF YARRABEE | 35p |
| ☐ | 02927 7 | NEVER CALL IT LOVING | 35p |
| ☐ | 02032 6 | SLEEP IN THE WOODS | 30p |
| ☐ | 00320 0 | THE BIRD IN THE CHIMNEY | 30p |
| ☐ | 01733 3 | SAMANTHA | 30p |
| ☐ | 12957 3 | SHADOW WIFE | 30p |
| ☐ | 12777 5 | LAMB TO THE SLAUGHTER | 30p |
| ☐ | 14993 0 | BELLA | 30p |
| ☐ | 15108 0 | WAITING FOR WILLA | 30p |
| ☐ | 15118 8 | BRIDE BY CANDLELIGHT | 30p |
| ☐ | 15256 7 | MELBURY SQUARE | 35p |
| ☐ | 14785 7 | CAT'S PREY | 30p |
| ☐ | 16056 X | AFTERNOON WALK | 30p |
| ☐ | 10787 1 | THE DEADLY TRAVELLERS | 30p |
| ☐ | 10786 3 | THE SLEEPING BRIDE | 30p |
| ☐ | 02925 0 | NIGHT OF THE LETTER | 30p |
| ☐ | 18189 3 | SPEAK TO ME OF LOVE | 40p |

*All these books are available at your bookshop or newsagent, or can be ordered direct from the publisher. Just tick the titles you want and fill in the form below.*

CORONET BOOKS, P.O. Box 11, Falmouth, Cornwall.

Please send cheque or postal order. No currency, and allow the following for postage and packing:

1 book – 10p, 2 books – 15p, 3 books – 20p, 4–5 books – 25p, 6–9 books – 4p per copy, 10–15 books – 2½p per copy, over 30 books free within the U.K.

*Overseas* – please allow 10p for the first book and 5p per copy for each additional book.

Name.......................................................................................................

Address...................................................................................................